D1134466

'You're a very seductive lady, and undoubtedly we still like one another enough to want to keep in touch, don't you think?'

Deborah moistened her lips. His mocking, lustful tone had lacked the emotion she craved to hear. A searching glance at his smouldering eyes told her that with just a little encouragement from her he'd see off the Captain and come back to her in minutes, not days. He very much wanted her—but not as he once had, as his wife. Next time when he returned to Woodville Place he would proposition her, and to her shame she knew if he did so whilst touching her she might be tempted to accept an offer to be his mistress.

AUTHOR NOTE

Regency Rogues—*Ripe for a Scandal. Ready for a Bride*

A roguish gentleman can be devastatingly attractive to a genteel lady—especially when she's already had a taste of loving him and regrets losing him.

In CHIVALROUS RAKE, SCANDALOUS LADY the heroine is unwilling to succumb to a rejected suitor's offer to be his mistress, despite being sorely tempted to do so. The vengeful rogue has a fiancée, and the heroine has a secret that should remain hidden if she is to salvage what remains of her reputation.

This second book in the duet, DANGEROUS LORD, SEDUCTIVE MISS, finds the heroine under threat from a gang of local ruffians. Then she is unexpectedly reunited with the hero many years after their youthful romance ended in a bitter parting. But is he a villain too? And does he present a greater danger... to her heart?

I hope you enjoy reading about how these couples overcome scandal and heartache to eventually find love and happiness.

DANGEROUS LORD, SEDUCTIVE MISS

Mary Brendan

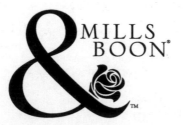

All the characters in this book have no existence outside the imagination of the author, and have no relation whatsoever to anyone bearing the same name or names. They are not even distantly inspired by any individual known or unknown to the author, and all the incidents are pure invention.

All Rights Reserved including the right of reproduction in whole or in part in any form. This edition is published by arrangement with Harlequin Enterprises II BV/S.à.r.l. The text of this publication or any part thereof may not be reproduced or transmitted in any form or by any means, electronic or mechanical, including photocopying, recording, storage in an information retrieval system, or otherwise, without the written permission of the publisher.

® and TM are trademarks owned and used by the trademark owner and/or its licensee. Trademarks marked with ® are registered with the United Kingdom Patent Office and/or the Office for Harmonisation in the Internal Market and in other countries.

First published in Great Britain 2010
Harlequin Mills & Boon Limited,
Eton House, 18-24 Paradise Road, Richmond, Surrey TW9 1SR

© Mary Brendan 2010

ISBN: 978 0 263 21477 2

Harlequin Mills & Boon policy is to use papers that are natural, renewable and recyclable products and made from wood grown in sustainable forests. The logging and manufacturing process conform to the legal environmental regulations of the country of origin.

Printed and bound in Great Britain
by CPI Antony Rowe, Chippenham, Wiltshire

Mary Brendan was born in North London, but now lives in rural Suffolk. She has always had a fascination with bygone days, and enjoys the research involved in writing historical fiction. When not at her word processor, she can be found trying to bring order to a large overgrown garden, or browsing local fairs and junk shops for that elusive bargain.

Novels by the same author:

WEDDING NIGHT REVENGE*
THE UNKNOWN WIFE*
A SCANDALOUS MARRIAGE*
THE RAKE AND THE REBEL*
A PRACTICAL MISTRESS†
THE WANTON BRIDE†
THE VIRTUOUS COURTESAN**
THE RAKE'S DEFIANT MISTRESS**
CHIVALROUS RAKE, SCANDALOUS MISTRESS††

The Meredith Sisters
†*The Hunter Brothers*
**linked by character
††*Regency Rogues*

MORAY COUNCIL
LIBRARIES &
INFO.SERVICES

20 31 15 37

Askews

RF RF

For Mum

Prologue

Coastal Sussex, circa 1828

'Do I have a choice in the matter?'

'You can refuse if you wish, my lord,' Colonel Montague replied stiffly.

The Colonel shifted to evade the glare of a pair of hawk-like eyes. The question directed at him had been uttered with an unnerving softness. If the fellow had bellowed at him, unleashing an anger he sensed was being tightly controlled, he might have preferred it.

Lord Buckland lounged back in the chair before coming abruptly to his feet, his bitter laugh shattering the tense silence that had developed. Having strolled to the window, he propped his tall frame against the crooked timber with a large brown hand. The view, had he chosen to pay attention to it, was quite picturesque. From his vantage point in the Colonel's office he could admire a quaint harbour scene complete with weatherbeaten old salts preparing fishing boats for sea, all set against a backdrop of mellow, autumnal hues. 'And what would be the consequence of such a refusal?' Lord Buckland demanded harshly over a shoulder. 'Will my mother and sister be ousted from their home and left destitute?'

'It's possible the crown might move to reclaim the Buckland estate.'

'It's more than damn well possible, and you know it.' Lord Buckland pivoted about and his amber eyes swooped on the Colonel's ruddy face. The fellow was embarrassed, and so he should be. A more blatant case of blackmail would be hard to imagine. And he had little choice but to knuckle under to it. 'The continuing comfort of my family is a very strong bargaining tool as you're well aware.'

'Be sensible, sir,' Gordon Montague said persuasively, as he fiddled a finger between his throat and his collar. 'Your brother has caused grave problems for you all. You've a chance to put things right and in doing so will keep your family's reputation safe. In addition, you've the prospect of earning a magnificent sum.' The Colonel's coaxing smile faded, for there was no reciprocal lightening in my lord's grim, sardonic expression on hearing that a king's ransom was to be had. He spread his hands appealingly. 'There's the matter of your brother's body, too. Surely you want it properly laid to rest? Sebastian will be given a Christian burial instead of remaining hanging on a gibbet till the crows have done their devilish work. Think of your mother's feelings and your sister's. Your father, God rest his soul, would have been desolate to know how things have turned out for you all. He would rely on you to do your utmost to ease their distress and contain a scandal.'

An acerbic smile tugged upwards a corner of Lord Buckland's thin lips. Inwardly he damned the Colonel to perdition for reminding him of what he couldn't forget. The duty to his family and the Buckland reputation—what remained of it—must determine his decision and therefore there was only one answer to give to the proposition that had been laid before him. He limited his agreement to a curt nod, simply a tightening of his mouth indicating his resentment at having been backed in to a corner.

'Do you want these?'

The Colonel opened a drawer in the desk to reveal some documents. 'There are papers here that might be of considerable use—names...places—'

'I need nothing,' Lord Buckland brusquely interrupted. 'I'll find my own way.'

'But...why? These may help.'

'Who else knows what's in that little lot?'

'Only the most loyal and trustworthy individuals.' Indignation brought ruddy colour in to the Colonel's cheeks.

'Tell that to the dragoon who last week had his head caved in on Hastings beach, betrayed, no doubt, by someone who had knowledge of what's in documents such as those. The soldiers were ambushed.'

The Colonel coughed and loosened his neckcloth at that reminder of the recent injury sustained by an officer on the south coast. He frowned at the tall man lounging back against the window, blocking the light with the athletic breadth of his shoulders. 'Are you saying you think we have a traitor in our midst?'

'I'm saying I'll trust no one, not even you, to protect me in this.'

'I'll report back that you'll do it, shall I?' The Colonel shoved the papers again out of sight.

'You may tell his Majesty that I'll need the wherewithal to get started,' Lord Buckland bit back. 'But then he knows I'm desperate for funds, doesn't he, or he wouldn't have me squirming beneath his thumb.'

Within a moment Lord Buckland was at the door and had

jerked it open. 'I'm staying at the White Hart in Lowestoft. You can get a message to me there. I'd like to journey south before the end of the week.'

Chapter One

'Your anger is understandable in the circumstances, Miss Woodville, but you must understand that there is little I can do.'

Deborah Woodville cast a glinting blue eye on the fellow seated behind the desk. 'I understand no such thing, sir,' she responded crisply. 'You are a local magistrate, are you not, and therefore responsible for upholding the law?' she reminded him of his office, hoping it might shame him into offering to do something to punish the vicious bullies who had set about one of her servants earlier that afternoon. Frederick Cook drove her carriage and he'd been knocked unconscious by two louts simply for remonstrating with them for using disrespectful language in her vicinity. The worst thing was that she knew it was she whom they meant to hurt. But she was a Lady of Quality and so far had been protected by her gentility in this rural backwater in East Sussex. Today the despicable cowards had vented their spite and frustration on her loyal manservant. But danger was coming closer and Deborah feared it might not be long before the ruffians breached the final barrier and laid their horny hands on her.

'I am privileged to hold the office of Justice of the Peace.' Roderick Savidge acknowledged his authority with a stately dip of his auburn head. 'But you must know how it is—the people hereabouts are close-lipped when questions are asked about their kith and kin. It would be impossible to get witnesses. Did you see it, Miss Woodville?'

'I did not; I have said I had gone in to the draper's shop and came out to find Fred bleeding in the road. When he came to, he told me he'd been attacked by two men who'd spouted abuse about me.'

'Can he describe his attackers?'

That was a tricky question to answer and her hesitation became more marked as blood seeped in to Deborah's cheeks. She was quite sure that her driver *could* describe them. She'd go further and say she believed he knew their names, but he would not identify them. Frederick worked for her and her mother and lodged with them at Woodville Place, situated midway between Rye and Hastings. But his parents and siblings lived in a village close by. Fred wouldn't want them to suffer the consequences should he stir an investigation into the villains who ruled the roost in this neighbourhood.

Mr Savidge gave a sigh that terminated in a sympathetic smile. 'I know the difficulties, you see, Miss Woodville, and understand why your servant has chosen to keep quiet,' he commiserated. 'Decent people might want to eject these felons from their midst, but they fear reprisals if they speak out.'

'But I do not fear reprisals, sir, and I shall say that I believe it was one or both of the Luckhurst brothers who beat Frederick. Will you apprehend them for questioning?'

'If you will forgive me, your attitude towards your safety— and you risk your mother's, too, of course—is not wise, Miss Woodville.' Mr Savidge frowned. 'As for apprehending likely suspects, it would be pointless issuing the warrants, my dear.' A patronising smile writhed on his fleshy lips. 'There is little chance of a conviction without a witness or even the victim's testimony to rely on. You will simply stir more enmity towards yourself and your kin by persevering with this. Fred's injuries will no doubt mend and perhaps he will in future think before he lets loose his tongue.'

'The risk of becoming increasingly unpopular does not worry me,' Deborah snapped, tilting up her shapely little chin in a way that denied the nausea rolling in her stomach. 'Why should Fred not voice his disgust for such boorish behaviour?' She knew she was dicing with danger, but she would not, could not, stand by and let bullies dictate her life or shape her character.

Mr Savidge picked up a little bell on his desk as though he would cover her complaints with its clatter. 'You will take tea, Miss Woodville?'

'No…thank you,' Deborah refused immediately. 'You have said you will not arrest the Luckhursts so I shall be on my way.' The fellow's eyes were lingering on her in a way she didn't like. She found his pale blue regard unsettling and she did not want to tarry a moment longer than necessary in his company. It seemed he had no intention of sending out the dragoons to investigate the assault on Fred and bring the culprits to court, so it was pointless remaining. She stood up and gave a single nod in mute farewell.

'You have done little to encourage the villagers to show good will towards your family, you know, Miss Woodville.' Mr Savidge had gained his feet whilst speaking and carefully replaced the little brass bell on the desk.

Deborah turned, her hand still gripping the doorknob. A sparking sapphire gaze was levelled on his worship. 'And I think you know, sir, why that is. We have endured much trouble and heartache at the hands of some of the locals. It is hard to like people who choose violence and lawlessness as a way of life.'

'Indeed, it was shocking what happened to your fiancé. But some years have passed now and the fellow responsible got his just deserts.'

Deborah knew that he was referring to an individual who had been nicknamed Snowy on account of his prematurely white shock of hair. It was generally held that he'd been responsible for Edmund's murder. The authorities had hunted the fellow but, before he could be captured and brought before a court, Snowy had been found dead in the lane. It had been murmured he'd come before another court: that of the smugglers themselves. They'd rid themselves of him rather than have the militia forcing entry to every house in the locality to discover if a neighbour was hiding him. No villager would want the authorities prying in cupboards and cellars for fear of what illicit goods they might find.

'Smuggling is entrenched in the communities hereabouts,' Mr Savidge began. 'City people don't always understand the ways and customs of coastal folk. Your late stepfather had a more…' he hesitated as though seeking the right word and then pounced upon '…*mellow* outlook on free-trading. A lot of the gentry in the vicinity feel the same way. Live and let live is a sensible motto for outsiders who intend to stay a while in these parts and dwell amongst the rascals.'

'I expect there is the added advantage of a barrel of brandy or a pound of tea as a reward for those prepared to turn a blind eye,' Deborah remarked sourly.

'I would advise you to keep such frank opinions to yourself, my dear.' Mr Savidge's bland tone did not quite correspond with a sharp glitter in his eyes.

'Had my fiancé not been murdered by those endearing rascals,' Deborah said scathingly, 'perhaps I might heed your good advice. But never will I be moved by the romantic myth of it all.

The Luckhursts and their ilk are brutal criminals and should be brought to justice.'

'It is not at all wise to say so, Miss Woodville,' Mr Savidge cautioned her. 'You and your mother are living alone with just a few servants to protect you.'

'Indeed, we are alone; it seems we cannot rely on the law of the land or its servants to come to our aid,' Deborah concluded damningly. With an angry frown creasing her ivory brow, she jerked open the door and exited the building.

The most galling thought, she acknowledged as she emerged into the autumn sunlight, was that his worship's attitude might be anathema to her, but it was undeniably logical. She *should* turn a blind eye, for she could no more stop the smugglers going about their business than she could control the tides that washed the shores they used for their illicit trade. But how could she forgive or forget when Edmund lay buried in St Andrew's churchyard, run through simply for carrying out his army duties?

'Debbie!'

Roiling thoughts rendered Deborah deaf to her friend hailing her. A second summons brought her head up and she spun about. A smile immediately lightened her delicate, fair features as she spied Harriet Davenport hurrying towards her.

Deborah clasped the gloved hands that Harriet had extended in greeting and the two ladies proceeded to walk arm in arm along Hastings Upper Street. The stiff breeze blowing off the seafront made them lower their bonnet peaks to protect their complexions from a briny buffeting.

'I saw you coming out of the magistrate's house,' Harriet began. 'Is Mr Savidge going to try to find those responsible for beating Fred?'

'I'm afraid not. He says it would be a pointless exercise.' Deborah sighed and tucked a wispy honey-coloured curl behind an ear. 'Mr Savidge regrets he has no assistance to give, other than to issue his opinions.'

'Which are?' Harriet asked expectantly.

'I should keep quiet and mind my own business.' Deborah pursed her lips ruefully. 'As I retired to bed last night I could see lights moving in the woods again. The smugglers were about their work.'

As Harriet heard her friend's comment, her teeth sank into her lower lip. 'Mr Savidge has a point, you know, Debbie,' she said carefully. 'We all know it is not right, but it is best not to cross them.'

'Indeed,' Deborah agreed with a grimace. 'What can be done if even the local magistrate is in cahoots with the felons?'

'Do you think he is?' Harriet gasped, her eyes widening.

Deborah shrugged. 'Actively? I doubt it. But I imagine he would describe his own attitude to those depriving his Majesty's treasury of funds as *mellow*.' She sighed. 'I know from experience that even people who can afford to pay full price for their luxuries are not averse to buying them cheaply.'

Indeed, she knew that very well; Woodville Place still had a residual amount of contraband stashed in its cellars and larders from her late stepfather's days.

After her father had died and her mother had married again, to a country squire, she had been loath to quit her fashionable Mayfair life at the age of nineteen and move permanently to a remote country house. She still would prefer to live in London, but over the years she'd grown to appreciate the natural beauty of her new surroundings. She'd become fond of her stepfather. George Woodville had been kind and generous to her and had been an amiable sort of chap. At first it would have been hard to find something in him to which she might object. But eventually she had.

She could clearly recall her first sight of the smugglers at close quarters. It had been on a midsummer night of unbearable humidity when the twilight barely dwindled, but remained till dawn. She had risen from her bed and settled on the windowseat to get some air. For some minutes she'd sat quietly, her chin resting in her cupped palms, listening to a soothing sound of distant surf rushing on shingle. A few bobbing lights had drawn her attention and alerted her to people approaching in the early hours of that pale, misty morning. Then she'd spotted the shape of a donkey cart lumbering up the incline towards their door and in its wake two more beasts laden with a keg slung on each fat flank. She'd watched, agog with curiosity, as fellows unloaded and rolled barrels towards the side of the house where a cellar opened in the earth. She'd caught fragments of a furtive exchange that had taken place between Basham and a burly fellow holding a flare who'd pocketed the cash handed to him by their manservant.

She had gone downstairs early to breakfast alone and her innocent questions had caused the serving girls to blush and giggle and scurry hither and thither with coffee and chocolate pots to avoid answering her. Basham had uncovered the dish of kedgeree for her with a flourish, then a wink and a tap at the side of his nose had warned her to ask no more. At nineteen she'd deemed herself a woman grown, not a child, and she had resented their attitude that it was some sort of secret from which she must be excluded. When she'd insisted on knowing what was going on, Basham had reported that back to the master of the house. Her stepfather had duly made a point of gently chiding her for her inquisitiveness about something that need not concern her. Bit by bit thereafter Deborah had pieced together the puzzle from overheard comments made by the servants and the locals. It became clear to her that not all thought it a shameful trade; a lot of people deemed the outlaws who ran contraband worthy of their pride and loyalty.

Her stepfather might not have held those fellows in high esteem, but he obviously gave tacit permission for their booty to enter his house.

That first introduction to the smugglers had been five years ago. Two and a half years later she'd become engaged to Edmund Green. It was to be a tragically brief betrothal. He had been killed within four months by one of the smugglers in an affray with the dragoons on coast watch.

Her solemn musing was interrupted as she spied Harriet's brother emerging from a large, elegant house set back from the road. Her expression turned wry as she saw he'd caught his vicar's robe in the gate and was fighting to free it from the hinge. Having adjusted his dress, the Reverend Gerard Davenport banged shut the gate with discernible irritation.

'Gerard seems to have finished his meeting with the bishop earlier than expected.' Harriet had also caught sight of her brother and waved at him. 'I hope he is going to take me to Rye market.' She gave her friend a smile. 'It is always nice when Susanna is from home,' she said, referring to her sister-in-law with a frown. 'It is like the old times when Gerard and I would go shopping or visiting without a sour puss sitting between us on the seat.'

Gerard Davenport had married for the first time when he'd just turned forty. His wife, Susanna, was only a few years older than her sister-in-law. Harriet was twenty-eight but she had always got on very well with her older brother, and they had lived in peace and harmony at the vicarage until Gerard had decided it was time to get a wife and family.

He'd found his wife too quickly, Harriet was wont to mutter. She knew very well that Susanna resented her presence in what she classed as her domain, but Gerard maintained his sister was welcome beneath his roof for as long as she wanted to remain there.

'Why do you not come to Rye, too, and forget all this unpleasantness for a short while?' Harriet suggested. 'Perhaps Mrs Woodville might like an invitation. An outing will do you both good.'

'I'd like to go with you,' Deborah said wistfully. 'But…Mama has been suffering with her heads recently. I sent Fred back with the trap.' She sighed. 'I told him to bathe his face and rest a while in case he again came over queer. I shall walk home…' Her soft lips remained parted as though she had more to say, but had been distracted.

Deborah had been intermittently flicking glances about at the street scene whilst conversing with her friend. She'd just noticed a gentleman emerge from the blacksmith's doorway and she continued to gaze in his direction so steadily that Harriet frowned at her.

'What is it?'

'I thought I recognised someone,' Deborah said with a hollow little laugh. Her heart had ceased beating for those few seconds she'd stared and wondered if it could possibly be him. The man had again gone inside the forge, and she was no longer able to scrutinise him from a distance. Now, as her lurching stomach steadied, she realised just how silly she'd been to imagine that Randolph Chadwicke would be so far from home. His home now, to the best of her knowledge, was in the Indies and had been so for many years. If he were back in England on a visit, she imagined he would either be found in Suffolk, where his family lived, or in Mayfair where he used to lease a town house. Perhaps he still did. She knew nothing of him now, nor did she want to. But once…once she'd been keen to know everything about him. She'd wanted him for her husband.

'How are you, Deborah?' Gerard asked solicitously as he joined them and slipped his sister's hand through the crook of an arm. He gave Harriet's gloved fingers a fond pat before launching into speech. 'I saw Fred mopping his face of blood this morning. He told me that some local ruffians had set about him. Would you like me to speak to Savidge about it to find out what can be done, my dear?'

A grateful smile rewarded the vicar for his offer. 'That's kind, Gerard,' Deborah said. 'But I have already been to see him.'

'Mr Savidge thinks that nothing should be done,' Harriet told her brother flatly.

'It's a dreadful to do when even the local magistrate is too scared of the villains to act.' Gerard Davenport sadly shook his head. He looked at Deborah for a response, but again her wide blue eyes were riveted elsewhere.

The tall gentleman had emerged from the smithy and she no longer was presented with his profile. He'd turned her way, causing a small gasp of disbelief to escape her soft lips.

Almost as though he sensed her eyes on him, he looked up. At first there was nothing, just the slightly sardonic, narrow-eyed interest of a gentleman who has caught an attractive young woman watching him. Then she saw the change in him, saw the hand that had been smoothing the sleek flank of the newly shod bay become still. He looked down before slowly raising his head to stare at her, and with such fierce intensity that Deborah felt her face flinch aside as though to evade a blow. A moment later she was aware of him approaching.

Chapter Two

'Miss Cleveland?'

It was a long while since Deborah had been addressed so and it brought with it a poignant memory of her time as the débutante daughter of Viscount Cleveland. At eighteen she'd been the toast of the *ton*, and newly single, having broken her engagement to the heir to an earldom.

He'd spoken before reaching her, a query accenting her name. He'd thought, too, that his eyes might be deceiving him, Deborah realised. A darting glance at her companions confirmed they were swinging interested looks between the two of them.

George Woodville had been her stepfather, not her sire, but since she'd arrived in Sussex with her remarried mother, people had seemed to assume she would want to be a Woodville too. Her father had been a peer of the realm, but he was not known in these parts, whereas the Squires Woodville could trace their prominence in Sussex gentry back as far as Cromwell's days. It had seemed trivial to Deborah to keep pointing out that her mother might now be a Woodville, but she was not.

Harriet was cognisant with her history and Deborah could see the young woman retrieving the relevant snippet from her mind.

She turned with her brother to gaze up at the ruggedly handsome stranger who had joined them.

'Why…Mr Chadwicke…what a surprise to see you,' Deborah uttered in a stiff, suffocated tone. It was not at all the first thing she had promised herself she would say should their paths ever again cross. But her good manners dictated that she remain polite in company. She could tell that her friends were impatient to be introduced to him, but his relentless golden gaze remained unnervingly on her face, causing colour to seep beneath her cheeks.

'I should like to introduce you both to Mr Chadwicke, he is…' Debbie hesitated and her uncertainty on how to continue caused a skewing of his narrow mouth. 'Mr Chadwicke and I…have mutual friends,' she resorted to saying. 'This is the Reverend Mr Gerard Davenport and his sister Harriet,' she concluded the niceties.

Randolph enclosed Gerard's extended fingers in a large brown hand and gave them a firm shake. Harriet received a courteous bow coupled with a murmured greeting.

'Are you related to the Somerset Chadwickes, sir?' Gerard asked brightly.

'I'm not,' Randolph replied. 'I hail from the east of Suffolk.'

'Ah,' Gerard said. 'A good part of the country; I have been to Yarmouth on several occasions and have found it most pleasant. But the cold winds nigh on cut one in half.'

'It can be bitter there in winter,' Randolph agreed.

At close quarters, and having surreptitiously studied him from beneath her bonnet brim whilst he conversed with the vicar, Deborah was astonished she had so easily recognised him. Apart from those hazel eyes seeming just as wolfish as she remembered, he looked quite different. His hair, once nut brown, had been made fair by a foreign sun and streaked here and there to colours close to caramel. His skin tone, too, was weatherbeaten and his features roughened. He looked to be a man who had been brutalised by life and the elements since last she'd seen him. There was no more of the debonair youth in him. Yet something in her first glimpse of his profile, of his physique, had been achingly familiar to her.

'Are you staying long in Hastings?' Deborah blurted as a silence developed between them all.

'I'm not sure, Miss Cleveland. Are you?'

'I reside here now, sir,' Deborah informed him levelly. 'I live at Woodville Place with my mother. My stepfather, George Woodville, died just over two years ago.'

'I had a communication from Marcus that your father had died,' Randolph said gently. 'I was very sad to hear that news. I knew, too, that your mother had remarried, but not that she was once again a widow. Neither was I aware you had permanently quit London for the country.'

'My stepfather kept a small town house in Chelsea. Before he passed away we used it quite often in the Season. Now I believe his son lives there.'

A silence again strained, but it seemed that Mr Chadwicke had no intention of taking his leave and returning to his horse. The blacksmith had emerged from his forge, looking for his customer; seeing him socialising, he'd tethered the magnificent beast more securely to a post before returning inside.

'Are you away from Suffolk to visit relatives in the area?' Gerard asked amiably.

'I have no relatives in the area,' Randolph once more told him. 'I've travelled to the south coast on a business matter.'

'And will it keep you here long, sir?' Harriet asked politely.

'Possibly,' Randolph replied succinctly.

After a pause that vainly begged a better explanation Harriet reminded her brother, 'Well…we must be going. You've promised to take me to Rye this afternoon and I've not forgotten. Are you sure you won't come with us, Debbie?'

'I must be getting along home,' Deborah replied huskily, but with a small smile for her friend. The ruthless golden gaze was again savaging the side of her face and instinctively she raised a hand to touch her hot cheek.

'Is there somewhere we can talk privately without being gawped at?' Randolph said whilst watching the vicar and his sister strolling away towards their dogcart.

Deborah, too, had noticed that they were under observation. In London well-bred people would mask their inquisitiveness behind concealing lashes or fluttering fans; these simple country folk employed no such sophisticated tactics. They stared quite openly as they passed by.

'Strangers always stir interest hereabouts,' she explained to him. Deborah knew, too, that undoubtedly news was travelling on the grapevine that her driver had been involved in a brawl whilst protecting her.

'Is there a tearoom we can go to?'

She had heard nothing from him in almost seven years. Now he wanted to sit and chat over tea!

Oh, there was much they could discuss that need not touch on the very thorny subject of their brief romance. They might swap news about their mutual friends, the Earl and Countess of Gresham. They could reminisce on the couple's glittering wedding when she had been a bridesmaid and Randolph had been Marcus's groomsman. It had been the last occasion they'd seen one another, seven years ago. The last time he'd kissed her passionately before forgetting about her.

'There is a teashop, but I'm not sure that visiting it, or prolonging this meeting, is necessary, sir,' Deborah rebuffed him coolly.

'Not necessary?' he ground out. 'Have we nothing to say to one another after so long?'

'If you had something to say to me, I imagine you would not have waited seven years to air it,' Deborah snapped. She took a deep breath and looked away, striving for composure. She would not give him the satisfaction of guessing that she'd pined for him for years after he went away. She would never let him know that she'd wanted to write to him in the Indies but had felt unable to abase herself and beg an address from his friend, the Earl of Gresham, so she might do so. Nor would she have needed to do so if Randolph Chadwicke had been true to his parting words on that glorious day when Marcus Speer had married Jemma Bailey.

At the reception, away from prying eyes in an alcove in the hallway of Marcus's magnificent mansion, Randolph had kissed her and told her that he must go away to sort out pressing family matters, but that he would write to her as soon as he could. Obviously he had never found the time or the inclination to put pen to paper and say where he was, or how he was doing, or when he would return and issue that unspoken proposal that had thrilled in the air between them. But no disaster had befallen him to prevent a communication. She had heard through her friends that Randolph Chadwicke was still in the Indies with his older brother.

'I didn't wait one year and well you know it,' Randolph muttered viciously through his teeth. He'd deliberately put too little volume in the words. He was equally keen not to reveal he'd been wounded by their ill-starred attraction. 'You sound as though you might have missed me, Miss Cleveland,' Randolph drawled as his eyes roamed over her classic pearl-skinned profile.

This time she heard very well what he'd said, just as he'd intended she should. A bubble of laughter met his conceit, but she swallowed the immediate denial that sprang to her tongue. It would sound false however she expressed it. 'Perhaps I did at first, sir,' she insouciantly agreed. 'But a lot of water has passed under the bridge since then.' A smile was forced to her lips. 'I was just a girl of eighteen when last we spoke.' She raised cornflower-blue eyes to his, held his narrowed gaze for a significant long second whilst adding, 'Now I am a woman.' Her brashness withered beneath lupine eyes. She felt suddenly uneasy for having implied something that was quite untrue, and she was at a loss to know why she'd done it.

'Despite all that water and experience you recognised me straight away,' he reminded her very quietly.

'As you did me,' she returned in a snap and then swiftly turned to stare at the sea sparkling in the distance. Her mind was in turmoil. She felt unprepared and unequal to dealing with this meeting. Once she had longed for it to occur; she had prepared in minute detail what she would wear and what she would say. But the event had sprung up defiantly when she'd believed the chance of it doing so had expired. She was at a loss to recall any of that witty conversation that had for years whirled in her mind, and her outfit was sensible rather than seductive. 'I didn't intend to sound brusque a moment ago,' she hastened on. What was she thinking of? *Seductive?* She no longer wished to attract him, she reminded herself. 'I have rather a lot to do. I expect you, too, have a lot to do as you are in the area on business.' She inclined her head towards the forge. 'I see Donald Smith is again look-ing for you. He is a stickler, so I've heard, for having his bills immediately settled.' She imagined Donald would not be too worried that this gentleman might abscond without paying. She ran a discreet eye over the impressive masculine figure beside her. His tailored jacket and snugly cut buff breeches were of obvious quality and the long leather riding coat that carelessly covered them looked to have been topstitched by a master crafts-man. She remembered that she'd always admired how well his lofty, muscular body suited formal attire when they'd socialised together at balls and parties.

But all that was gone and forgotten. Charming and elegant he might have contrived to be, but she knew it all for a sham. He'd been a practised flirt and she'd been naïve enough to take his empty promises seriously. She extended gloved fingers. 'It is nice to have met you again, Mr Chadwicke. I hope your business in the area goes well.' It seemed he was not going to match her polite farewell. A firm clasp tightened on her hand as she made to slip it free after an appropriate time had passed.

'I have to go home now. My mother will wonder what has become of me.' Deborah again wriggled her fingers against the warmth of his palm whilst scouring her mind for a polite yet meaningless remark. 'Of course, if you find business ever again brings you this way, sir, you must come and see us.'

He looked down at those fidgeting digits and slowly released them. 'Thank you for the invitation,' he said softly. 'I shall call on you tomorrow afternoon.'

'I didn't mean this time—' Deborah blurted before her pearly teeth nipped at her lower lip. She hadn't intended to sound quite so inhospitable, but she wasn't sure she could cope with again being tormented with his presence. This impromptu meeting had set her pulse accelerating alarmingly; she couldn't countenance sitting and politely taking tea whilst brooding on memories of what had happened seven years ago. The disturbing knowledge that just ten minutes of his company had the power to stir to life embers of emotions she'd believed withered to ashes made her heart constrict beneath her ribs. 'It would be better to leave a social call till your next trip to Sussex,' she insisted, dipping her head in readiness to step away.

'Why next time? I should like to see the Viscountess before I leave the area.'

'She is plain Mrs Woodville now and not always in the best of health.'

'Then I should certainly like to have the opportunity to pay my respects to her, if I may. I remember both your parents with fondness.'

Deborah looked about as though hoping something might catch her eye and allow her to distract him.

'Where is your house?'

'Oh…not far. It takes me only about twenty minutes if walking briskly towards Rye.'

'You have no carriage or servants accompanying you today?'

'I did set out with a vehicle and a driver…' Deborah hesitated, feeling oddly reluctant to disclose to him the tale of her servant's misfortune. She concluded there could be no harm in recounting what had happened to Fred. 'My driver was set about by some bullies whilst I was shopping.' She grimaced in a mix of regret and disgust at the memory of it. 'I sent Fred on ahead in the trap so he might rest in case he is concussed.'

'I'll walk with you,' Randolph said, quietly adamant.

'There's no need,' Deborah immediately countered. 'I'm quite able to look after myself. But thank you in any case for your concern.'

'I'll walk with you,' Randolph repeated with such grit in his voice that Deborah blinked nervously at him. As though to impress on her that he meant what he said, he took her elbow and moved her determinedly with him towards the forge.

Once the bill had been paid, and Donald had tugged at his forelock several times before ambling back in to the smithy, they set off along the lane that led to Rye with the magnificent stallion clopping docilely at his master's heels.

At first they proceeded in silence, both seemingly deep in their own thoughts. Debbie's feverish mind had been occupied in searching for an innocuous topic of conversation that would skirt any past intimacy between them, yet be absorbing enough to fill the twenty minutes that stretched ahead. The most obvious subject was settled upon. Their mutual friends would provide all that was needed to fill the time until they reached Woodville Place.

'I have recently had a letter from Jemma—'

'What caused those louts to attack your driver?'

They had spoken together and fell silent together too. Deborah realised she'd had no reason to fear he'd been brooding on their past and might increase her uneasiness by referring to it. She was unsure whether to feel relieved or indignant that Fred's misfortune seemed of more interest to him.

Randolph indicated with a polite gesture that she should carry on.

'I…I was just saying that I have recently had a communication from Jemma. She and Marcus have been visiting relations in Ireland since the early summer. They hope to return by late November and have invited us to join them at Gresham Hall for the Christmas holiday.' Deborah slid a look up at him. 'Do you regularly keep in touch with Marcus? I imagine you know they have a son as well as a daughter?'

'The boy is named after me…at the end,' he qualified wryly, a smile twitching his lips.

'John Solomon Bailey Randolph Speer,' Deborah recited softly the name of their friends' infant son. 'He must be toddling about now. His sister, Violet, is nearing her fifth birthday,' she added, naming her sweet goddaughter.

'You are one of Violet's godmothers, I believe,' Randolph re-marked, slanting a look down on the top of her bonnet. He could see just a glimpse of her beautifully carved profile. A lock of honey-gold hair had tumbled forwards to dance against her cheek as she walked. Randolph's left hand clenched as he suppressed the urge to brush back the curl, caressing her complexion. Once he would have touched her and she would have welcomed it. But not now. He'd sensed the frostiness in her from the first word she'd spoken to him. Whatever infatuation she'd had with him had long gone. Perhaps he shouldn't have expected a woman as young and as stunningly lovely to wait for him while he went overseas. But, of course, she hadn't waited, had she? he savagely reminded himself. She'd quickly forgotten him, and in time had become engaged to an army officer. But for the unlucky fellow's demise she'd be a married woman.

She was presently tolerating his company because of good man-ners and because they shared mutual friends. Now he was back in England it was likely they would from time to time be thrown together whilst guests of the Earl and Countess of Gresham. She saw potential embarrassment in their forced proximity and was struggling to feel indifference for him. Unfortunately he knew he'd never manage to have such lack of feeling for her, much as he might want to.

Not for the first, or the thousandth, time in his life Randolph cursed his brother Sebastian to damnation. But for his selfish, licentious ways he wouldn't be in this part of the country at all and Deborah Cleveland would still be just a shadow in his past. Gone…if not completely forgotten. Now she was again by his side and it seemed the most natural place for her to be. An unbidden curse broke beneath his breath at such maudlin romanticism and with enough volume for Deborah to hear his frustration.

'I was asking about the men who set about your servant,'

Randolph reminded her to cover his lapse. 'Did some sort of quarrel erupt between them?'

'Yes,' Deborah said and gazed into the distance, uncertain whether to admit that she'd been the unwitting cause of poor Fred getting a beating.

'Over what did they quarrel?' Randolph probed, a ghost of a smile acknowledging her reticence in informing him.

Deborah sighed. 'As you are new to the area you probably know nothing of the horrible things that go on around these shores,' she began. 'My servant was simply protecting my reputation by remonstrating with some ruffians for being disrespectful. He got a beating for being loyal to me.'

Randolph stared straight ahead, his eyes narrowed to slits against the afternoon sun low in the sky. 'And why would these ruffians want to be abusive about you?' he asked exceedingly softly.

'Because I hate them, and I make no bones about letting them know it,' she returned forcefully. 'I'm not going to act blind, deaf and dumb so that they may carry on unchallenged. But for them I would now be Edmund's wife.'

A firm grip on her arm spun her about so she stood before him. 'Explain exactly what you mean by that,' he roughly demanded. His hands were on her shoulders, drawing her close; through the cloth of her cloak he could feel her quivering.

'My fiancé was on coast watch and they killed him.' Deborah's voice shook with distress. 'More recently another dragoon, Lieutenant Barrow, was wounded. He has a dreadful head injury and it is feared it will prove fatal.'

Randolph's hands dropped away, then were again refastened on the soft tops of her arms. 'Your fiancé was killed in a clash with smugglers?' he said hoarsely.

Deborah nodded and her huge blue eyes glistened at him.

'I'd heard from Marcus that you were betrothed to an army officer and that he'd been killed on duty,' Randolph said softly. 'That's all I knew. I wasn't aware how he'd died.'

'He was murdered by the outlaws who infest this area,' Deborah said querulously. 'They hate me because I won't forget or keep quiet about it.'

Randolph pulled her close, stilling her agitation against the warm, solid strength of his body. A hand was raised to tilt up her chin; slowly it slid to cup a cheek and to keep her looking at him.

Deborah felt her breath wedge in her chest. For a moment it seemed the years were peeled away and she was dressed not in sturdy outdoor clothes and chipstraw bonnet, but a pastel silk gown with gardenias threaded in her hair. She was not in an autumnal setting, serenaded by birdsong, but in the Earl of Gresham's pale marble hallway with strains of a lilting melody drifting from the ballroom. But the gaze that was bathing her face with golden warmth was the same and her lids drooped as she anticipated Randolph's lips bruising hers with a passion she recalled had left her feeling weak and dazed and so wonderfully happy. A second later the spell had been whipped away.

'Hope we're not interrupting...' sneered a male voice.

Chapter Three

'You are very much interrupting,' Randolph returned in a lethal tone. He moved Deborah behind him and anchored her there with an unshakeable hold on her wrist. 'So go away.'

'You!' Debbie spat whilst squinting against a gilded western sky to see the youngest Luckhurst brother grinning at her. She'd immediately recognised the owner of that coarse voice. Behind him were two other men of about the same age whom she'd noticed accompanying him on other occasions. 'I know it was you who set about my driver, Seth Luckhurst—' she began, before pressure on her wrist insisted she keep silent. She heeded Randolph's warning and her teeth sank into her unsteady lower lip to stem further wrathful accusations. Thereafter her loathing was limited to glaring at the three men who were emerging from a thicket a few yards away. All were dressed in rough country garb, although a neckerchief knotted about Seth's throat brightened his drab figure.

'Are you deaf as well as stupid?' Randolph enquired mildly. 'I said your presence is unwelcome. Do you not understand English?'

A look of surprise passed between the men. They were used

to issuing threats, not receiving them, but all of them were ready for a fight.

'Don't reckon it's us wot's stupid.' Seth smirked as he swaggered closer. 'You're not from round here, are you, friend? If you was, you'd know not to cross me.' One of his thumbs jabbed arrogantly at his chest. It rose to tip his hat back on his head in a cocky gesture, then both brawny fists were jammed on his hips. 'If you fancy being a hero for Miss Woodville, I'll give you a fight. Or you could just get going, y'know.' Something about the stranger's cool confidence was unsettling Seth Luckhurst despite the odds being stacked very much in his favour. 'It's her I'm after. I need to…talk to her,' he finished on a lewd chuckle.

Randolph gave a sigh, as one might when one's patience is being tested to its outer limit. 'Unfortunately you can't,' he replied with weary courtesy. '*I* want to talk to her and my need is greater than yours.' He let go of Deborah's wrist and started to shrug off his leather coat as though readying himself to take up Seth's offer of a fight.

Deborah immediately sought and gripped hard at one of his hands, unsure whether she did so to seek his security or to stop him brawling. He had little chance of success against three adversaries. She was as worried as much for Randolph's safety as she was for her own. A finger traced a soft, secretive caress on her palm—a wordless instruction that she remain quiet and trust him. Randolph turned to his horse to deposit the garment over the saddle and pivoted back with a pistol in each hand.

An immediate gasp parted Deborah's lips. She'd not even seen him remove the weapons from their repository, so coolly and smoothly had he handled them.

'Be sensible and be on your way.' Randolph's suggestion held an amount of tedium.

Seth rubbed a nervous hand over his bristly jaw. 'There's three of us and you've only got two shots.'

'And both of them are levelled on you,' Randolph told him with a smile. He could tell that Seth was the ringleader and the others deferred to his authority. He seemed a common enough bully and Randolph suspected Luckhurst would crumble when his own life was in serious peril.

'Shoot me and they'll get you,' Seth blustered, but he'd backed away a pace.

'Sensible move,' Randolph drawled his praise.

Seth stopped on seeing his cronies peering at him askance. Turning tail so quickly would do nothing for the reputation of the Luckhursts. He and his brother, Zack, were feared as the area's most brazen villains. If Zack found out what had gone on, he'd beat the living daylights out of him. Seth adjusted his hat and, beneath its lowered brim, ruminated whether his accomplices would blab that he'd retreated from a stranger who spoke and dressed like a town fop.

Sensing he was wavering, Randolph helped the fellow make a decision. A shot rang out, making Deborah start and suppress a scream and Seth bellow in rage as his hat flew backwards off his head. It landed, tattered and smoking, on a grassy mound.

'Missed.' Randolph tutted and gave a sardonic smile. 'I'll need to practise.'

'You'll pay for this,' Seth snarled. His usually rubicund cheeks had turned ashen in alarm. He knew very well that the fellow could have put a bullet between his eyes had he chosen to. He was obviously a proficient marksman and therefore a fellow to be wary of. From town he might be, but he was certainly no novice gunman. Seth turned and, furiously swiping the ragged hat from the ground, stomped back towards the shrubbery. His cronies fell into step behind him, looking uneasy. Before he disappeared into the thicket Seth turned and glowered at Randolph. 'Stupid thing you just done. I'm going to come looking for you and when I find you…'

'I'll make it simple for you. I'm staying at the Woolpack in Rye. Ask for Randolph Chadwicke from Suffolk.'

Immediately on hearing that three tousled heads almost collided as the men immediately conferred. Seth straightened, arrowed another suspicious stare at Randolph. A moment later they'd disappeared and soon after came the sound of hooves hitting hard ground.

Randolph paced away from Deborah, the loaded pistol still raised as though he suspected they might arc about to return on horseback in a surprise attack.

As the sound of the gang's retreat died away Deborah's shoulders slumped in a release of tension and a sigh shuddered out of her. A moment later the enormity of what had happened—and how much worse it could have been—hit her like a thump in the stomach. A sob burst in her chest and she crossed her arms over her middle, inclining forwards as though she felt sick.

As soon as he noticed her stifled anguish Randolph returned swiftly to her side. An arm remained raised, levelling the loaded gun in readiness whilst the other enclosed her in a comforting embrace and pointed the spent weapon skywards. A moment later he had deposited both weapons whence they came and swung into the saddle. Reaching down, he circled an arm around her narrow waist and scooped her up easily in front of him as though she were weightless.

Simultaneously Deborah smeared the wet from her eyes and sucked in a startled breath. She could never in her life remember being handled so roughly. Spontaneously she squirmed as though she might slide down the animal's sleek flank to the turf.

A brawny arm girdled her midriff, preventing her moving, then jerked her back against his solid torso.

'Be still,' Randolph growled against her ear. 'Trust me, if they decide to come back mob-handed and overpower me, you won't like what it is they have in mind for you.'

Deborah could feel her cheeks starting to prickle and burn, and not simply from the warm breath that had just bathed it. She knew as well as did Randolph it wasn't conversation those villains had had in mind for her this afternoon. The terrifying thought made her shudder and her hands pressed at her stomach as though to suppress the nausea rolling there. Seth and his cronies might not have happened upon them by unlucky chance as they walked towards Woodville Place. It was not unusual for her to stroll home using this route. Had Seth been watching her since Fred drove off in the trap? Had he plotted to ambush her with the intention of physically punishing her for reporting him to the magistrate? If so, he must have put his plan into action before he saw her set off home with an escort. He certainly had not been ready for the challenge Randolph presented.

'They won't cow me,' Deborah announced with a shaky attempt at bravado. 'I'm not frightened of them.'

'Well, you should be.' A large hand caught her sharp little chin and tilted her head so he could scan her profile beneath a shadowing bonnet brim. He tightened his hold as she tried to twitch her face free. 'Has he tried to intimidate you like this before?'

Deborah shook her head, her golden tresses swaying against his abrasive cheek as he inclined towards her to catch her quiet response. 'It's just been nasty looks and comments and so on, although on one occasion he did try to grab me when I passed him in a lane near Hastings. Our maid Lottie was with me that day. But that didn't stop him.'

'And?'

'I knocked away his hand. It was about six months after Edmund was murdered by one of those brutes. Luckhurst was probably just showing off to his friends. He said he'd marry me so I wasn't left on the shelf. They all started laughing.'

'You don't go out alone in future.'

Deborah swivelled about to frown at him. No man had spoken to her with such curt authority since she was a teenager. And of course her father had had a right to dictate to her. She was a viscount's daughter, an only child who had been reared to be confident and independent. Since her stepfather had died, and her mother had grown increasingly nervous and prone to her migraines, Deborah had taken over the reins at Woodville Place. She made decisions that affected the lives of her and her mother and their few servants. She was her own mistress. Who did Randolph Chadwicke think he was, ordering her about? But for a quirk of fate the hiatus in their acquaintance might not have been breached today...or any other day in the near future. They were now strangers to one another. She raised sparking sapphire eyes and drew a breath in readiness to forcefully remind him of all of it, but a grim smile told her he had no need to hear her lecture—he could guess the gist of it.

The stallion was prodded into action and the sudden motion threw her back against him. She felt his arm tighten, anticipating her rejection, but after a moment resting rigidly against him, she felt her body involuntarily relaxing. Soon she'd curved into him for warmth and lowered her bonnet against the wind whipping at her complexion.

By the time their ride was at an end Deborah was feeling very subdued and not a little guilty.

The horse ambled in a circle, once, twice, in front of rusting iron gates that stood ajar at the head of a leafy avenue that wound to Woodville Place. She realised Randolph was giving her an opportunity to invite him to take her right up to her door before he had to insist he do so.

'Would you like to have a cup of tea and a bite to eat, sir, before you set on your way again?' she asked in a small voice.

'Why…thank you, Miss Cleveland, I should very much like that.' Randolph's answer was ironically formal and suited to a light dialogue conducted in a drawing room rather than one addressed to the back of her head as she perched, rather windswept, atop his trusty steed. Overhead, branches of a stout oak tree formed a canopy of drily rustling leaves. The breeze strengthened, causing a few scraps of curled russet foliage to drift down and settle on her skirt. In front of her Randolph's hand brushed them idly off, then refastened on the reins. She stared, as one fascinated, at long brown fingers intertwined with leather, feeling suddenly shyly conscious of her hips snugly settled between his muscled thighs. She could feel her cheeks becoming warm from the intensity of his scrutiny; she knew his eyes were constantly on her. There was so much more to be said. She owed him an apology and her gratitude, for, without him… She dared not think what might have happened to her.

During the gallop home, safe in Randolph's arms, she'd come to appreciate just how fortunate she'd been. But for his presence by her side today she might be lying beaten and abused in a ditch by the wayside. She felt deeply ashamed that earlier she'd implied that, if he visited her and her mother at Woodville Place, he'd be unwelcome.

'You will say nothing to my mama of what went on, will you?' Over a shoulder she slanted up an appealing look at him. It was the first time she had properly studied him for any length of time. Earlier her sliding glances had quickly darted away. But now she gazed and, whilst waiting for his answer, she realised that he wasn't so very changed in looks from the man she'd thought she'd marry when a tender eighteen years old. The grooves bracketing his mouth and radiating from his feline eyes weren't extremely ageing, she decided. His hair was now long and light and his visage far darker and leaner, but he still resembled the handsome gentleman she'd wanted to be her husband.

'I'll not tell your mother Seth Luckhurst has designs on your virtue.' Randolph's tone sounded quietly ironic.

'His design is to keep me quiet,' Deborah stressed on a blush. 'He has no liking for me.'

'He doesn't need to have a liking for you, Deborah,' Randolph returned as one explaining something that ought to be obvious. 'Don't ever go out again without a chaperon.'

Deborah limited her mutinous response to making a tight little pout of her mouth. Of course she knew his advice was sound and sensible. Still it rankled that, if she took it, her freedom and independence—things she cherished—would be lost to her. The lout who'd forced her to change her habits deserved no such victory.

'Does your mother know that your driver was beaten today?' Randolph asked abruptly.

A forceful shake of the head preceded her words. 'I told Fred to avoid her and go straight away to his quarters and rest. If Mama finds out that Seth is threatening me, she will suffer very badly with her nerves.'

'What did Luckhurst say about you that caused your driver to remonstrate with him?'

'I'm not sure…'

'I think you are,' Randolph contradicted. 'What did Luckhurst say?'

Deborah twisted her fingers in her lap. 'Fred truly would not repeat it and, as he was in pain from his injury, I did not insist he tell me. I guessed from his embarrassment that it was something lewd.'

'I imagine you're right. So are you going to promise to heed my warning and only go out accompanied in future?'

Deborah looked up and, as their eyes held, she felt a sudden yearning to have him again put his arms about her and comfort her. For all her bold talk of standing up to the bullies, she felt a coil of fear unfurl in her belly. Soon Randolph would again be gone from the area and she would have no champion to scare off the likes of Luckhurst for her. She sensed rather than saw his amber eyes drop to her softly parted mouth and her breath caught in her throat as she realised he need only incline forwards a little to lock together their lips.

'Will you soon be gone from here?' she whispered, her eyes riveted to the shady chin just a few inches away.

'I don't know.'

'What business…?'

Her query was curtailed by the finger he put to her lips to silence her.

'Promise you won't go out alone,' he demanded harshly.

She nodded.

'Say it.'

'Promise,' she muttered with bad grace.

The finger that had hovered a fraction away from her lips returned to gentle a reward on her plump pink skin. Abruptly he took up the reins. A second later he'd urged the horse in to a sedate trot towards the house.

Chapter Four

'I've brought a guest home today, Mama.'

Julia Woodville had been tackling a Gothic tale with some apathy so was happy to hear someone novel might brighten her mundane routine.

Usually she spent the mornings at her sewing and taking a constitutional in the garden. The weather was now too fresh to spend a lengthy time outdoors so today she'd limited her stroll to the paths on the southern side. The spare time till luncheon had been whiled away at her writing desk. She liked to keep in touch with her friends in London. She better liked having their replies to learn what was going on in the *beau monde*, although their gay news always made her sadly yearn to be a part of it.

The afternoons were customarily employed in reading. She enjoyed scanning the ladies' journals and appreciated a good book. But the romance Deborah had got her from the circulating library this week was not one to hold her interest. Julia Woodville gladly let it drop to her lap. Myopically she squinted at her daughter and at the fellow stationed behind her.

Deborah approached her mother's chair positioned close to the log fire. Having removed her straw bonnet, she tossed it to the sofa and combed a few fingers through her tangled flaxen locks

to try to bring some order to them. She was conscious she probably looked unattractively dishevelled after the thundering pace
Randolph had set on the short ride to Woodville Place. Her other
chilly digits were held out to the glow in the grate. It was a glori-
ously bright yet invigorating day in mid-October. Draughts were
stirring the curtains at the casements, making warmth from the
flames very welcome within the parlour's solid stone walls.

'Who is it, dear?' Julia hissed in an undertone. 'Is the vicar
again come for tea?' Julia Woodville's failing eyesight allowed
her to see little more than a gentleman's silhouette. Yet she could
read the print in her books very well. She peered past her daughter again, feeling a mite deflated. The vicar was a nice enough
chap, but his sister was better company and this fellow seemed
to be alone.

'No, it is not Gerard. It is an acquaintance from London. He
is presently in Sussex on business.'

Julia's interest re-ignited with the information. It was her constant wish that they might return to the metropolis and live a
mean approximation of the wonderful life they'd once known.
She'd accepted that they could never recapture the sumptuous existence her first husband had provided for them both, but a small
neat villa on the fashionable outskirts would suffice, she'd told
Deborah. Unfortunately their funds would not suffice, Deborah
constantly told her, even for that modest dream to be realised.

Now that the visitor had come closer Julia could see that it
was indeed not the vicar. Gerard Davenport was nowhere near as
tall and broad as this gentleman seemed to be. But she couldn't
fathom his identity. His features were still indistinct, although
he seemed to have a good head of light-coloured hair.

'It is Mr Chadwicke. I expect you must remember him. He is
a friend of the Earl of Gresham.' Debbie introduced him rather
breathily. 'I expect you remember that when we lived in London

with Papa he would sometimes visit us with Marcus.' Deborah knew that mention of the Earl of Gresham was likely to disgruntle her mother. Julia Woodville had never quite come to terms with the fact that her daughter had spurned an earl. Even knowing that Marcus had been as keen as Deborah to end their betrothal had remained a minor setback to a grand match in Julia's mind.

'Yes, I do remember him,' Julia whispered after a long pause. She picked up her book rather agitatedly, then put it back in her lap. It was opened once again.

Deborah turned and gave Randolph a rather apologetic smile. She knew her mother tended to suffer with her nerves depending on her mood, but that didn't excuse this rather rude reception. When they'd lived in town Randolph had been a visitor to their Upper Brook Street mansion. At times he'd arrive alone, but more usually he'd call with his friend, Marcus. She could only recall her mother greeting Randolph charmingly in the past. Surely he could have done nothing in the interim to upset her?

'How are you, Mrs Woodville?' Seemingly unperturbed by her inhospitable welcome, Randolph approached Julia's chair to courteously offer her a hand,

'I'm well enough, thank you, sir.' Having given a limp shake to his firm fingers, Julia drew her shawl closer about her. 'You are back, then, from foreign lands.'

'I am,' Randolph concurred. 'It is good to be home.'

'And that brother of yours? Is he home too?' Julia once more looked agitated and the book was picked at with fidgeting fingers.

'Sebastian is dead, Mrs Woodville.' The information was given tonelessly.

That news caused Julia to look thoughtful. 'Must we remember to address you as Lord Buckland? Or did your brother get himself a son?'

'I have a nephew and a niece,' Randolph informed her in the same neutral, polite way.

'So you ended up with nothing at all, then…' Julia appeared not to require a response to that. She flicked pages in her book as though hunting for an interesting excerpt.

Deborah had listened to this exchange with her jaw dropping in astonishment. Her mother seemed to be acting very oddly this afternoon. But it was not just her mother's unfathomably churlish attitude that had startled her. In just a few short minutes she'd learned a good deal about Randolph's relations that had come as a shock.

When they had been close friends years ago, Randolph had been happier to speak about his sister than his brother. At the time Emilia Chadwicke had been a schoolgirl of about ten. Deborah guessed that she now would be about seventeen and preparing for her début. His father had long been deceased but, as far as she was aware, his mother was still alive and living in Suffolk with her daughter.

As for Randolph's older brother, she'd heard rumours that Sebastian Chadwicke constantly caused trouble for his family. Randolph had confirmed his brother existed and was a nuisance, but Deborah had discovered very little else about him—Randolph had always seemed reluctant to discuss him. Deborah's friend, Jemma, was married to Randolph's friend, Marcus, so little snippets had come her way over the years to add to her suspicion that the fellow must be a very bad sort. In contrast to his errant sibling, Randolph had always been sought after in society and had been known as a personable gentleman. Debbie could recall feeling glad that Randolph had not been unfairly treated because of his brother's notoriety. Yet now it seemed her mother was doing just that.

The news that Sebastian Chadwicke had died had not come

her way, neither had she been aware that the fellow had at some time married and produced children. But then, after seven years apart, she no longer had any right or reason to make enquiries through their mutual friends about Randolph's life or his kin. Neither had it been very right of her mother to pry. But having done so, at least she should have offered a brief condolence on learning of Randolph's loss, no matter that the deceased was rumoured to have been a rogue. It was very out of character for her mother to overlook etiquette.

'I bumped into Lottie in the vestibule and asked her to bring some tea, Mama,' Deborah brightly announced to break the quiet. 'And Mr Chadwicke has kindly agreed to stay and dine with us later.'

'Yes, indeed he must,' Julia agreed, as though feeling a little guilty over her previous lack of manners. In a quite sprightly manner she got up from her chair and smoothed her pearl-grey gown. 'It is nice to see people from the old days. Sometimes I think I should love to have a chat with a friend about Almack's or the latest rage drawing audiences at Drury Lane. Such wonderful parties we would attend! Vauxhall! Now there was a treat! Although it could be a little…scandalous…' She gave a meaningful nod, her features momentarily animated by mischief. 'Did you enjoy visiting the pleasure gardens, Mr Chadwicke?'

'I did, Mrs Woodville. I remember having a very enjoyable evening there with you all.'

'Indeed, we did have a good time!' Julia corroborated. 'Of course, your chum, Marcus, didn't accompany us when he should have done. He was newly engaged to Deborah at the time,' she remarked with a faraway smile at the fire. 'But you were kind enough to take his place and escort us on that occasion.'

'It was my pleasure to do so, ma'am,' Randolph said, his eyes gliding to Deborah and lingering there.

'It was bad of Marcus to stay away—'

'You cannot blame him for that, Mama,' Deborah interrupted on a constrained laugh. 'At the time he was falling in love all over again with his future wife,' she softly reminisced, very aware of a pair of predatory eyes on her.

'At the time you were his future wife,' Julia reminded her daughter pithily.

'But I was glad that he didn't want me!' Deborah's tone was sharpened by impatience, as usual, on hearing her mother snapping at her for having turned down the chance to be the Countess of Gresham. Her eyes darted to Randolph and for a moment were engulfed by a warm, honeyed look.

Lottie appeared, bearing the tea things. The young maid slid the tray on to polished mahogany and looked expectantly at Deborah. A small gesture from Deborah indicated that the girl was not needed to carry out the ritual of pouring.

'Have you lately been in London, Mr Chadwicke?' Julia asked, her tone bright with anticipation. She enjoyed hearing the newest *on dits*.

'I'm afraid not, Mrs Woodville,' he answered.

'Oh…' Julia murmured with patent disappointment. 'Well, never mind. After you have had tea you must take Mr Chadwicke to see the gardens, Deborah,' she said. 'We have a sunken garden, you know, sir. My late husband, Mr George Woodville, was a keen gardener. He knew the names of every shrub and there are acres of them to choose from. There is a pond, too, with a fountain and fish the size of pheasants.'

'Are you not having tea, Mama?' Deborah watched as her mother continued past her to the door.

'I shan't; I had some tea and seed cake not long before you arrived home and I don't want to spoil my appetite. We must give our guest a good dinner this evening. I shall go and see what our Mrs Field has got in the still room.' She paused. 'I believe Basham was out shooting earlier this week. There should be plenty of game if the beef is all gone.'

Had Deborah cared to take a look into the corridor whence her mother had just disappeared, she would have seen the woman heading for the stairs rather than the kitchens. But she was too conscious of Randolph's overpowering presence, and the apology owed to him for her mother's bizarre behaviour, to follow her parent and find out what on earth was troubling her this afternoon.

'I…I'm sorry my mother seemed a little unwelcoming at first,' Deborah blurted as soon as the door had closed on Julia Woodville's departing figure. 'I assure you she doesn't mean to give offence.'

A crooked smile acknowledged Deborah's plea on behalf of her mother. Randolph had his own suspicions why the woman might not want him around without his friend, the Earl of Gresham, rendering him acceptable.

People of Julia Woodville's age knew that the Chadwickes had for generations regularly turned out a few reprobates. She knew, and no doubt her first husband, Viscount Cleveland, had also known, that a number of his paternal ancestors had been to blame for passing bad blood on to his brother, Sebastian. Had his great-great grandfather not been such a scoundrel, the barony, and the thousands of Suffolk acres that came with it, would have stayed with the crown.

'You will have some tea, sir? Oh…and there are some cinnamon biscuits, too,' Deborah said, spotting that Lottie had had the foresight to include them. Having received Randolph's wordless assurance that her mother's attitude had not bothered him, Deborah approached the tray and occupied her nervous hands with cups and saucers.

'Thank you,' Randolph said. He approached the fire and held out his palms.

'Oh…please sit down if you would like to, Mr Chadwicke.' Deborah pointed a silver teaspoon at the twin fireside chairs. Once he had settled his large frame in one of them she handed him his steaming tea. Solicitously she moved a small circular table closer so she might put the plate of biscuits within his easy reach.

She took the chair that her mother had vacated opposite him, so that the fire was between them. Having taken a sip of her tea, and a nibble at a biscuit, she placed both down in a rattle of crockery. It was a good while until the hour to dine. Usually she and her mother would eat dinner at eight o'clock and it was not yet five. On those days they were not particularly hungry they might ask Mrs Field to simply prepare a buffet supper to be set out in the cosy parlour.

Deborah turned her face to the mellow autumnal light filtering through the glass, thus escaping a gaze that was as relentless as midsummer heat. 'Would you like to take a stroll in the gardens after tea, sir?' she asked politely whilst watching a blackbird on a branch cocking his head at her.

'I'd like you to stop calling me sir and Mr Chadwicke,' Randolph said softly. 'Have you forgotten my name, Deborah?'

'Indeed I have not, sir,' Debbie returned coolly as she turned to look at him. 'Neither have I forgotten that using it would imply a closeness that we no longer have. Many years have passed since we were friends.'

'I'd like us to again be friends.' When his gentle remark made Deborah appear to resume her interest in the garden, he continued suggestively, 'I remember very well the last time we met. It was at Marcus and Jemma's wedding.'

Deborah picked up her teacup and took a gulp from it. Oh, she knew very well what was on his mind. He was remembering how she'd shamelessly clung to his neck and had revelled in being kissed and caressed into insensibility behind a marble pillar. Perhaps he imagined that for old time's sake she might again be persuaded to allow him to take a few liberties whilst he was in the vicinity.

To jerk her mind away from arousing memories she focused on the incident that had coupled them together far more recently. The business with the Luckhursts was in its own way equally disturbing to her peace of mind. Because of it there was much she still had to say to him. Her thanks and apologies were overdue. He had saved her from coming to harm, yet she had accepted his escort home, and his protection, with very bad grace.

She knew, too, that she ought to offer her condolences on his brother's demise. But she would skirt about mentioning their past or when he would be leaving the area. She had been in his company for only an hour or so after many years spent apart yet, oddly, she knew how easy it might be for her to again feel his absence. That silly thought was chased away; in its place she firmly put a reasonable explanation for such mawkishness. Naturally his presence had thrust to the forefront of her mind her salad days when, as a débutante of eighteen, and believing herself in love with Randolph Chadwicke, she'd had a scintillating life as the pampered, popular daughter of Viscount Cleveland.

'I have not properly thanked you for your assistance this afternoon,' Debbie briskly rattled off. 'I also must say sorry for having been rather…prickly towards you. It was a great surprise to see you and I…well…I did not intend to seem churlish. My mother, too, was probably similarly flustered by being confronted with a ghost from the past.' It was a paltry effort and she inwardly winced on acknowledging it. Hastily she picked up her tea and took a sip.

'Was the last impression I made on you so bad?' Randolph asked huskily. 'My understanding was that we parted on reasonably good terms.'

She could sense the smile in his words as he dared her to recall their exciting tryst in Marcus's hallway. *Reasonably good terms* hardly did justice to describing the passion they'd shared away from prying eyes.

'My understanding was that your absence abroad would be reasonably short.' A languid hand attempted to make light of her spontaneous retort. Again she'd not managed to control her lingering hurt and anger over it all. 'It seems at the time we both were under a misconception.' Idly she twirled a flaxen curl about a finger. 'It was a long time ago and is now unimportant.' Before he could respond she fluidly changed the subject. 'I must convey my condolences on the loss of your brother. Did he pass away recently? Had he been ill?'

'It was a few months ago. He had been suffering a malaise for a considerable time,' Randolph added carefully.

'Did living in a hot climate contribute to his poor health?' Debbie asked, her voice resonating with sympathy.

'It did him no good at all to go there,' Randolph answered bluntly. 'Twice he suffered bouts of malaria.'

'I'm very sorry he died. He must have been still quite a young man.'

'He had just turned forty-one.'

'Your poor mother; she must be very sad. I imagine she was worried about you, too, whilst you were in the Indies.'

'I escaped any major illness,' was Randolph's succinct reply.

'I know your brother was reputed to be a roguish character, but nevertheless he was a son and a brother. You have a nephew and niece, so his wife and children must be missing him too.'

'I also must offer you my condolences.' Smoothly Randolph

altered the course of their conversation so it focused on her. 'You mentioned earlier today that your fiancé was killed by the smugglers.'

Deborah nodded, a frown creasing her smooth, ivory brow. 'It occurred more than two years ago. Edmund was on coast watch. There was an affray between the dragoons and a gang of smugglers in a lane leading to the coast.'

'Was the culprit brought to justice?'

'It was reported that a fellow nicknamed Snowy fired off the gun that fatally wounded Edmund.' A glaze appeared in Deborah's eyes as she recalled the awful time. 'Snowy was later murdered,' she resumed huskily. 'The smugglers would sooner kill one of their own than have the dragoons snooping about in the villages looking for a suspect.' She sighed. 'There was no proper trial…save the one his colleagues put on. One cannot be sure that it was Snowy who was responsible for Edmund's death.'

'Did you meet your fiancé in London?'

Deborah shook her head. For a moment she remained silent, for she was tempted to tell him to mind his own business. But if she divulged a little of what had occurred to her in the intervening years, perhaps he might tell her what he had been doing; she knew she had a curiosity to know it. 'My stepfather was a sociable sort of chap. When the militia were billeted close by he would offer hospitality. Occasionally he would hold small parties for neighbours and the officers. It was at such an event that Edmund and I were introduced.' Her voice tailed away and she looked at him. 'And you, sir?' she asked with an admirably neutral tone. 'Have you a fiancée or a wife and children?'

'No…' Randolph said quietly. 'Once I thought I had met the right woman, but I was mistaken. Now I'm happy to remain a bachelor.'

'I see,' Deborah said in a stifled little voice. 'How very sad for you.'

'Indeed, I'm deserving of your pity…let's talk about something more cheerful,' he suggested silkily. 'I had the impression that your mother would like to visit town.' Randolph had placed down his cup and saucer. He relaxed back in to his chair and a booted foot was raised to rest atop a buff-breeched knee. Idly he splayed long brown fingers on a Hessian's dusty leather. 'Do you go to London very often?'

'Unfortunately not. But you're right; my mama would love to frequently visit town,' Deborah answered him automatically, although her mind was in turmoil. She knew very well what he'd hinted at. Once he'd believed he'd wanted to marry her, but then he'd gone away and discovered that he'd found it easy to forget her. A burning indignation roared in her chest. Yet of what could she accuse him? He'd never told her he loved her, neither had he promised to marry her. And he certainly hadn't forced her to kiss him. She'd been a very willing participant in that! The most she'd had from him were compliments and complaints that she was a seductive little miss who could drive him wild with desire. It was probable she'd had a lucky escape. Had he not gone away when he did she might have let him properly seduce her. The consequences of that didn't bear thinking about. But she was determined not to let him know that any of it bothered her.

'It is my mama's greatest wish that we return to town to live.' Her voice sounded shrill despite her attempt to keep it light and level.

'Are you also keen to return there to live?'

'I certainly miss the gaiety and the friends I had there,' Deborah answered, more composed.

'If you returned to London, you'd avoid the necessity of living amongst the likes of the Luckhursts.'

'I shan't allow them to drive us away,' Deborah retorted with a defiance that made him cock a dark brow at her. Had he told her he found her attitude immature he could not have made his opinion plainer. 'We have some friends here,' she continued doggedly. 'Harriet and her brother are nice people. So are Mr and Mrs Pattinson. Not everybody hereabouts is in league with the smugglers. Evil will triumph if good people are too cowardly to combat it.'

'Certainly,' he agreed drily. 'But a lot of decent folk don't consider contraband a bad thing, but a benefit.'

A defeated little grimace was Deborah's acknowledgement of the truth in that statement. Her stepfather had been a good man, yet he had happily paid to have his cellars stocked illicitly.

'Why do you not return to London to live?' Randolph asked. A few brown fingers curled to rest close to his narrow mouth as he waited for her reply. After a silent moment he prodded, 'Is there more to it than a battle of wills with the smugglers?'

Deborah got to her feet and collected the cups to put on the tray. She spun about to face him, feeling an odd unwillingness to admit that she—once an heiress with a magnificent dowry—now could not afford to live in London. Yet she had nothing to be ashamed of. She had not squandered her inheritance; it had been taken from her. Again she had an inclination to tell him that he had no right to ask. But then that would imply that she cared what he thought. And she didn't.

'When Papa died the whole estate was entailed on the next male heir. I have no brother, as you know. There was no close relative on the paternal side who might have felt morally obliged to treat us generously. A distant cousin—a gentleman we haven't met who resides in a castle in Scotland—took the title and estate. Mama was very well provided for in my father's will, and my inheritance was held in trust. Unfortunately it was one that could be breached.' She shrugged, clattering crockery.

'When your mother remarried her assets became Mr Woodville's,' Randolph guessed.

'Indeed,' Debbie muttered, her fingers tightening on the edge of the table until the knuckles showed bone. 'And Mr Woodville had a son and a strong belief in primogeniture.'

A silence ensued and whilst Debbie stared fiercely through the window Randolph watched her.

'You have enough to live on?' he eventually asked quietly.

'Oh, yes. Mr Woodville left Mama enough to carry on living here comfortably, if we are careful. When she has passed away the house and estate will go to his son, Norman. In order that I would not be left destitute, he also left me a bequest of a few thousand pounds to tempt a prospective husband. It is not quite the sixty that my father had wanted me to have.' She turned with a smile on her lips. 'Well, as we have finished tea, sir, shall we now take a stroll in the gardens?'

Chapter Five

Once in her chamber Julia went directly to the small anteroom
where her writing desk was positioned close to a window. When
seated in that spot she had a splendid view of the rosebeds and
lawns that flowed in an undulating emerald swathe to a stream
edging an area of deciduous woodland. The trees were a beautiful sight to behold, garmented in shades of gold and red. At
present the charming view did not lure Julia's interest, rather her
desk did. She sat down before it and got from a pocket in her
grey gown a key. She used it to open the bureau, then, having
found the little spring with a finger, she put pressure on it until a
secret compartment came open. Gravely she gazed at the contents
within. An unsteady hand trembled forwards to withdraw a few
letters tied with ribbon.

'Oh…Gregory, he has come,' she whispered. 'He seems angry
with her, too, despite his courtesy. But I think he still wants her.
We should not have done it,' she murmured to her beloved first
husband. 'Our Debbie did not make the excellent match she deserved. Nice Edmund Green is lost to her, too. She is a spinster…
soon to be twenty-five. A beauty still, indeed she is, but past her
prime.' She pressed pale fingers to her watering eyes. 'Now you
are not here and I alone must decide what to do. What shall I

say if she asks if letters arrived for her? Must I deny it all? Shall I burn them or hand them over with excuses?' She dropped the unopened letters back whence they came. 'Will they think the letters were innocently lost and accept it as fate's way rather than our way of telling them their love was not to be?'

An hour or so later Julia woke from her fitful slumber with a start. A thought had been pricking at her semi-consciousness. Now it surfaced and made her gasp. She had forgotten to visit the kitchens and tell Cook they had a guest to dine. She used her elbows to get upright on the coverlet where she had been napping.

A woman's musical chuckle was heard coming from outside and it drew Julia from the bed to the window. The sun was setting in the west, filtering through autumn-hued trees and turning the eastern boundary to a fiery panorama. A movement on the southern path caught her eye and she watched as the handsome couple strolled. With a woman's eye she noticed straight away that her daughter had not taken Mr Chadwicke's arm whilst promenading. They were side by side, and smiling, but a good space was between them. Despite their time alone, and their amiable appearance, no intimate conversation had taken place. Julia knew, to her shame, that she was glad their pride held them apart. She hoped he would leave and go about his business without making any mention of his letters.

Deborah had been a touch formal with him. Julia had sensed that immediately, in spite of her daughter's attempt to conceal her emotions behind good manners. But Julia was sure that Mr Chadwicke still had a hankering for Deborah. She was not so shrivelled that she could not recognise when a man had a certain twinkle in his eye. She craned her neck as the couple began to disappear from sight in the direction of the walled garden. She imagined Deborah was intending to show him the parterre and the fishpond situated beyond the iron gate.

Drawing back with a sigh, Julia was about to turn away when a movement to the north of the plot caught her attention. Instinctively she shrank back in fear as though to conceal herself behind the heavy curtain. A fellow was lurking and appeared keen to secrete himself behind a huge yew whilst peeping in the direction that her daughter and Mr Chadwicke had taken. Julia knew the burly individual was one of the Luckhursts. He and his brother were alleged to be notorious criminals, although it seemed they always managed to escape arrest. When she'd been shopping with Deborah in Hastings Julia had seen them brazenly swaggering about with their cronies. She had never liked the way the younger one smirked at her daughter with a mixture of lechery and belligerence on his coarse face.

On moving to Sussex with her second husband Julia had initially felt an indifference to the fact that they lived amongst smugglers. But since her daughter's fiancé had been killed, she had been thrust into awareness of the true price of contraband. Deborah loathed the smugglers and let everybody know it. On many occasions Julia had cautioned her daughter to guard her tongue. One never knew who might be listening.

Blood began to pump deafeningly in Julia's ears. Why was Seth Luckhurst in the garden spying on Deborah? Had her daughter recently challenged him again over his wickedness? Again she peeked out. For a moment she was mesmerised by the brawny fellow who was glancing this way and that. He seemed to be checking if the coast were clear before making his move. Julia skittered backwards away from the window as she saw him look up. She was frightened he might have spotted her. She collapsed on the edge of the bed, her fingers threaded tightly together. A calming thought occurred to her: their guest might be the person drawing his interest. Randolph Chadwicke looked a well-to-do fellow with his handsome appearance and stylish apparel. Perhaps the miscreant had been following him. Was he watching for him to leave so he might ambush him and rob him of his valuables? A moment later Julia was again fretting for her own safety. Anybody could see that Mr Chadwicke had a lofty height and a fine pair of shoulders on him and would put up a good fight. It was more likely that Luckhurst was watching for their guest's departure so he might burgle Woodville Place. A coil of fear tightened in Julia's stomach and she sprang up and rushed to the door.

'There is no one out there now, Mrs Woodville, you have my assurances on it.'

'But are you sure, sir? They are a wily lot and know how to hide themselves away. He was loitering behind the yew hedge on the north perimeter.'

'We have checked thoroughly,' Randolph again reassured her. He took a look over his shoulder at Basham who, it seemed, had the position of general factotum in the household. 'Your manservant will confirm that we have made a good search of the grounds.'

'But the felon might return when it is dark,' Julia insisted in a squeak. 'It is almost dusk now.'

'We intend to check again later,' Randolph reiterated soothingly, 'And take flares to light the way.'

'I'll get the flares prepared, m'm,' Basham immediately offered. 'Anybody out there up to no good, we'll find them sure enough.' He made a fist and shook it in a meaningful manner.

Julia looked unimpressed by her manservant's brave statement. Basham was a trusted employee who had been in residence long before she had arrived at Woodville Place. Unfortunately his youth was now far behind him. At almost fifty-six years old, and with his stockiness due more to middle-aged spread than to muscle, Julia knew he was no match for the young thug who had been spying on them. Fred Cook, the coachman, was more of an age to be useful in a scuffle. 'Is Fred in his quarters? Why was he not helping you in the search?' Julia demanded peevishly.

A significant look passed between Randolph and Basham. Both knew that Fred Cook was indeed in his quarters…with a cold compress on his head. By the morning he was sure to be sporting two very black eyes.

When a bloodied Fred had crept in through the side door earlier, Basham had soon been apprised by the youth how he'd come such a cropper. He'd discovered, too, that Miss Woodville didn't want her mother worried over it all. The few servants left at the house accepted that the daughter rather than the mother held sway at Woodville Place, and they were grateful for it. Since the master had passed on, his widow had grown increasingly unpredictable and nervous. Nevertheless, the worrying news that one of the Luckhursts was on the prowl had sent Basham directly to find out if his only male colleague was yet in a fit state to be of assistance. He'd found Fred still groaning in pain from his beating earlier that day, and more likely to be a hindrance than a help in a brawl.

In the event he'd not needed him. A gentleman had miraculously turned up who Basham reckoned could take on the Luckhursts single-handed if he chose to. Elegant and refined Mr Chadwicke might appear to be, but Basham sensed he was also an intensely dangerous fellow and the sort of cool character who was always needed in a crisis, but was rarely to be found.

When Mrs Woodville had flown down the stairs earlier in a high old state Basham had been on the point of exiting the drawing room, having just replenished the hearth with apple-scented logs. Miss Woodville and Mr Chadwicke had been entering the house, having returned from their walk. The ensuing clamour of crisscrossing demands and answers had been cut through by Mr Chadwicke's authoritative tone. Within a very short time the guest had got the gist of what ailed the hysterical woman. A moment later Basham had been sprinting after his tall figure as Mr Chadwicke went on the hunt for Luckhurst leaving Miss Woodville with the task of calming down her mother.

'You must take another sip of your brandy, Mama. It will fortify you.' Deborah had just returned to the parlour with a bottle of smelling salts that she'd fetched from upstairs. She hurried to where Julia was reclining on the day bed, held out the glass of cognac and urged her mother to take some. The other hand held the dark bottle in readiness to be thrust under her mother's nose.

Having sipped her drink, and snorted strongly at the salts being waved below her nostrils, Julia coughed, then again collapsed back against the velvet upholstery. 'That villain is going to try to break in and steal everything we own,' she cried faintly. 'He'll overpower Basham and Fred and ravish the maids...and you...'

'Hush, Mama,' Deborah chided, her cheeks heating. 'You are overwrought.' She took one of her mother's hands between her palms and chafed it. 'Mr Chadwicke has checked everywhere with Basham. If it was Seth Luckhurst, he was probably just... curious about Mr Chadwicke.' Deborah's cornflower-blue eyes were angled upwards to tangle with Randolph's narrowed, watchful gaze. An unspoken message passed between them. 'We saw Seth Luckhurst earlier when I met Mr Chadwicke in town. You know how the locals are—they are suspicious of strangers. That oaf probably came to get a better look at him in case he's a Revenue Officer in disguise,' she gently teased her mother.

'I did draw his attention, Mrs Woodville.' Deborah's innocent quip had caused Randolph's sensual lips to slant sardonically. 'Luckhurst seemed a suspicious sort. I expect it was inquisitiveness that brought him here.'

Julia seemed a little reassured by Randolph's endorsement of her daughter's theory. She put away her bottle of hartshorn and scrubbed her moist eyes with her handkerchief. A moment later she again looked agitated. 'Oh…and I have forgotten to tell Mrs Field that you are to dine with us! How bad of me!'

'It's of no matter, ma'am,' Randolph gently stressed. 'I am staying at the Woolpack in Rye and they do a good roast—'

'No…no!' Julia interrupted, flapping a hand. 'You must stay! You were invited to dine and you will. It is the least we can offer you for all the help you have given.'

'Shall I…?' Basham jerked his head in the direction of the exit, miming his willingness to run an errand.

'Thank you, Basham,' Julia said. 'Please tell Mrs Field she must quickly stoke up the range. We shall have game and roasted vegetables and some fruit tartlets and cheeses. Are there pickles? Oh, I suppose I should go and see for myself what we have.' Julia appeared to have recovered her composure and was soon determinedly heading, with Basham in tow, for the door.

Before she quit the room she turned and looked at the young couple. Her thankfulness for Randolph's help had momentarily made her forget his intercepted letters. She'd forgotten, too, she'd wanted him soon to leave. His presence now seemed more of a benefit than a threat. 'There is some brandy and whisky on the sideboard in the dining room, Mr Chadwicke,' she announced magnanimously. 'If you prefer, there is sherry or port in the cellar. Deborah will make sure you get whatever you fancy, you have only to ask her for it.'

There followed an excruciating silence during which Deborah's complexion grew hotter and brighter because a pitilessly amused pair of eyes refused to budge from it. She rather thought she could guess at what it was he fancied and she had no intention of allowing him enough time to bring it to her notice.

'I'm so sorry you have been embroiled in all this, sir,' she fluidly said. 'I'm sure you must dearly wish you'd never stopped to have your horse shod in Hastings today. You have had nothing but trouble ever since.'

'I'm glad I stopped when I did,' Randolph quietly contradicted her, a sultry humour still lurking far back in his eyes.

'I can only imagine your horse was very lame for you to say so,' Deborah weakly joked. 'No sane gentleman would welcome being thrust unexpectedly in to the role of protector…'

As her words faded and her blush re-ignited, Randolph gave her a ruthless smile. 'I'll willingly offer you my protection, Deborah. As for my sanity…I'll admit that once I was mad about you,' he finished with savage self-mockery.

'And my mother?' Deborah returned coolly. 'May I tell her that you are offering to act knight errant for us both?'

'Of course,' he said softly. 'Anything you want…'

'When did you start to care about what I want?' she returned sourly.

'A long time ago.'

'For a short while.'

'I took the hint that you'd prefer it that way,' Randolph returned in a lethal drawl—he'd heard very well her muttered sarcasm.

Deborah tore her gaze away from eyes that had narrowed to hawkish slits. 'We appear to be at cross-purposes and talking in riddles, sir. Please do sit down and I shall go and see how long we must wait for dinner.'

She started for the door, but from beneath long, lush lashes she saw him take a lazy pace to block her way. At the first hint of his skin scuffing hers she snatched her hand free of the lean dark fingers encircling her fragile wrist bones.

'Don't rush off just as we're talking, Deborah. You might not be interested in solving this particular riddle, but I am.'

'Would you like a brandy, sir?' she asked with cool civility. She raised her icy blue gaze to his. Desire was burning at the backs of his eyes, enlarging the pupils and blackening their tawny depths. He might have changed his mind about proposing to her seven years ago, but it seemed he couldn't quash his desire for her as easily.

'Whatever I fancy is what I was offered,' he reminded her in a voice that was velvety and made her spine tingle.

'And that is?'

'If I tell you, I imagine you'll bring me hemlock.'

'It might be wise then to let me choose. I'll fetch you a brandy.' Despite her intention to act distantly, her lips twitched in amusement. It was a poignant reminder of times, long ago, when he'd made her laugh with his dry, self-deprecating sense of humour. With an exaggeratedly servile little bob she started forwards to run the errand.

'I'm still not sure I trust you not to poison me.' Randolph said dulcetly. 'Can you think of a way to convince me you'll be kind to me?'

'I'm afraid not, sir. But if it'll put your mind at rest, I'll taste the brandy first.' She'd paused for a moment to answer him, but now resumed walking towards the door. He moved, too, just as she'd known he would. What she hadn't anticipated was her reaction to his pursuit this time. Instead of altering course to avoid him, she felt overpowered by his confidence. The scent of cool air and cologne that clung to his clothes pleasantly teased her nostrils and the strength of his virility seemed to paralyse her reason.

This time when he arrested her with his hard fingers, her lush dark lashes fell naturally to screen her eyes. When he turned her about so she was facing him, her breath caught in her throat and a heady excitement wedged it there. She felt herself sway involuntarily towards him, her face tilting up at a perfect angle to collide with his as it descended. Their mouths came together in a perfect blend of shape and size.

For a while after he had gone away, whilst still optimistic of him contacting her, Deborah had fantasised about the moment he would return to claim her. He would storm in and insist they waste no more time in becoming man and wife. Then he would kiss her with a courteous yet imperative passion that weakened her bones and made her feel as though molten honey raced through her veins. For those were the wonderful sensations she'd experienced at their friends' wedding reception. In a chilly, marble-flagged hallway, dressed in a flimsy silk bridesmaid's dress, he'd warmed her by fusing together their mouths and bodies until she'd felt she was burning with rapture.

But this was nothing like that magical memory! His mouth had moved on hers with a speed and force that startled her, as did the immediate touch of his tongue as it worked at her lips to prise them apart. When she resisted his probing and her face attempted to jerk free of his punishing assault, his hand sprang from her spine to her nape. Long pitiless fingers speared into her hair, curved on her scalp, preventing her evading him. His other hand caught at her chin so he might artfully manoeuvre her jaw apart and plunge his tongue within.

A mix of anger and humiliation made a small sob break in her throat, and immediately he let her go. Deborah heard the low oath that escaped him as he dropped his fists to his sides, then jammed them into his pockets.

'I'm sorry,' he gritted out. 'That was unforgivable of me.' He turned and in two rapid paces was at the door. 'Convey my sincere apologies to your mother,' Randolph sent over his shoulder. 'I regret I can't stay to dine this evening.'

'But you must stay!' Deborah reflexively cried through fingers that had sprung to soothe her bruised lips. 'My mother is expecting you to keep to your word,' she qualified her frustrated demand as he turned to blast a fearsome look at her. 'You promised you would again check the grounds for interlopers. If you go without doing so, she will be anxious and not get a wink of sleep.'

At that moment the woman Deborah was fretting over entered the room looking a picture of serenity, until she spied her guest so close to the exit.

'Are you leaving us, sir?' Julia asked, a trepidation trembling in her voice that validated her daughter's fears.

'Mr Chadwicke was about to go and find Basham and the flares so that he might go on watch.' Deborah's eyes were bright as stars as wordlessly she pleaded he at least oblige her with that small favour before he left them to fend for themselves.

'Oh, you need not go on patrol just yet, sir.' A happy sigh of relief escaped Julia. She clasped a hand on Randolph's elbow and urged him back into the room with her. 'I have told Basham we will eat before you venture again outside.' She shivered at the thought of the chilly autumn night air, and the reason their guest must endure it instead of remaining close to the fire. Randolph's arm received a pat that conveyed Julia's gratitude. 'Dinner will not be so long after all. Lottie took the initiative and conveyed to Mrs Field that a guest was expected to dine. Mrs Field—God bless her common sense—anticipated what I might choose to put on the menu. They have the meal already underway and Basham is lending a hand preparing the pheasant and duck, which he has a wont to do in any case. He is a real help in the kitchens at Yuletide. Do you like to shoot, sir?' Julia looked up at Mr Chadwicke. Finding his stern countenance turned in her daughter's direction, she swung a glance between the young couple. Finally it dawned on her that the atmosphere in the room was thick enough to slice. Julia studied her daughter, noticing her pallor and agitation as she clasped her quivering hands behind her back.

'Oh…you have not got a drink, sir,' Julia rattled off. 'I shall fetch you a brandy—'

'I shall get the decanter, Mama.' Deborah swiftly halted her mother's attempt to diplomatically depart. Her vivid eyes dropped away from a sardonic preying gaze. Gracefully she passed him with, 'I was just about to do so. Mr Chadwicke has only just let me know what it is he wants.'

Chapter Six

'What business brings you here to Sussex, Mr Chadwicke?' Julia asked conversationally whilst slicing in to a chunk of tender pheasant. She daintily chewed the morsel whilst awaiting his reply.

'Sheep, Mrs Woodville.'

'Sheep, sir?' Julia echoed, her mouth motionless whilst she digested that shocking information.

Deborah, too, was surprised on hearing his reason for being in the area. She ceased toying with her food and looked up and, for the first time since they'd started dinner, she allowed her eyes to be captured by his. Throughout the first course of pea-and-ham soup she'd been dodging an agate gaze that seemed to glitter at her through flickering candlelight. But she'd been acutely conscious of him seated opposite, at his ease, eating and conversing so pleasantly that she must have imagined that a few short hours ago he'd been so angry he'd been on the point of storming out of the house.

'The Kent Marshes have long been famous for the quality of the wool produced from hardy breeds of sheep,' Randolph started to explain. 'The animals I'm interested in seem to thrive in bleak conditions. They might suit the pastures close to the

Suffolk seaboard where I have property. The landscape is as flat and desolate as the salt marshes hereabouts and the climate in winter similarly harsh.'

Having listened to this information, Mrs Woodville still appeared to be rather startled by it. For a quarter of a century she'd lived a cocooned life in Mayfair as the wife of Gregory, Viscount Cleveland. When she'd remarried she'd found that her second husband possessed a more bluff character than her first. George Woodville had been a country squire born and bred, yet he'd still delegated most estate business to Basham.

Julia had known Randolph's parents years ago and had liked them very much. When his father had been killed in a carriage accident in early middle age, and Sebastian took the reins, nobody could have guessed what havoc he would wreak on the Buckland reputation and fortune. Randolph had always been a personable chap undeserving of the taint of his brother's existence. But unfortunately, when they'd lived in London and all were friends, his brother *did* exist. That connection meant Randolph had not been considered a worthy enough candidate for their only child's hand and, had he made a formal approach, they would have had to conquer the embarrassment of telling him so.

They had decided that intercepting any communication might be a relatively painless way of protecting their daughter from an alliance with a disreputable dynasty. On that matter Julia and Gregory had been in full agreement. Much as they'd liked Randolph, when his letters had arrived from the Indies they'd known for sure the reason Deborah had aborted her engagement to the Earl of Gresham. They'd had their suspicions for a while; one only had had to look at the two of them together to know where Deborah had settled her heart. But the thought of their beautiful, vivacious débutante daughter being sister-in-law to a fellow who had been known to cheat and lie and engage in all sort of devilish activity had been insupportable, especially when other men of wealth and standing had been offering for her following Marcus Speer's withdrawal.

However, Julia had continued to deem Randolph a nice enough fellow, and her expectation of him now was much as it would have been then: that he might be brought to a rural area to invest in land or property, not to attend a local cattle market.

'Well,' she said, raising her sparse eyebrows and looking a little lost for words, 'I would not have guessed you to hold farming so dear to your heart, sir.' She again turned her attention to her plate and set about a crisp roast potato. She encompassed her daughter in a little nod. 'Being town folk, we know little about livestock. You must excuse our ignorance.'

'I wouldn't expect either of you to hold a conversation on animal husbandry, Mrs Woodville.' Randolph smiled. 'I admit to having little expertise in the matter myself. Ordinarily my steward would deal with it. He is not well enough to travel at present and to undertake the task.'

'Is it vital you purchase these animals now, Mr Chadwicke?' Deborah probed, having listened and carefully considered what he'd said. 'Will the matter not wait for your steward's improvement?'

'It is important, yes,' he answered smoothly as he placed down his cutlery. Instead his fingers skimmed the fragile stem of his wine glass. 'Transporting and settling the ewes as soon as possible is best for successful spring lambing. And it is likely Roper will not improve. The physician thinks the lung disease might prove fatal.'

'I'm sorry to hear it. He is quite old?'

'No, he is quite young—just a few years older than myself, I'd say.' Randolph's lips moved in a vestige of a smile as he lifted his glass.

'Are you quite young?' Deborah queried with a hint of inso-
lence. 'I had you for older than Marcus...perhaps near forty.'

'I expect it's the hard life I've led that makes me appear de-
crepit at just thirty-five,' he mildly replied. He put the glass to
his lips and before sipping said, 'Whereas you, Miss Cleveland,
seem to have changed very little in seven years.'

'Perhaps not in appearance, sir...' Debbie returned sweetly, if
with significance. She sensed her mother's observation and shot
a glance sideways. The woman had picked up on the intimate
inflection in their conversation and was studying her from beneath her brows.

'Do you presently rear sheep on your estate?' Deborah reverted
to her line of questioning. She was like a dog worrying at a bone.
She wasn't sure why, but she felt disinclined to believe the tale
she'd just heard from him explaining his presence in Sussex. The
Randolph Chadwicke she recalled from years ago had been a
sophisticated urbanite, not a country dweller happy to roam far
and wide to inspect and purchase livestock. Neither did a gentleman of means usually undertake such tasks. He was dressed
smartly. His horse looked to be a magnificent thoroughbred. He
hardly appeared to be on his uppers and unable to despatch a
knowledgeable hireling to Kent to examine the local flocks if
his steward was too ill to fulfil his duty.

She had an idea of her own why he had travelled to the south
coast. If she were proved wrong in it, she must acknowledge
her conceit. Nevertheless she still gave credence to her theory
that he might have come to Sussex to find her. The mystery was
what she could possibly have done to stoke in him such enduring
vengefulness. Had he waited for seven long years, and for his
return to England, before finding out from Marcus her location
and setting out with an axe to grind?

The punishing kiss he'd forced on her earlier had confirmed

what she'd suspected from the first moment their eyes had collided in Hastings Upper Street: he was angry with her for a reason she could not fathom. Knowing she was innocent of deserving such treatment, it now angered her. Of the two of them she was the one entitled to claim to be the injured party over any past slights. Yet in time she had subdued her hurt over his abandonment and found a future husband in Edmund. Today, despite her shock at seeing him, she had striven to maintain a semblance of civility. So had he at first; and then, when they were alone in the parlour and his resentment and lust had got the better of him, he'd shown his true colours. The fact that afterwards he'd said he regretted doing so simply added to Deborah's suspicion that he was striving to maintain a façade.

Earlier, she'd brought the decanter of brandy to the parlour and handed it, and him, over to her mother's care. She knew that her mother's genuine fright about the possibility of Luckhurst returning, and Randolph's innate gallantry, would persuade him not to leave unfinished the task he'd promised to undertake. In order that no further friction could arise between them she'd excused herself by saying she would like to freshen her dress before dinner.

In the interim she'd had an hour or so to turn over in her mind what had occurred that day. She couldn't deny that he'd acted as her saviour on the walk home, or that he'd promptly and willingly gone to rout Seth Luckhurst from the grounds of Woodville Place. But despite his spontaneous protectiveness she'd still not managed to shake off her sense of disquiet about his motives in turning up at all.

At eight of the clock they had taken their places at the stately yew dining table. Thankfully Lottie had had the sense to set the places reasonably close and not scatter them to the corners of the vast polished board so they must squint at each other through candle flame and converse loudly or not at all.

When Randolph eventually answered her question, so mild was his tone, and so sunk in contemplation was she that Deborah simply blinked at him with deep blue eyes.

He smiled slightly as he reminded her of her enquiry. 'I believe you were asking whether my trip here was strictly necessary.' Randolph's eyes were narrowed, faintly amused. He was letting her know that he was aware she thought his motives dubious. 'I have some sheep, but their number was severely depleted last year when the sea wall was breached and a good deal were lost in the ensuing flooding.'

Deborah stuttered a mumbled commiseration and gave her plate her attention, busying herself with spearing a potato. He, too, carried on ostensibly enjoying his meal but she knew his eyes frequently settled on her whilst he ate and slowly she became more certain he'd sensed her suspicion.

Once she'd thought she knew Randolph Chadwicke well…well enough to want to marry and spend her life with him. Now he was a stranger—a man she found intriguing, but also unnerving. The notion that he might be here in Sussex because of her made her breath catch in her throat in dizzying excitement, yet at the same time a ripple of apprehension sprinkled ice along her spine.

'I believe I recall reading in the newspaper at the time about that natural disaster,' Julia burst out to terminate a lengthy silence. Her eyes skipped from her daughter's lowered profile to Randolph's saturnine features, half-covered by a slowly revolving crystal glass.

Randolph lowered his goblet to the table and, seeing his hostess staring at him, gave her a smile.

'How awful it must be to have one's land and property destroyed by the sea,' Julia carried on whilst a subtle glance begged a little assistance from her daughter.

'The marshes about Rye have flooded several times,' Deborah contributed. She'd understood her mother's tacit plea to lighten the atmosphere. She also didn't want Randolph to think that she doubted everything he'd said, or that he could intimidate her into keeping quiet. 'The locals still talk of a bad storm some hundred years or more ago when all was washed away for miles inland. The sea wall was breached on that occasion. You can clearly see where the massive waves marked the walls of the church and that stands on quite high ground.'

'Churches and other important buildings close to the coast were often built on manmade mounds in the hope they would escape the sea's vengeance.'

'Vengeance, sir?' Debbie echoed faintly.

'Salt marshes were once seabed. Some believe the sea will have back what man has stolen from it.' He picked up his glass and in a swallow emptied it.

'Shall we talk of something cheerful?' Mrs Woodville hastily intervened, once more attuned to the tension in the air. 'After dinner, and after you have kindly done your duty outside, sir...' it was a reminder softened with a coy smile '...we could play a game of cards. Or you could sing for us, Debbie. My daughter has a fine voice and can play the pianoforte tolerably well, too—'

'I don't think we should impose on Mr Chadwicke's time any longer than is necessary,' Deborah sharply interrupted. 'He has been delayed already and must want to return to his lodgings in Rye.' Her mother's next announcement made her soft lips spring apart in shock.

'Oh, but Mr Chadwicke must stay the night.' Julia frowned at her daughter as though chiding her for her lack of manners in not anticipating that. 'We cannot expect our guest to travel on at such an hour. I have already asked Basham and Lottie to prepare a guest chamber.'

'Thank you for your consideration, ma'am, but I should return to Rye this evening.' Randolph's voice was firm, his narrowed eyes fixed on Deborah's stricken countenance.

'But the villain might return in the early hours when we are asleep and murder us in our beds,' Julia hissed, low and fearful. She hadn't needed to give much thought to whether she'd sooner Randolph went on his way before a mention was made of his letters. She'd much rather he stayed and continued to protect them. Post from foreign lands was notoriously irregular. If he cared enough now to raise the matter, he and Deborah were sure to settle on a mundane explanation for the loss.

'Mama, you are overwrought,' Deborah interjected quickly. 'We have Basham and Fred to protect us in the unlikely event that a felon should try to break in.'

'Oh…Fred will be of no use!' Julia flapped a hand in disgust. 'He is in a fine old state. He has been fighting again. I saw him earlier creeping on tiptoe to the kitchens when he thought I might not spot him.' She snorted at the memory of the youth's derisory attempt to evade detection. 'I asked him how he'd got such a beating. He looked sorry for himself, I can tell you. Basham sent him off upstairs with a flea in his ear, then told me what had happened. It seems the blacksmith's daughter has been flirting with Fred although she's walking out with another young fellow. Naturally trouble ensued from it.'

'It's not Fred's fault…'

'It's not the first time this has happened.' Julia spoke fretfully over her daughter's defence. 'He has an eye for the girls. A few months ago he was in a brawl with another fellow over Lizzie Smith. Now he's fighting for her again. Perhaps we should let him go before he causes real trouble.'

'No.' Deborah pushed away her plate quite violently over polished wood. 'I know he had a scuffle in the village once before, but this time it was not his fault.' Deborah's eyes skimmed on Randolph's and she knew they were both thinking the same thing. Basham had tried to protect his mistress and his colleague by fibbing about how Fred acquired his injuries. Unwittingly the old retainer had worsened the situation. The last thing Fred deserved was to lose his job after his heroic defence of her. 'I know what went on and I can assure you that Fred did nothing wrong,' Deborah announced with finality.

'Well...even so...' Julia's words faded away and she looked quite taken aback by the vehemence in her daughter's voice. A beseeching glance at Randolph preceded her next words. 'I would be most obliged if you would stay just this one night, sir. We are women alone but for one able-bodied manservant. Basham is loyal and very willing, but he is no longer a young man.' Her voice quivered with anxiety and she pressed fidgeting fingers to her cheek. 'I should hate him to be crippled in defending us.'

'If it will ease your mind...and your daughter's...I will remain overnight.' Randolph's eyes fixed deliberately on Deborah for an answer.

When Julia saw the direction of his gaze she gave her daughter a surreptitious, emphatic nod designed to hurry her response in case he changed his mind.

'I think it unnecessary, but if you will sleep easier, Mama, I...'

'Well, that's settled, then,' Julia quickly said as her daughter's stilted agreement tailed off. 'Ah...good—pudding is arrived.' She pounced on the distraction of the arrival of another course.

Basham and Lottie had discreetly entered the room and begun loading the sideboard with sweet pastries, fruit and nuts and cheeses, together with dishes of creamy syllabub. Once they had unburdened their trays they approached the table and, with permission, started to take away the used crockery.

The meal was finished quite quickly. Deborah had lost her appetite; in fact, her insides had tilted on knowing that Randolph was to sleep under the same roof. But how could she deny him the offer of a bed for the night after all that he had done for them? She could hardly announce she thought he had designs on her virtue and might make a clandestine visit to her room in the early hours.

It seemed Randolph, too, had eaten his fill, for he politely declined anything else despite Julia's insistence that he try a blackcurrant tart.

'Perhaps a dish of syllabub,' Julia persevered, already rising from the table to fetch it from the sideboard.

'Thank you, but, no,' Randolph said before his hostess was fully on her feet. 'I have had more than enough and thank you for a fine dinner.' He pushed back his chair. 'If you both have no objection I shall go now and see if Basham is prepared to go on watch. I ought to call at the stables, too, to make sure that my horse is bedded down comfortably for the night. I might be gone a while.'

'Of course, sir,' Julia said. 'Good of you to show such concern for our safety,' she added humbly as though she'd never dreamed of pressurising him to do so.

As Randolph rose, bowed politely, then strolled to the door, Julia dug in to her dessert, avoiding her daughter's fierce glare.

'You must take some port when you return, Mr Chadwicke,' Julia called affably. 'It will warm you after the night air.'

'How could you do that, Mama?'

'Do what?' Julia asked innocently, savouring the syllabub on her lips.

The bow of Debbie's soft pink lips was lost to a tightly compressed line. After a moment she contained her anger well enough to splutter, 'Do you think it was seemly to ask Mr Chadwicke to stay the night?'

'I think it would have been unseemly not to have done so,' Julia answered tartly. 'The fellow has done us a very good turn in offering us his protection. You of all people should know how necessary it is to have a strong young man about the place. Have you forgotten how wicked and brutal are those Luckhursts and their cronies?'

'Of course I have not forgotten, Mama,' Deborah stressed in a ragged whisper. 'Nevertheless, it was unnecessary to make Mr Chadwicke remain here overnight. He has gone for the second time in a few hours to put your mind at rest that no villain is skulking outside. Are you expecting him to be at your disposal for the duration of his stay in the area?'

'Don't be silly...' Julia flushed. 'In any case, he doesn't mind.'

'I think he does mind...and so do I.'

'You are too wrapped up in yourself, miss.' Julia made her point with a silver spoon. 'It would do you good to think of me and my nerves once in a while.' She pushed away her half-eaten syllabub and put a hand to her forehead. 'The throb has started,' she whispered weakly. 'I shall need to lie down before I get giddy.' A moment later she was midway to the door with a remark tossed over a shoulder. 'Once you were friends with Mr Chadwicke. I find it hard to believe that you cannot bear to entertain him for just one evening so we might sleep easier in our beds.'

'Where are you off to, Mama?' Deborah threw her napkin on to glossy wood and stood up. She knew her mother suffered with migraines, but she doubted that this was a genuine malaise.

'I am going to bed.' Julia sighed. 'If I take a draught I might get to sleep before I start to feel quite poorly.' She tottered about by the door. 'When Mr Chadwicke returns, offer him my goodnights and a nightcap of port or brandy. It is the least he deserves.' She opened the door, then hesitated as another thought occurred to her. 'Don't go off too soon, Deborah, and leave the fellow twiddling his thumbs with only a decanter for company. If he gets too deep in his cups, he'll be no good to us if the Luckhursts come back.'

Julia had remembered that as young bucks about town Randolph Chadwicke, Marcus Speer and many of their chums had had rackety reputations. Many a scandalous rumour had started over the amount of wine and women they'd got through. 'Perhaps you might enjoy a game or two of piquet, to while away the time,' Julia suggested.

'Yes, of course, Mama,' Deborah muttered beneath her breath at a closing door.

Chapter Seven

'He won't be back, not alone anyhow,' Basham announced knowledgeably, raising his flare so he might take a peer about at murky shrubbery. 'Likes o' Seth Luckhurst don't do fair fights. That one'll want henchmen around him 'fore he gets in a tough tangle. Coward, he is. Bully, too. His brother's a bit different. More his own man, if you know what I mean. But vicious and wicked as sin the two of 'em are, and they like to let us all know it.' He swept a sideways look up and down Randolph's powerful physique. His eyes returned to linger on a shadowy profile outlined against the night sky. A sliver of moon and a flickering flame had carved his visage to eerily planed angles of light and shade. It was as though the fellow hadn't heard, nor cared, for a word he'd said about the local villains who could terrorise on a whim.

For the second time that day Basham's nape prickled as he sensed a strange menace about this reticent gentleman, poised still and silent beside him. He was listening, he realised, like a nocturnal animal might when it's on the prowl. 'Seth got to meet you earlier, didn't he, when you escorted Miss Woodville home?'

A single nod answered Basham. Randolph's narrowed eyes

remained on an impenetrable darkness that lay beyond the pool of gold in which they stood.

'Mark my words, sir, Seth won't be back on his own, not if he's got it into his head to do mischief. Let's hope he ain't—'

'You take the southern side and I'll go towards the north boundary,' Randolph interrupted Basham's one-sided dialogue. Tilting the flare so it illuminated a few yards of grass, he quit the stone-flagged terrace and set off at a stroll in the direction of the yew hedge.

So…he had been spotted trespassing earlier that afternoon, Seth Luckhurst realised as he watched the two disembodied lights gliding on opposite sides of the garden. He'd thought he'd glimpsed the widow watching him from a window and, as he'd slipped away back to the village, had heard men's voices in the distance and wondered whether his presence had brought the stranger and some servants outside to investigate.

Seth's fleshy lips curled as he watched the glow on his left go behind the yew hedge. If the stranger was behind that torch, Seth reckoned he'd been right about him from the start. He was just a foppish fool who thought his quarry was an idiot too. Only a dunderhead would return to loiter in the same place as before. As the crescent moon was lost to cloud he peered into blackness; both flares had disappeared and he slunk a little further behind the stout trunk of the oak on the fringe of woodland. Behind him he could hear the sound of the stream as it tumbled over rocks and rushed to feed the river.

Earlier that day, after his run in with the fellow who called himself Chadwicke, Seth had sent his cronies on their way, then turned back to lie in wait at Woodville Place. He'd hoped Miss Woodville's escort might drop her off at the top of the drive and give him a chance to ambush her before she entered the house.

But not only had Chadwicke taken her to her door, he'd gone in with her too. Obviously they were acquainted and Seth guessed they'd met before in London. He knew a bit about Deborah Woodville's past: that she'd been a fine lady who'd lived in a fancy house until her rich father had died.

Seth's lust for Deborah Woodville had been steadily mounting for some years. In fact, he'd had a fancy for the uppity wench from the first time that he'd set eyes on her shopping with her mother in Hastings. They'd been new to the area and he'd made it his business to find out about her. But he'd been sensible enough to know not to interfere with a woman under the protection of an influential pillar of the local community. After Squire Woodville's death his stepdaughter had got betrothed to a dragoon and, again, Seth knew that it would be suicidal to draw the wrath of the militia down on his own and his brother's heads by going after her with every intention of tumbling her.

When the betrothal was announced, he had mentioned to his brother that he had a yen for the Woodville girl. His brother had then impressed on him, very painfully, that she was out of bounds and he should continue to relieve himself with the local tavern jades. Zack had also scoffed with much uproarious hilarity that Deborah Woodville was a fine lady from Mayfair and way out of his league. Seth had known that was true, but her angelic looks and haughty way simply increased his need to bring her down.

Apart from her lovely face and lush body there was another reason why Seth had an itch where Deborah Woodville was concerned: she needed to be taught a lesson. The piquancy of quenching his lust whilst simultaneously disciplining her made his loins heat and throb with anticipation. Since her fiancé, Edmund Green, had been killed, she'd been a thorn in the side of every smuggler.

Just that afternoon he'd found out that she'd demanded a

warrant be issued for his arrest because he'd beaten her driver. She'd caused trouble in the past with her accusations, but never had she gone this far in speaking out against them to the authorities. Luckily the magistrate had known not to stir trouble for him. Even the local judiciary could be persuaded not to upset the smuggling brethren.

Seth had come back tonight not to spy on her, but to see if the stranger was still a guest of the Woodvilles. He'd told Zack what had gone on that afternoon, expecting some support and loyalty from his brother. What he'd got was a beating for not heeding Zack's warning to keep away from the Woodvilles. He'd returned here from the village with a bruised jaw and a burning need to know more about the fancy cove who called himself Randolph Chadwicke.

The slight sound behind made Seth twist about, but he was too late to dodge the snaking hand that gripped ferociously at his throat and slammed his skull against bark, knocking him out.

Icy water brought him coughing and spluttering to his senses. He tried to escape it plunging into his stinging nostrils, but couldn't move his head more than an inch. After a moment he realised that the weight on his neck, holding him face down in the stream, came from a man's booted foot.

'You're making a habit of annoying me, Seth Luckhurst,' Randolph said quietly, 'and it has to stop.'

Seth bucked and wriggled to escape the pressure on his neck. He bared his teeth in fury and mortification for he was as helpless as a speared fish. His show of defiance did nothing but fill his gaping mouth with freezing water. He coughed and choked and floundered about.

'Let me up,' Seth spluttered. 'I'll kill you; I swear it. Let me up…I'm drowning.'

'I want you to stay away from Miss Woodville and her home. Do you understand?' The callous force on Seth's neck had intensified, as had the soft savagery in Randolph's voice.

'You're drowning me,' Seth bubbled, with mounting hysteria.

'Do you understand?' Randolph repeated.

Seth wobbled his head about.

'I can't hear you.'

'Yes!' Seth screamed in a gurgle.

Randolph lithely stooped and gripped the back of the man's sodden collar, hauling him upright. He easily evaded Seth's wildly swinging fists and rammed him, gasping and squirming, against the oak behind which he'd hidden.

'If I find out you've been here trespassing again, or making a nuisance of yourself anywhere in the vicinity of Miss Woodville or her mother, or any of her servants, you'll wish very much that I'd let you drown just now. Do you understand?'

Seth tried to lift his face up and away from where bark dug painfully in to an already bruised cheek, but the brutal fingers tightened on his neck so he could do no more than croak an agreement through his crushed windpipe.

Randolph let him go and stepped back a pace. Immediately Seth whipped about, his lips drawn back against his teeth in a bestial snarl, his fists primed.

Randolph looked untroubled by the risk of an imminent attack. 'I see somebody's already given you a lesson recently,' he said with muted amusement as he spotted the bruise that ran the length of Seth's jaw. 'Was it Zack?'

'What do you know about Zack?' Seth spat with a mix of sullenness and suspicion, his fists dropping a fraction.

'More importantly, what do you know about me, Seth Luckhurst?' Randolph returned. 'I suspect the answer to that is nothing or you wouldn't be here putting me to this bother.

Unfortunately I haven't the time or inclination to presently rectify your ignorance. In time you'll find out and you should heed very well what you hear about me.'

Seth shook his shaggy head to clear water from dripping into his eyes. The moon escaped its cover and he blinked rapidly, staring at the granite features of the tall man standing poised to strike at any time. Despite his elegant clothes and his cool correctness he didn't seem like a dandy from a drawing room now. With some alarm Seth finally accepted that he was in the presence of a deadly opponent and that if he made an aggressive move he'd be punched pitilessly to the ground.

As shocked comprehension began to drop Seth's sore jaw towards his barrel chest, Randolph gave him a sour smile. 'So, perhaps you've guessed a little bit about me. Unfortunately it's true. So be off with you before I change my mind about being lenient.' Randolph gave an idle dismissing flick of his head. 'And heed well what I've said. Don't ever come back here if you value your life.'

'Are you a free-trader?'

'Let's leave explanations for another day. I've told you where to find me. In case you've forgotten, I'm staying at the Woolpack in Rye. Now get on your way.'

Instinctively Seth moved to obey, then stopped when he realised his mistake. A moment later inquisitiveness overcame caution. 'What's Miss Woodville to you?' He jerked a nod at the house. 'She hates all smugglers. A dragoon she was about to marry was murdered by one of us.'

'Which one of you?'

'Ah, now, that'd be telling,' Seth said with a sly squint.

'I'd like you to tell me.' The gleam of menace in Randolph's eyes belied the lazy humour in his voice. He took a step forwards.

'Snowy, he was called. It got took care of before the search for him started and dragoons started banging on doors,' Seth quickly supplied. 'You can't be her kin; if you were, she'd have nothing to do with you if I'm right in thinking you a free-trader. So if you're not related, what is she to you?' he dared to ask.

'Miss Woodville is under my protection, as are all the people she cares about. That's all you need to know.' Randolph's eyes were a hawkish gleam between narrowed lids.

Still Seth stared at him as though he was ruminating on what he'd been told to make sense of it.

'Let me simplify it for you,' Randolph drawled on a skewed smile. 'She's mine. Do you understand me now, Luckhurst?'

A leer contorted Seth's scowl, but he was unable to completely conceal his frustration. Every time he thought the haughty beauty was becoming vulnerable, and he might have a chance to have her, a fellow appeared to give her shelter. But this was no regular arrangement with rings on fingers. He knew what Chadwicke meant now—the lucky dog was slyly bedding the little wanton. And her so high and mighty and looking like butter wouldn't melt in her mouth.

'Be off, then, before I give you the beating you deserve.' Randolph made another languid advance.

Seth matched his movement with spontaneous aggression before he remembered… With puffed chest he swaggered past and disappeared into the woodland.

Randolph rubbed a thumb over a bruised knuckle and pulled in mild irritation at his cuffs on realising they were dripping wet. He shook his hands to dry them, then plunged his fists in to his pockets. His head dropped back to study the stars through a canopy of dry, whispering leaves. He stood quietly like that for some moments until he heard twigs cracking beneath clumsy running feet and a corner of his mouth tugged into a grim smile. He turned back towards the house, collecting the torch from behind the yew hedge as he went.

'Thought I heard a noise coming from the woods,' Basham puffed out as he came towards Randolph at a limping jog. 'Got here quick as I could, sir.' Basham swerved a look past Randolph's tall figure. He squinted warily at the looming fringe of trees in the distance as though he expected a marauding horde might burst forth. He then glanced up at the face of the fellow standing at his ease in front of him. Mr Chadwicke had come from that direction. If he'd had a run in with somebody in the woods, he'd obviously come off best and hadn't needed any help whatsoever. He looked as cool and unruffled as he had when they'd set out on watch over an hour ago. 'Was there anybody about, sir?' Basham blurted, but less stressfully.

'Whoever it was has run off.' Randolph started across the lawns with Basham trotting unevenly in his wake. 'He turned tail quickly.'

'Well, if it was Luckhurst, he wouldn't want that getting out, that's for sure.' Basham chuckled. 'Thinks himself a champ, does that one. But as I said before he's a coward when push comes to shove.' After a pause to get his breath, Basham resumed, 'If it was a fellow out on his own, and he scarpered real quick, it was probably a poacher. I've had to scare a few away this past fortnight. Since the master's been gone we don't shoot or fish as much as we used to.' He sucked in a breath and slowed to a walk whilst casting a jaundiced eye on the fellow covering the ground in a deceptively lazy pace. With a sigh Basham speeded up again to a hobbling run. 'Place is teeming with wildlife now we don't have the shooting parties we once had,' he carried on. 'Of course, the chance to snaffle a few brace of pheasant 'n' hare draws the poachers time 'n' again—'

'No doubt you're right about it being a poacher,' Randolph

interrupted Basham as he started up the stone steps. 'I know the fellow was by the stream. Perhaps he fancied doing a bit of night fishing…'

A hint of dry humour in Mr Chadwicke's words caused Basham to tilt his head to get a better look at his profile and see what amused him.

'It might be wise to say nothing to your mistress about a poacher,' Randolph cautioned. 'Mrs Woodville is already upset about what occurred this afternoon. There's no point in worrying her again needlessly.'

Basham looked thoughtful at that. He knew this fellow would soon be gone. If Mrs Woodville got a bee in her bonnet that someone was seriously snooping about the place, he'd be sent out alone tomorrow evening, and probably every evening for the rest of the week. Basham rubbed nervously at the bridge of his nose. As Mr Chadwicke said, no need to say anything and worry the ladies unnecessarily.

Chapter Eight

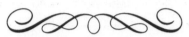

'Have you been waiting up for me?'

Deborah blinked in incomprehension as a shadowy masculine face close to hers shimmied out of focus. Her eyelids felt cumbersome but she forced them to again lift so she might properly see him. Through the fog in her mind she remembered moments ago a touch on her cheek and realised that his brushing fingers had brought her to her senses. She struggled to sit straight in the fireside chair where she'd drifted into slumber. Her warm, curled position, with her legs tucked under her, was too comfortable to be completely abandoned. The glow in the grate had already made her complexion rosy; now its bloom deepened. How long had he been watching her sleeping before he'd stroked her awake?

'Will you go to bed now if I promise to go and sleep in the stables?'

'What? No…you…you must not do that!' Deborah garbled, pressing her knuckles to her eyes. 'You have been invited to stay the night, sir.' Her words seemed awkward to eject, her tongue clumsy in her arid mouth.

'That doesn't answer my question, Deborah,' Randolph softly

said. 'I know you'd sooner I was miles away. Can you deny you hoped I'd return to Rye tonight?'

Indeed she could not, but never would she admit to it. He'd again done her and her mother a very good turn. Repaying him with honesty was beyond her breeding. Her intelligence was still dulled by sleep, so she shied away from participating in a verbal duel and settled instead on ignoring his challenge.

'You were a long while,' she murmured whilst a few unsteady fingers raked back pale tangles from her brow. 'Was there something suspicious that needed investigation?'

'You've nothing to fear. If I understand the likes of Luckhurst, he'll be about now in the local tavern.'

'Do you understand the likes of him?' Deborah frowned and a bleary blue gaze was raised to his face.

'Yes…I understand him.'

'He might instead be on the beach collecting kegs.' Deborah sighed sleepily, feeling reassured by his indolent attitude.

'True…he might be up to his nefarious activities,' Randolph concurred with half a smile.

After her mother had gone to bed Deborah had asked Lottie to direct Mr Chadwicke to the parlour when he returned from outside, after which duty the maid had permission to go to bed.

When an hour had passed, and no sign of him, she hadn't known whether to feel indignant or relieved at the possibility that he might have chosen to be shown to the guest chamber rather than join her in the parlour. Having decided to tarry just ten minutes more for him and give him the benefit of the doubt, Deborah had taken a few fortifying sips of port to liven her up; she had begun to feel quite light-headed with fatigue. Unfortunately the alcohol had had the opposite effect and the last thing she recalled was a cosy contentment settling on her as she watched the slowly swaying pendulum on the wall clock opposite. She stared at it again now as it chimed eleven times. She had dozed for almost an hour.

'My bedchamber faces the woods. Sometimes I see the lights moving in the trees when contraband is coming ashore,' she told him, smothering a small yawn with slender fingers.

'There's nothing out there now to worry you. Apart from an owl hooting, everything is quiet and still.'

'An owl?' A slight shiver undulated through Deborah and her fist, rubbing at her eyes, fell to her lap.

'Does an owl bother you?' he asked, gently amused. Slowly he moved a hand to her face to remove the persistent curl that again had flopped forwards to corkscrew on her lashes.

'Of course not.' She gave a tiny diffident smile. 'But Basham has told me a bit about local history. The smugglers of old— owlers, they were named—would use the call of the owl as a signal. I expect some still do.'

'It's not very original or secret then,' he remarked wryly.

'No…but…'

'It was definitely an owl,' he reassured her with a finger brushing against a soft pink cheek. 'It was sitting watching me from a tree and looking very wise too.'

He was still crouching down in front of her chair, his face level with hers, mere inches separating them. From beneath a curtain of inky lashes she noticed that his tawny eyes, half-concealed behind his lids, had dropped to her slightly parted mouth. He looked quite wise, too, she realised with a thrill of alarm, and able to swoop as quickly as could that owl. Quickly she brought together her lips and turned her head towards the port bottle and glass. The table was still between the two chairs, positioned precisely where she had left it earlier that day when she had served him tea.

'My mother has gone to bed with a headache, but has asked me to convey her thanks and her goodnights to you,' she announced breathily. 'Also she'd like to offer you a nightcap to warm you.' Now her faculties were reviving Deborah could sense the fresh scent of frost that clung to his clothes. She sent a darting glance sideways at him and with clearer vision noticed that the raw night air had stolen colour from his tanned complexion, and made lank the long, fawn hair that trailed on his high collar.

'You look chilled, sir,' she said with husky concern. 'You should take some port and warm yourself by the fire.'

In a fluid motion he stood up and a few paces brought him to the hearth. He held his palms towards the meagre flames and with the toe of a damp boot stirred a little more life into the smouldering embers. A log was selected from the pile and pitched on to fledgling flames.

'Are you tolerating my company to please your mother?'

'Have you heard of the owlers?' Deborah asked, ignoring his harsh demand. She was more mentally alert now and didn't intend to allow any leading questions to draw them into a passionate dispute. With a hand still weak from sleep she upended the weighty bottle of port. Glass and bottle clattered clumsily together, drawing his attention. An instant later long fingers had sprung to cover hers, steadying them, before the rocking goblet toppled over.

A soft cry of dismay escaped her and she twisted on her knees on the seat so she might quickly attend to the blood-red droplets she'd caused to spatter the mahogany.

Randolph extracted a linen handkerchief from a pocket and dried her stained fingers before he let it drift on to the spillage.

He had squatted down in front of her chair again and watched her until she capitulated and allowed her eyes to be dragged to his golden gaze.

'I know I acted like a lecherous brute earlier today, but you've nothing to fear from me, Deborah. I swear it won't happen again. Nevertheless, I think it best I sleep in the stables.' He smoothed the satiny skin of her wrist, soothing her quivering. 'It's as much for my benefit as yours,' he added with a rueful smile at his caressing thumb.

'There is no need to go outside, sir, I have a lock on my door,' Deborah artlessly rattled off whilst dabbing at spilled port with her free hand.

'And every intention of using it tonight, I'm sure,' Randolph muttered sardonically. A mirthless sound grazed his throat, then he lifted her fingers, skimming her warm knuckles against his cool lips. Swiping the bottle and glass from the table, he came upright in a fluid movement, casually pouring a measure of port as he did so. In a swallow he despatched it and the glass and bottle found the mantelpiece in a thump. A double-handed grip enclosed the marble edge before he shoved himself back and turned to face her. 'There…your duty's done,' he said with hard irony. 'You've waited up, thanked me, given me a drink and as I imagine a goodnight kiss is out of the question…what else is there?'

'I'll have Lottie wash this for you tomorrow.' Deborah kept her face averted as, done with mopping, she carefully folded the stained linen. His gentle amusement on having found her asleep was obviously evaporating and a stronger emotion was taking its place, causing him to be sarcastic.

'It's not important,' Randolph said roughly and started for the door.

'Where are you off to?' Deborah rose up on her knees and twisted about on the seat to watch him. 'You surely can't really intend to spend the night outside.'

'Why not? I've done so before. Straw makes a reasonable bed.'

'But you can't!' she cried and emphasised her indignation by thumping the back of the chair with a small fist. 'Do you know how upset my mother will be if you do that? How insulted she will feel if you spurn her hospitality and choose to bed down with the horses?' With a hint of desperation she offered, 'I should like it if the evening ends more appropriately. You were offered a little entertainment after dinner. It is not too late for a game of cards, if you would like...'

'Or you could sing for me,' Randolph suggested. Pivoting about, he sent a frustrated look up at the ceiling. 'Your mother said you have a sweet voice. A bedtime lullaby might be nice. God knows I could use a little soothing from you, Deborah.'

She knew the savage mockery in his tone had been directed more at himself than at her. She sensed, too, that he was suffering from an exasperation that equalled her own inner writhing. He had questions he wanted to launch at her just as she had some she wanted to fire his way. But it had been a frantic day and she knew she needed to refresh her mind with rest before embarking on a conversation that was sure to be punctuated by bitterness. She didn't want to regret her impatience, or her ineptitude, tomorrow when accusations were aired—as surely they would be—that begged answers and apologies. She understood that he was restricting himself to barbed hints for the same reason. They both were unwilling to yet attack the thorny subject of their past. Seven years, interspersed for them both, Deborah supposed, with episodes of happiness and heartache, now distanced the young people who once had ardently kissed on their friends' blissful wedding day from the people they were now.

'As you don't want diversion then I shall go to bed.' Deborah sighed in defeat and sank back on to her heels in readiness to get up.

'I didn't decline everything,' he drawled, an amused glitter far back in his eyes. 'But I'll forgo the game of cards.'

It was not hard to guess his meaning. Deborah's small, pearly teeth sank into her lower lip, as much to stifle a retort that he seemed to quickly have forgotten his promise to curb his lechery as to stop its quiver. She knew that, in part, she'd invited such a remark in not choosing her words more carefully; she knew, too, it was his intention to try to provoke her with his innuendos. She might be a genteel spinster, but she could counter his ironic suggestiveness. 'If you're asking for a performance, sir, I think you should reconsider. My mother tends to greatly overstate my talents.' She gave him a tight little smile. 'Far from soothing you, my lack of skill might have an unnerving effect.'

'I'll risk it to have you stay a while longer with me. I'm sure eventually we'll find something mutually enjoyable to do.'

'I'd sooner retire at once than risk disappointing you, sir,' Deborah returned with faux sweetness, but a twitch of her lips betrayed her incipient smile. Years ago they would banter like this. She could tell from his subtle smile he, too, was recalling those arousing contests whilst dancing, walking, as though quite alone, despite their accompanying friends. Then she had been a debutante, an heiress protected from a serious seduction by her youthful innocence. Of course, he'd held her in respect and affection too. By his own admission it was only later he'd realised he'd misjudged his feelings for her. Now it was different. No misconceptions or mitigations remained and that brutal kiss earlier was an indication that he'd deal quite ruthlessly with her in any sensual game.

Their eyes locked across the few yards of heady atmosphere separating them. She'd stopped him leaving, but what now? Deborah knew, despite his promise, that with just a tiny encouragement he'd breach the space and touch her again. Perhaps he might find that soothing, but she knew she would not. The thought of enduring another callous assault made her tongue tip moisten her lips as though she anticipated such balm being soon needed.

Randolph's eyes tracked the circling movement on her full pink lips. A tug at the corner of his mouth acknowledged that he understood her anxiety and the reason for the solid wall of tension building between them.

'Go to bed,' he said hoarsely as he approached. He passed her chair to snatch up the port bottle from the mantelpiece and pour a measure.

Deborah sat back on her heels to watch him as he slumped down in the chair opposite. Negligently he thrust one long leg out whilst the other foot tapped impatiently against the boards close to the chair. He upended the goblet before twirling the empty vessel idly by its fragile stem. A moment later he was up again and refilling his glass at the mantelpiece.

'Go to bed Deborah. Sleep well.'

He hadn't turned about to give his goodnight, but she realised he would know by the sound of the door closing behind her that he was alone.

'I shall sleep very well, I assure you,' she responded, but for a reason she could not fathom refused to be dismissed. She stayed exactly where she was.

'Good…I'll envy you your rest and your sweet dreams,' he murmured drily, his eyes on the glass's balletic dance as it spun between his fingers.

Still she was reluctant to go and scoured her mind for something, anything to say. 'Our guest chamber is comfortable. Why should you not sleep well?' She had tilted her head to get a better view of his impassive profile. Suddenly a draught rattled the sashes as though ghostly beings sought entry. Her eyes were drawn to the casement cosily covered by closed curtains. A shiver rippled through her as the timbers trembled again and gave vent to a wordless whispering.

The sinister sound had drawn her mind to danger. That in turn caused a sudden notion to send Deborah's insides tumbling and her heart hammering. She'd imagined he might have been hinting that his desire for her would keep him restless; perhaps she flattered herself too readily. 'Do you think you will need to keep alert tonight…in case…of trouble?'

'I told you there's nobody out there, Deborah.' He put down the glass and turned to face her. 'Go to bed.'

A quiver undulated through Deborah that now had nothing to do with the wind sobbing through the sashes' cracks and crevices. The numbing effect of her catnap had completely dispersed. She cast her mind back to dissect what he'd said when she'd asked him what he'd found outside. Now that she concentrated on his answer, she concluded that it could have been ambiguous.

'Did you see someone out there earlier?' she asked with earnest directness. His silence made her demand, 'Please tell me! If you will not, then Basham will. I shall go and find him.'

'And rouse him from his bed for no reason?'

'You haven't actually confirmed that nobody was prowling around in the grounds after dark,' she retorted in exasperation.

Swiftly he came to her chair and squatted in front of it. 'Do you think me a liar, Deborah?' He dropped his face towards his clasped hands. 'I have said I'm going to Kent to buy sheep and I've also said that there's no risk to your safety tonight. Do you believe me?'

'Say he wasn't out there.' With impulsive audacity a small hand spanned his shady chin and jerked it up. 'You saw Seth Luckhurst, didn't you? Didn't you?' Stormy sapphire eyes scoured his features as though she might read the truth there if he would not utter it.

He held her eyes with a studied lack of expression until hers darted away and her palm, too, sprang away from the skin abrading it. Her gaze suddenly focused on the wet cuff of his jacket. It was positioned on a breeched knee and was discolouring the buff twill beneath it. Her small palm curved over the damp sleeve, feeling its clammy coldness infiltrate her flesh. A blemish on his knuckles, where tiny beads of blood had welled beneath the skin, drew her eyes. Taken together they were suspicious signs of some harm having recently befallen him. The graze looked to be fresh and unattended, and his apparel, apart from his boots and cuffs, looked to be dry.

Randolph stood slowly, but Deborah wasn't done with him yet. As he moved away a pace she snatched at his dark digits. They were raised so she might inspect the damage to his fingers. It was indeed a new injury and she flung away his hand and clashed questioning eyes on his sidelong, lupine gaze. He returned to the chair opposite and again sat down.

Determined to have her answer, Deborah scrambled to get a foot to the floor and this time go over to him. Immediately she put weight on to those toes, and a soft cry escaped her. Deadened by her having sat curled up for so long, the foot twisted and she stumbled back against the chair arm. Pins and needles shot fierily along her veins, making it feel as though she were attempting to balance on jelly.

Randolph was out of the chair and had closed the space between them in a single stride. He caught at her arm to give her support and steady her.

'I fear I have been curled up on this chair for too long,' she said bashfully. A grimace slanted her lips as she once more tested her weight on her foot. She accepted that staying to interrogate him further would be foolish. At the moment Luckhurst—drat him—seemed the least of her troubles. The throb in her foot was worsening. 'I will bid you goodnight, sir.' She made to pass him, but it was as though she trod on air. She hopped a step, wincing as she tried to keep her tender ankle off the floor. A muted gasp of frustration cluttered her throat as she again swayed towards the chair for support. Before her snatching hands could gain purchase on the upholstered wings, she was swept off her feet and was being carried towards the door.

'I can walk, sir,' Deborah gasped in alarm when she had regained sufficient breath to do so. 'Please put me down at once.'

'I think you've just shown you can't walk, let alone climb stairs.' A sultry amber gaze bathed her face. 'But it is high time for you to get to bed. Better that than we bicker until dawn light.' Randolph slid forwards the hand beneath her thighs so he that might grasp the door handle. Ignoring her suffocated plea that he let her go, he'd soon covered half the distance to the stairs, Deborah wriggling for liberation in his grip.

'No…please…somebody might see,' she mouthed urgently against his ear as he started up the treads so quickly that she might have been feather-light. Her small hands clutched the solid muscle of his arm, digging in as though she could force him to do her bidding. When she gained nothing by spearing ten nails into the superfine wool covering a powerful bicep, she again hissed, 'Please…put me down!'

'Right or left?' he asked softly.

Her appealing gaze earned her nothing but a ruthless smile.

'Right or left at the top?' he repeated, low and vibrant. 'I'm not going to set you down halfway up, Deborah. You might topple over and crash to the bottom. That would bring your mother running, no doubt about it.'

She knew then that he'd not be deterred from carrying her

to her chamber. Her heart was thundering and she was sure he must feel it beneath that warm hand that was nudging the curve of a tender breast. Causing a noise by arguing with him was unthinkable, and he knew it—the sound of raised voices was sure to bring everyone out to investigate. She clamped together her lips in frustration. If they remained quiet they were sure to go unobserved. It was almost midnight. Her mother had gone upstairs hours ago and the draught she'd taken had probably sent her immediately to sleep. Lottie would by now have retired, as would Mrs Field. Basham and Fred would be in their quarters, too, at this time of night.

He'd stopped at the top and she knew he was waiting for her instruction. 'Right,' Deborah admitted in an angry mutter. Her mother's chamber was only yards away. He swung that way with a speed that was unsettling—deliberately so, Debbie imagined, as she found it necessary to snake her arms around his neck. She rammed her face against his shoulder to stifle a hiss of shock at his sudden manoeuvre and pointed to a door halfway along the corridor.

Slowly Randolph removed the arm beneath her thighs, but the other retained its clasp about her waist. Slowly she slid against his body, held fast with her feet just inches from the floor and her back to her chamber door. He let her drop down another inch so that her toes tentatively touched the rug.

'Does it still hurt?' a husky voice asked.

The sensation of his hot, hard body pressed intimately against hers stole away her breath. She gulped and set one foot down, then the other. Bravely she tried to ignore a twinge felt in her left foot. It was certainly less painful than previously it had been.

'Thank you, I can manage now,' she murmured. She glanced up into a shadowy face and what she read there made one of her hands slip behind her back so she might quickly let herself into her room. Her searching fingers closed over warm flesh and she realised he'd got to the door handle first.

'You will find your bedchamber is in the opposite direction. It is to the left at the head of stairs.' The directions were ejected in an unsteady whisper. 'It is about halfway along the corridor and you will know it by a portrait of a wolfhound hanging by the door. I hope you will use it and not insult us by sleeping in the stables.'

Randolph's fingers slipped about capturing hers, and he took their entwined hands to the small of her back, forcing her away from the door and against him. She glared up at him. He smiled down at her. He was daring her to make a noise and arouse attention. He had her just where he wanted her, she realised. The throbbing heat of his arousal was against her abdomen, his solid thighs merging with the softness of her curvy hips. He could do whatever he would to her now and she must allow it or cause a scene.

As his face approached Deborah felt mesmerised, unable to avoid or welcome the inexorable touch of his lips on hers. Her eyes closed as silky smooth warmth caressed her lips in a goodnight kiss that was unexpectedly sweet and unexpectedly brief.

'Don't forget to lock your door.' The dry advice drifted back to her as he shoved his hands in his pockets and strolled away.

Chapter Nine

Dawn light was filtering through a chink in her curtains when Deborah finally managed to fall into a doze. But she'd been curled cosily on her side, gratefully sinking into oblivion, for only minutes when she was jerked to wakefulness by a noise from outside. She blinked rapidly at the stripe of colour on her bedroom wall, put there by the blush on the eastern horizon. A moment later she'd rolled on to her back and was staring at the ceiling.

He was leaving, just as she'd guessed he might as soon as the sun began to rise on a new day. He had fulfilled his promise to stay the night and was now free to go on his way.

Last night when finally she had got into bed—having first dragged a brush through her tangled curls and a tepid washing cloth over her face and hands—she had very much hoped sleep would immediately overtake her. But too much excitement had occurred in one day and chaotic thoughts continued to circle in her mind, denying her the rest she craved.

After Randolph had left her by her door she'd gone within and stared at the heavy black iron key in the lock before turning it with trembling fingers. For some moments she had remained there, her eyes closed as she savoured the sensation of his mouth caressing hers far too briefly. She had wanted more, had felt his loss as soon as he'd unsealed their lips. She suspected it had been his intention to deliberately torment her with a little taste of the seductive sweetness he could bestow, if he chose to.

Whilst lying quiet and still in bed, her mouth still pulsing from his kiss, Debbie had listened intently for him to retire. He hadn't used the guest chamber. There had been no soft click of a door closing along the corridor. But neither had he gone outside to the stables as he'd said he might. She'd been equally convinced of that. He had, she imagined, done his duty by returning to the parlour and the port bottle, to pass five hours by the dying embers of the fire.

There came an unmistakable clop of hooves on cobbles to distract her reflection. She tensed, straining to listen, and heard the heavy snorting breath of a horse. What did she care if he left without saying goodbye? Let him go…

She threw back the covers. In a trice she had darted to the window to peer towards the stable block.

Basham was up and dressed early, too, but it was the tall distinguished figure standing with their manservant who drew Deborah's gaze. She drew back the curtain a fraction so she might get a better view of him.

He had on the long leather riding coat that he'd worn yesterday when first she'd seen him in Hastings. Something he'd said to Basham made the old retainer grin broadly, then Randolph swung easily into the saddle. The magnificent stallion looked to have spent a peaceful night, even if its master had not. The beast pranced and circled energetically and Deborah pushed the curtain back further, craning her neck to get a last glimpse of him as the spirited animal took him out of sight. He might have immediately set off along the avenue to take the road east to Rye. But he'd controlled his mount and brought it back to the stables.

Whilst patting the bay's strong, sleek neck he turned his head and quite deliberately took a look up at her window. She knew he'd seen her, and that it would be better to stand still than attempt to scramble aside and confirm her excruciating embarrassment. That would amuse him. When he continued to stare at her she felt her face blazing. She raised her hand a little as though she might wave and brazen it out. Had she not, of course, risen early as a courtesy to see him off? Her fingers clenched at waist height and the fist disappeared behind her back. He smiled then...and it was so slow and sardonic it made her insides squirm. He tipped his head; it was a minimal movement, just for her, and hadn't alerted Basham to the fact that she was spying on them from her window.

Deborah let the curtain fall back into place and twisted about, her chilly hands springing to her feverish cheeks to soothe them.

'You were quite a while outside with Mr Chadwicke yesterday evening. Was there anything suspicious going on in the grounds?'

Basham continued to pour coffee into Deborah's cup. 'Took a while, miss, 'cos we did a thorough search.'

'And did your thorough search turn up anything?'

'I saw nobody at all,' he stoutly replied. He returned the silver pot to the sideboard and made to leave.

'And Mr Chadwicke? Did he see anybody?' Deborah asked, halting Basham by the door.

'Do you suspect something?' Julia launched that question at Deborah. She had detected something disconcerting in her daughter's tone. 'You said Mr Chadwicke took some port before bed, and you had a conversation. Would he not have said if anything untoward had occurred?'

'He might not have wanted to alarm us. He knew he would be leaving today and would not be here to protect us,' Deborah quietly pointed out.

'Surely he would have warned Basham of his suspicions so that he could continue to be vigilant,' Julia persevered. 'Basham has said he's not aware of anything sinister. I'm sure Mr Chadwicke is the sort of fellow who would do his utmost to help us if he could.'

'I'll fetch more toast, m'm.' Basham found an opportunity to slip from the room.

'I hoped Mr Chadwicke might stay long enough to have breakfast with us.' Julia dipped her knife in to the jam pot and liberally applied strawberries to her toast. 'It is bad of him to go off without saying his goodbyes.'

'Basham gave you the note he'd left for you.' Deborah took a sip from her coffee cup before adding, 'You said in it he expressed his thanks and his farewells.'

'It is not the same,' Julia responded a trifle testily. 'We have so few visitors. It would have been nice had he stayed longer. I'm glad you brought him home with you yesterday.'

'You were not glad at first,' Deborah reminded her. 'In fact, Mama, I thought you acted quite rudely towards him.'

That bald complaint caused Julia to stare at her daughter open-mouthed, her toast hovering just before her lips. Quickly she took a bite and chewed to cover her confusion. 'Well…you know he has bad relations,' she mumbled through her napkin, dabbing at her lips.

'He has *one* bad relation. Or rather he had one,' Deborah said. 'Could you not have shown a bit of sympathy on hearing of his brother's death?' she chided. 'I know Sebastian was reputedly a wretch, but…'

'You don't know the half of it, miss.' Julia looked to have

recovered from the shock of being taken to task by her daughter. 'The late Lord Buckland was a devil.'

An arch appeared in Deborah's eyebrows as she silently requested the details.

'Sebastian Chadwicke fled abroad to the Indies to escape arrest,' Julia suddenly blurted. 'It was rumoured he did so to avoid being hanged for murder.'

'Was it a duel?' Deborah rocked the coffee back and forth in her cup. She was not that surprised to know the extent of his crime. She'd heard whispers years ago that he'd fought over a Covent Garden nun. She knew, too, that gentlemen who duelled and killed their opponent often fled abroad for some years to allow the furore to die down.

'Nothing quite so noble,' Julia said sourly. 'Your papa would not tell me it all, but I gathered it was some sort of criminal activity in which he was involved. Sebastian was always in trouble and a constant source of worry to his parents. I remember them as nice people. But the whole family was tainted by the shame Sebastian brought down on their heads. Those poor people had to accept that even liberal folk would at times have to shun their company.'

'Did you and Papa shun their company?' Deborah asked.

'We always welcomed Randolph. You know we did.' Julia wiped agitatedly at her fingers. 'You know he used to come with Marcus and was always included in our circle.' She gave a quivering smile. 'I still *do* like him and would have him visit again before he leaves the area.'

'But he has already left. He went early and I expect he is now in Kent.'

'We might catch him at the Woolpack in Rye. I can despatch Basham with a message.'

'He has business to attend to, Mama. I doubt he will want to come back.' Deborah gazed at her cloudy coffee, knowing she stupidly longed for the statement to be untrue. How much did he desire her—enough to interrupt his business, and return to Woodville Place to see her? Inwardly she scoffed at her conceit. One wooing kiss from him and already she yearned for another. She doubted he did. He'd said yesterday that he was content to live his life as a bachelor, but she knew he wouldn't lack for female company.

Randolph Chadwicke had been a notorious rake, as had his friend Marcus Speer before he married Jemma Bailey. On one of those occasions that her mother had alluded to, when he had been included in their circle and escorting her at the pleasure gardens, several women—not all of them ladies—had been blatant in displaying the fact that they found him attractive. If he needed a woman to quench his lust—soothe him, he might say, she reminded herself with an acid little twist of the lips—no doubt he would find a willing partner. Perhaps when back in the metropolis it might be one of those fawning flirts who'd bumped her hips against him when he was at Vauxhall, then looked surprised to have got his attention. With a sigh Deborah flexed her ankle beneath the table; for it felt a little stiff.

'Is your ankle any easier?' Julia asked, having noticed her daughter's fidgeting.

As soon as Deborah had entered the breakfast room that morning Julia had naturally been curious to know what mishap had occurred to cause her daughter to limp. Julia had seemed relieved to know that nothing more sinister than pins and needles was to blame for Deborah's stumble. Now, one minor injury led her to ponder on worse scenarios. 'You will not go in to town and stir up anything with those Luckhursts, will you?' Julia picked at crumbs on her plate before raising her eyes to give her daughter an anxious look. 'What does Luckhurst want with us?' she fearfully asked, having brooded for a few moments and found no solution to the suspicions tormenting her.

'I told you yesterday, Mama, he is probably just curious about Mr Chadwicke.' *And I, too, am curious about him*, Deborah thought as she sipped at lukewarm coffee. With a little grimace of distaste she replaced the cup on its saucer and pushed the set away.

Yesterday she'd not had from him the answer she'd wanted: that Luckhurst had not been prowling about their grounds. But she was sure Basham would not lie and he had said he'd spotted no interlopers whilst on watch. Was she being too suspicious? But it was natural for her to feel insecure after Luckhurst had tried to ambush her. He had ogled and leered at her before; he'd made crude comments about her figure and how he'd like to handle it. Never before had he and his cronies lain in wait for her to pass by on her trek home. She knew that Randolph's warning that she should not go out alone in future was very sound advice. There would be no more leisurely walks back from town for her. She had promised him she would not do so quite half-heartedly at the time. But now she accepted that to invite such trouble would be utterly foolhardy.

Restlessness again assailed Deborah. Having barely eaten a morsel, she pushed back her chair. With just a twinge in her ankle slowing her pace she approached the window of the morning room and took a look out. It was another beautifully mellow autumn day. Later in the week, when her foot was sound, she would take the carriage—if Fred were fit enough to drive it—and visit Harriet at the vicarage. She hoped she would find Harriet's sullen sister-in-law still away from home. Although she was always polite to her, Susanna seemed to cast a gloom on the atmosphere. Deborah bucked herself up. She would keep herself busy and not dwell on Randolph Chadwicke again. It was absurd to think that she might pine for him to return to Hastings when they had not seen one another for so long.

She was feeling bereft because, in common with her mother, she realised it was at times beneficial to have a strong male presence about the place. One of the reasons she'd accepted Edmund's proposal was to ease her mother's mind about their vulnerability at Woodville Place when so many rogues resided in the neighbourhood. And of course Edmund had been a good, kind man who had loved her. She had very much hoped the affection she felt for him would grow into love, but had lost him before she could find out.

Henceforth she supposed she should avoid visiting Hastings at times when Seth Luckhurst was likely to be there. Market day was one occasion that would draw him every week. It was sensible; it was also craven behaviour, and every fibre of her being rebelled at the thought of adopting it.

'What's this? A welcoming committee?'

Randolph had ducked his lofty frame under the low beam at the entrance to the Woolpack's taproom.

On hearing that drawling question, Seth Luckhurst spun about so swiftly he spilled some ale and almost unseated himself from his stool. His brother swivelled on his seat in a less agitated fashion to stare at the stranger. The two henchmen who accompanied them unwound from where they'd propped their elbows on the battered, blackened bar.

Zack Luckhurst was the first to regain composure and approach Randolph.

Randolph was not fooled by Zack's false smile or his firm handshake. A sweeping glance took in the men in the room. None of them trusted him, and Seth, in particular, hated him.

'Seth's been telling me that you two had a bit of a disagreement yesterday.' Zack slung a cautionary look sideways at his sullen brother as he heard a muttered cursing.

Seth continued to glower from beneath his wiry brows. He took a swig from his tankard and watched the proceedings over it. He'd told Zack how this fellow had humiliated him and was hoping this time for some support and loyalty from his brother. He couldn't understand why Zack wanted to find out more about the cove. Seth reckoned they should just haul him outside and give him the whipping he deserved.

'I think we understand one another,' Randolph said easily. 'Seth now knows not to upset me on certain matters.' He followed that up by addressing Joss Barker, the innkeeper, who was sitting behind the bar polishing brasses as though deaf and blind to whatever mischief the Luckhursts might be concocting on his premises. Having given his order for a hearty breakfast of eggs and venison steak to be taken to the back parlour, Randolph again turned his attention to Seth. Following an ironically comprehensive head-to-toe inspection, he concluded, 'You seem no worse for wear and up and about bright and early.'

'We wasn't expecting you to turn up so bright 'n' early,' Seth returned with seething resentfulness. 'What with you looking after Miss Woodville 'n' all, we reckoned you might be spent 'til noon.'

A chorus of sniggers erupted from the two henchmen and Zack, too, chipped in a lusty chuckle.

Emboldened by his cohorts' reaction, Seth became increasingly ribald. 'I wouldn't let that one off lightly, if you know what I mean. I'd make her earn her keep if I was looking after her.'

'But you're not. I am.' A corner of Randolph's mouth just moved; his eyes remained as cold and flinty as tawny agate. 'And as I told you yesterday, you forget that at your peril.'

'Seth's told me you're mighty friendly with the Woodville

lass.' Zack attempted to defuse the tension by slapping a hand on Randolph's shoulder. He'd spent just a few minutes in the stranger's presence, but instinctively he realised this was not a fellow you took for a fool. Randolph Chadwicke was clearly cultured; he was also unnervingly forthright and confident. Unlike his dense brother, Zack had a wily intelligence and knew when to proceed with caution. 'If you can thaw that ice maiden, good luck to you, my friend.' His eyes and tone became crafty as he added, 'Deborah Woodville's a beauty that'd turn any man's head. But you should know she's caused a lot of trouble for certain people round these parts.'

'Certain people? I take it you're referring to the smuggling fraternity.'

'What d'you know about smuggling, Mr Chadwicke?' Zack asked, sliding a sly look from beneath bushy brows at the nonchalant fellow standing opposite. He was annoyed to discover that despite being almost six feet tall he was some inches shorter than Chadwicke and was obliged, whether seated or standing, to look up to him.

'What do I know about smuggling?' Randolph gave a sour smile. 'More than you, I'll warrant, and not necessarily from choice.'

Zack and Seth exchanged glances. 'What's that supposed to mean?' Zack enquired.

'It means that I'm not intimidated by you, Zack Luckhurst, or your oafish brother. You and your motley crew have a way to go yet before you reach anything like the Trelawneys' standard.'

'*Trelawneys?*' Zack and Seth chorused together.

'You know Ross Trelawney?' Seth gaped at him, stunned out of his sulk at having been branded an oaf.

'I know his brother Luke, too. Ross told me about your enterprise when I was with them recently.'

A slow, satisfied grin split Seth's face. The thought that the Trelawneys had knowledge of his existence, let alone had mentioned him, was a very high accolade.

'They had nothing good to say,' Randolph drawled scathingly, having noticed Seth's barrel chest puffing in pride.

'So...you understand about certain things, then,' Zack said with a fierce squint. But he, too, was delighted to know they'd come beneath the notice of such eminence. 'You know nobody can be allowed to betray the fraternity. You'll understand why your...lady friend...has been a bother to us and needs taming.'

'You've been a bother to her,' Randolph countered with a negligence that was belied by his steady feline gaze. 'I'll warn you once only to cease troubling the Woodvilles.'

'Are you going to let him threaten us?' Seth surged up off his stool with a belligerent snarl, fists balling at his sides.

Zack sent a ferocious scowl at his brother and swiped out in a way that made Seth duck. One of Zack's horny hands went to his chin and began massaging bristles. He, too, had a burning need to make it clear that the Luckhursts were top dog in these parts. Unlike his younger brother, Zack was able to appreciate that sometimes wit was a mightier tool than was muscle. It would be easy enough to make some enquiries and find out if what this fellow had said was truth or fantasy. Zack suspected that Randolph Chadwicke was a successful and dangerous free-trader from East Anglia. He'd had his orders and had been warned to be on the look out for a stranger who might try to take over. He didn't know how his paymaster had found out a rival was coming, but he suspected the fellow had now arrived, and with the Trelawneys' backing.

The Trelawneys had been the most notorious smuggling clan ever on the south coast. The brothers were now all legitimate businessmen and as rich as kings, but their epic reputation and exploits had been written into folklore and were passed on at every hearth from father to son.

Zack was suspicious; he was also driven by self-interest. He was wily enough to consider whether benefits were to be had from transferring his allegiance. His current paymaster was a man who wanted to remain anonymous. He communicated with the Luckhursts only by note or messenger. Snowy had run messages for him. Zack had come to his own conclusions as to why old Snowy had met his end over Edmund Green's murder when all his colleagues knew he hadn't done it. Snowy had known too much and had had to be silenced.

'I don't care who he thinks he is, or who he thinks he knows,' Seth suddenly bawled. He'd grown impatient waiting for his brother's rumination to end. 'How do we know he's Trelawney's pal?'

'My word should be enough.'

The brothers pivoted together towards the door, jaws dropping. Randolph also turned with a smile curving his mouth.

'I was expecting you yesterday,' Randolph said as Ross Trelawney sauntered forwards.

The two men warmly shook hands, then, as a figure passed the open doorway, Randolph said, 'Ah…breakfast at last.' He'd noticed the innkeeper carrying a tray laden with steaming victuals towards the back parlour.

'I hope you've ordered enough for two,' Ross said as he followed his friend back towards the exit. With no more than a cursory look cast on the bar's other occupants, the two friends ducked their tall frames beneath the crooked doorframe. With the Luckhursts gawping after them, they were soon strolling down the passage behind the stout figure of Joss Barker.

Chapter Ten

'Oh, that's a shame!' Harriet Davenport looked quite glum to
have just learned from Deborah that Mr Chadwicke had already
gone about his business in Kent, and would probably not return
to the locality. 'I would have liked to see him again.' Her dark
ringlets tumbled forwards as she leaned to conspiratorially whisper, 'I thought him very handsome.'

Deborah placed down her cup and saucer and smiled at the delicate bone china. 'Yes…he is…' she agreed, albeit reticently.

'I thought he seemed as though he had a great deal he wanted
to say to you,' Harriet commented archly with a sideways peek
at her friend. She picked up the plate of seedcake that was on
the table and offered it to Deborah.

Deborah took a small piece, avoiding her friend's eye. 'Is
Gerard with the bishop today?' Usually when Deborah visited
the vicarage her friend's brother came out of his study to say
hello, but so far there had been no sign of him.

'He is, and I must say, Miss Woodville, that's a shameless
attempt to change the subject.' Harriet clucked her tongue with
mock exasperation. 'I see I must act quite vulgarly inquisitive if
I'm to find out anything at all. Did Mr Chadwicke once have a
tendresse for you? If you say not, I shall find it hard to believe.

The fellow could barely keep his eyes from your face when he joined us in Hastings that day. And what wonderful eyes they are too.' An exaggerated thrill prettily shimmied Harriet's shoulders. 'I'm sure a wolf must look less predatory than Mr Chadwicke.'

Deborah could not prevent a little laugh bubbling in her throat. She knew exactly what Harriet meant! 'Doubtless he was staring at me for the same reason I kept looking at him.' A rueful smile tipped her full lips. 'We both were astonished to meet under such odd circumstances. The last time we socialised was at our friends' wedding, in Mayfair, seven years ago.'

'You must have made quite an impression on him then, for he certainly had not forgotten you. He recognised you straight away. I'd say he's very much hoping to get to know you again.' Harriet cocked her head for a reaction to that remark. When Deborah simply took a nibble of cake, she persevered, 'Will you allow it?'

'I doubt I will need to give the matter much consideration,' Deborah replied, brushing cake crumbs from her fingers. 'I know Mama is keen to have him back again—as our protector—but I think he is probably already in the next county. If our paths again cross it will be whilst guests of the Earl and Countess of Gresham.'

The possibility that they might meet again at Yuletide made a flutter of excitement stir Deborah's insides. Randolph had not indicated whether he would be visiting their friends when she had mentioned that she had received from them an invitation. Now he knew she would be at Gresham Hall at Christmas, would he be persuaded to go too?

'Will you report to the magistrate that Luckhurst and his cronies tried to waylay you on that afternoon?' Harriet had given a little disappointed sigh on having her romantic ideas punctured, and had turned her mind to more practical concerns. 'It was dreadful of the brute to try to cause yet more trouble on the very same day he'd beaten your driver.'

'It was Seth's intention to punish me for reporting him,' Deborah said gravely. 'A waste of time it was, too, to have taken such a risk! Mr Savidge found excuses to avoid arresting those beasts over Fred's injuries; he will certainly do nothing about Seth Luckhurst laying in wait to ambush me. I would not be surprised to be accused of being at fault for walking home alone.' An agitated gesture displayed her vexation.

'It might have been far worse for you had Mr Chadwicke not insisted on escorting you home.' Harriet's brown eyes became clouded with mingling disgust and horror.

'I know…' Deborah's answer was followed by a protracted sigh of relief that fate had intervened that day.

Deborah had arrived that afternoon at the vicarage, fully anticipating her friend's probing questions about Mr Chadwicke. She'd known that Harriet would be keen to discover what had occurred once she and Gerard had departed for Rye market. Deborah had no reason not to tell her friend most of it…but some parts were too thrillingly secret to share with anyone, even her good friend.

Harriet cocked her head. Suddenly she got to her feet and approached the window. 'Gerard is home. He is early today. Will you stay and have supper with us, Debbie?'

'Thank you, no.' Deborah replaced her cup on the table and glanced at the wall clock. 'Fred drove me here in the trap. He still has aches and pains from his beating. Besides, I promised Mama I would not be out too long. I should like to visit the churchyard before we set off home.'

Harriet nodded in understanding. She knew that Deborah often took the opportunity to tend the resting places of her stepfather and her fiancé, both at peace beneath the shelter of the sycamores in St Andrew's graveyard.

As Deborah was pulling on her gloves in readiness to leave, Gerard entered the parlour and straight away launched into, 'How nice to see you, Deborah. I have just bumped in to your friend Mr Chadwicke in Hastings. I must say he is a nice chap. He stopped and passed the time of day, although I could tell he was busy and wishing to get on.'

'He is in Hastings?' Debbie echoed faintly.

'Indeed he is, although he tells me he will be travelling to visit his friend.' Gerard deliberately widened his eyes to show that he was impressed. 'He is friendly with Viscount Stratton who has a vast estate in Kent. I know the viscount has a farm. Perhaps he will let Mr Chadwicke purchase a few of his sheep. He told me he is interested in obtaining some hardy breeds for his Suffolk estate.'

'Yes, I know,' Debbie muttered sourly.

'Mr Chadwicke dined and stayed overnight at Woodville Place.' Harriet sought to bring her brother up to date with events. 'Seth Luckhurst has been making a dreadful nuisance of himself and has been stalking Deborah,' she recited forcefully. 'Mrs Woodville spotted Seth prowling around in the grounds of Woodville Place, but luckily for them Mr Chadwicke scared him off before he could get up to any more mischief.'

'Thank goodness he did so.' Gerard shook his head, despairing of Seth's wickedness. 'But I have to say I thought it odd Mr Chadwicke wants to buy sheep.'

'He told us he lost a good deal of his flock in sea flooding,' Deborah explained.

'He gives the appearance of being a refined gentleman, and used to his comforts. I'm not surprised he has influential friends.' Gerard nodded sagely.

'We share some such friends,' Debbie supplied with a wry smile. 'But people can have a change in circumstances,' she added in more subdued tone. She had no idea if Randolph was no longer as comfortably off as once he'd been. He looked to be thriving, but appearances could be deceptive. His brother's wild ways might have had financial as well as social repercussions for all the Chadwickes.

She and her mother knew only too well how a luxurious lifestyle could be suddenly whipped away by a stroke of fate. Her father's death, and her mother's remarriage, had set in motion a sequence of events that had drastically altered their lives and set their finances on a downward path. But she would not blame her mother for marrying George Woodville. Her mother had needed a husband's love and support and the squire had made Julia very happy during their short marriage.

Deborah knew only too well she had no right to criticise the loss of family cash. Even before his death, her father's wealth had been depleted by his generosity to her. He had spared no expense launching her into society; a lavish new wardrobe had been provided containing every imaginable garment, shoe and accessory; a new bottle-green landau and two pairs of magnificent chestnut horses had been purchased for her and her friends' particular use that Season; and, to top it all, a magnificent ball with over two hundred invited guests had been held to mark her début. To her shame she knew that the most costly sum had been wasted on her aborted engagement to the Earl of Gresham. Despite Marcus Speer's insistence that he must contribute to all money paid out on preparations for a wedding that would never take place, her father had been adamant that he alone must bear the brunt of the losses—and they had been considerable, Deborah knew that. But her dowry had been kept safe, or so she'd thought...

'Perhaps Mr Chadwicke will tell us more about himself when he is our guest.'

That news drew a startled look from Deborah, and a gasp and a delighted smile from Harriet. That very morning Harriet had urged her brother to ask Mr Chadwicke to pay a call if he was still in the vicinity.

'He has agreed to come to a little soirée early next week before he sets off for Kent.' Gerard swerved his eyes to Deborah. 'I hope you will not think it an impertinence, but I told him I expected you and your mother would accept an invitation.' Gerard had turned to his sister and thus missed Deborah's stuttered reaction to that.

'We must make an occasion of it,' Harriet said gaily. 'I think we should ask the Pattinsons too. We could have a buffet supper and afterwards perhaps Mrs Pattinson might be persuaded to play the pianoforte; I have heard her do so very well. I know Squire Pattinson likes a game of whist and Deborah is an excellent piquet player...'

'That sounds capital!' Gerard enthused, quite infected by his sister's mood. 'And I have more to tell you. A Captain Stewart has arrived to take the place of Lieutenant Barrow,' he beamed. 'I think we should invite him and perhaps one of his officers as well. We must let the dragoons know we support them and their fight against blackguards such as the Luckhursts.' Gerard stepped to the fireplace and rubbed together his chilly palms, then held them to the glow in the grate. 'I think this Captain Stewart means business. Only a week in the job and already a father and son from Bexhill, caught red-handed with twenty kegs of Geneva, have been confined in one of the Martello towers. Soon they will be up before the magistrate, then on their way to Horsham gaol.'

'Is there any news of Lieutenant Barrow?' Deborah asked in

a rather breathless way; an erratic thump had started beneath her ribs as soon as she'd learned Randolph was still close by. It was some while since he'd left Woodville Place and she'd believed him already miles away. In an attempt to calm her frantic thoughts she concentrated on the plight of the injured dragoon.

'I learned today from Savidge that the Lieutenant is still unconscious,' Gerard advised her. 'He has a high fever and is delirious, but still clings to life.'

'Yet nobody has been brought to account for it,' Deborah said with a despairing shake of the head.

'From what Gerard has said about Captain Stewart, it seems things might change now he has arrived to take charge,' Harriet chipped in whilst giving a soothing pat to her friend's arm. Harriet knew that Deborah's rage at Edmund's murder had been little alleviated by the passing of the years.

'Captain Stewart seems a forthright, conscientious sort of chap.' Gerard clasped his hands behind his back. 'The bishop introduced us this morning and I took to him straight away. He said he intends to investigate Lieutenant Barrow's assault as a matter of urgency. There will be warrants issued soon, mark my words.'

'Not before time,' Deborah muttered as she set her bonnet on her sleek golden chignon and tied the strings.

'It is good that this new officer is prepared to tackle the smugglers. Unfortunately, as soon as word gets about that a serious investigation is under way, a great number of men will abscond rather than risk being apprehended for questioning,' Gerard said solemnly.

Deborah and Harriet exchanged a look on hearing that. They knew very well that once those men and their wages were gone, the wives and children they left behind would be forced on to parochial relief or even the workhouse. Deborah had now lived

long enough in this coastal community to know that the consequences for the fugitives' families could be tragic.

Fred Cook frowned as he gazed at the bleak landscape. He
turned up the collar of his heavy-caped coat and stuffed his fists
into his pockets.

Deborah pulled at a few more fronds of bell-bind that were
twined about the headstone on Edmund's grave. She slanted a
look at her restless manservant as he stabbed the toe of a boot
into a clod of earth and peered about.

'I see you are waiting to go, Fred. Are you in pain from your
bruises?'

''S'not that, miss. It's getting late.'

'The sun's not quite set.' Debbie took a glance to the west
where a shimmer of light hovered on the horizon.

'Don't do to tarry in these places at twilight,' Fred said, squinting this way and that through his yellowing eyelids. He took a
walk to the left and then to the right, weaving between the stumps
of granite that jutted out of the grass at odd angles. Over the
years the elements had caused many of the headstones to sink
and slant. 'Noose-head Ned's been seen riding about the lanes
and the churchyard.'

A musical little chuckle met that. 'Fred Cook!' Deborah softly
chided. 'You don't believe that yarn about ghostly beings.'

'You might scoff, miss,' Fred mumbled in agitation. 'But Lizzie
Smith's seen him not so long ago. Went into hysterics, she did.
She was coming back from Rye fair with Billy Critchley. Took
her an age to get over it. She says she still ain't properly over
it.'

'Billy Critchley isn't the fellow Lizzie is supposed to marry,'
Debbie pointed out. 'Perhaps she concocted the tale as a diver-

sion when it was found out she'd again been walking out with another fellow.'

Fred's cheeks turned as colourful as the bruise that spanned his jaw. He too had come under Lizzie Smith's roving eye. Instinctively he rubbed his chin as he remembered the punch he'd received from Harry Jones who was soon due to marry the little flirt. 'A few others in the village have seen Noose-head Ned riding about,' he said earnestly. 'It's said he keeps appearing by Pump Cottage 'n' you know that's where he once lived. Folk say he's trying to go back home. Horrible he is, too, they say, moaning, 'n' groaning, 'n' looking like he just got dug up.'

'The smugglers like to put these silly tales about,' Deborah said as she stood up and dusted her palms together to remove gritty soil. 'It's their intention to frighten people to stay indoors so they can go about their night-time activities undisturbed.'

'Maybe…' Fred said grudgingly with a peer about. A cloud had covered the horizon, prematurely ending the day. 'But I don't reckon it do to tempt fate, 'specially round the graveyard, or Pump Cottage, 'cos that's where Lizzie said he rose up in front of 'em, wailin' 'n' swinging the rope about his neck.'

'And what did Billy Critchley have to say about Noose-head Ned?' Deborah asked, suppressing a smile.

'He never said nothing. He said he weren't there. Lizzie accused him of running off and leaving her on her own.'

Deborah ruefully shook her head. 'Poor Lizzie. She should think herself lucky that Harry Jones still wants to marry her. It seems Billy Critchley has proved himself an unworthy rival.' With a chuckle she took Fred's arm and let him assist her over the mounds and hillocks back to the path. A few minutes later the trap had started on the mile-long journey back to Woodville Place.

Chapter Eleven

Susanna Davenport was shamelessly matchmaking!

Deborah slipped a glance from beneath a screen of lashes to where the vicar's wife sat, her auburn head tipped coyly towards Captain Stewart. She was conversing with him whilst darting glances at her sister-in-law, apparently unconcerned by Harriet's discomfiture. It was common knowledge that Susanna hoped to oust Harriet from her territory by finding her a husband. She had, it was gossiped, been putting her mind to it for the duration of her marriage.

Within a few minutes of Deborah and her mother stepping over the threshold of the vicarage Harriet had cornered them to impart some bad news. Glumly she had said that her sister-in-law was back from Devon too soon. Gerard Davenport, however, had seemed pleased at his wife's early return and had watched her fondly as she sallied to and fro, declaring she was delighted to have such a gay homecoming.

Presently Harriet was seated at the card table between Squire Pattinson and his wife, and opposite Captain Stewart. Deborah could clearly see the spots of mortified colour on her friend's cheeks. They were spreading to form a fiery blush as Susanna continued to regale the dragoon with her sister-in-law's charming domesticity.

'The hussy is trying too hard! Captain Stewart looks embarrassed!'

That hissed remark came from Julia Woodville, who was sitting next to Deborah on the sofa.

'I think poor Harriet is suffering more than he is,' Deborah replied in an angry murmur muffled by her glass. She put her drink down on the table, about to get up and go to intervene. She wasn't sure if she would be successful, but she could try to turn the conversation before Susanna provoked Harriet into doing or saying something she was sure later to regret. Deborah knew her friend well enough; Harriet would take only so much of Susanna's baiting before she retaliated.

'No doubt Mr Chadwicke will be next in her firing line. I noticed Susanna acting girlish around him at supper.' Julia's rumbled remark delayed Deborah's departure from the sofa. 'I wonder why her husband doesn't have something to say about her flirting with him. Not that Mr Chadwicke's given her a scrap of encouragement. I will say that for him.' A subtle peep at her daughter lingered long enough to gauge a reaction.

Her mother's comment caused Deborah to sway her blond head sideways to find a pair of tawny eyes watching her…as they had been for most of the evening.

Deborah had the distinct impression that Randolph had guessed the gist of the whispered conversation between her and her mother. As though to prove her right, he strolled away from Sergeant Booth, with whom he'd been stationed, and took a seat next to Harriet at the card table. Immediately he started to chat to her whilst dealing the cards. Deborah shifted backwards on the cushions, determined not to follow him although she knew that, of the two of them, she'd first had the idea to go to Harriet's aid.

Her eyes lingered on him for a moment, admiring his air of lazy elegance. He looked wonderfully distinguished in a superbly cut grey tailcoat, yet there was a casualness about him that made his presence in the vicarage's small drawing room quite appropriate. Other guests seemed also struck by his magnetism and several pairs of eyes had tracked his movements during the evening.

Moments after Randolph had seated himself Susanna had eagerly transferred her attention to him. Seeing his moment to escape, Captain Stewart declined another game and made his excuses to quit the group. As soon as he was up from the table he made a beeline towards Deborah and her mother.

'Are you enjoying your posting to Sussex, Captain?' Julia asked as the fellow sat down close by in a wingchair positioned opposite the sofa.

He smiled, his eyes lingering on Deborah's perfect features. 'I am, ma'am, thank you. It is nice to feel so welcomed.' He took a glance at his host, who was now chatting to his colleague. 'This is a fine gathering and I'm pleased to have had the opportunity to meet you all this evening. Sergeant Booth appears to be enjoying himself too.'

'And we are pleased to meet *you*, sir, and your junior officer.' Julia tapped at his scarlet sleeve with her fan to emphasise her point. 'We are particularly pleased to know that you are here to keep those Luckhursts and their ilk under control.' Julia smoothed her satin lap with fidgeting fingers. 'They are dreadful rogues. One—the younger and the worst—was trespassing on our land just a short while ago and looking very shifty.'

Captain Stewart's eyes reluctantly relinquished Deborah's heart-shaped visage. 'Did you report the intrusion to the magistrate?'

'There is no point in doing so, Captain Stewart,' Deborah said, giving him the opportunity he wanted to again transfer his attention to her. 'Mr Savidge seems unwilling to challenge the smugglers.'

'Indeed? What makes you think so, Miss Woodville?' His steady stare caused colour to highlight Deborah's sculpted cheekbones. 'Is there a specific incident to which you refer?'

Deborah hesitated; she wished she'd thought more carefully before she'd spoken. Her mother still did not know that Fred had come by his injuries whilst protecting her from verbal abuse. Neither had Julia any idea that Seth had lain in wait for her, or that she had been lucky to have Randolph's protection on that occasion. Deborah was acutely aware that this was not the right time for any of it to come out.

'I've heard Mr Savidge believes that the locals protect their own, and it is difficult to collect evidence against the perpetrators,' she said carefully.

'Perhaps I can persuade him to take a more robust attitude towards criminals, and his duty in bringing them to justice.'

'Have you any news of Lieutenant Barrow?' Deborah quickly carried on, feeling more unsettled than flattered by his unwavering regard. He was a well-built, good-looking man of about thirty years old, she judged. She'd known from the moment that they had been introduced earlier that he found her attractive. The gleam in his eyes was intensifying and Deborah knew, following a flitting glance to her left, that her mother had also noticed his interest in her.

'He has regained consciousness, thankfully,' Captain Stewart informed her.

'That's wonderful news,' Deborah softly exclaimed, turning to beam her relief at her mother.

'He has still a long way to go before he is fully recovered,' the captain added pessimistically. 'The hunt for those responsible goes on.'

'I've heard a rumour the culprit fled abroad.'

Deborah had known that Randolph had risen from the card table after playing a couple of hands. Despite conversing with the captain, she was peripherally aware of where Randolph was and to whom he was speaking, just as she knew she was constantly under his covert observation. As he'd moved out of sight she'd imagined he had gone to join the group of gentlemen who were discussing some tomes on the bookshelves situated to the rear of the sofa. She had not expected to hear his husky baritone voice so close to her, or to sense the weight of a hand on the back of her chair, a hairbreadth from her exposed shoulder. He was so near she could sense his warmth bathing her cool, nude skin. To her shame she realised she yearned to sway closer to it.

'Perhaps he did flee abroad. But there are people in the vicinity who were accessories to the crime. They will not escape punishment.' Captain Stewart had looked over Deborah's head to speak to Randolph, confirming that he had positioned himself just behind her.

Randolph had been the last guest to arrive at the vicarage this evening and, apart from a mild exchange, curtailed by her mother's more enthusiastic greeting for him, they had barely had an opportunity to converse.

Deborah had been aware, before her mother mentioned it, of Susanna's immediate interest in Randolph. She had clutched his arm to steer him hither and thither to ensure that introductions were made between the guests, although Gerard had already performed the office. On glancing across, Deborah realised that Susanna's eyes were trained again on Randolph and she was ignoring Harriet's game attempt to revive the card session since Sergeant Booth had joined them at the baize table.

'So you hail from East Anglia, Mr Chadwicke,' Captain Stewart said, whilst his eyes lingered on the long, dark fingers splayed on velvet, a fraction distant from nudging a sculpted ivory shoulder.

'I'm from Suffolk,' Randolph said easily. 'And you, Captain? Where were you previously stationed?'

'At Whitby—I had command of the coast watch there and was in league with the Revenue Officers to crack down on the smugglers plaguing the area.'

'Were you successful against the rogues, Captain?' Julia asked, agog with interest.

'Indeed—we had a very great victory just a few months ago in the summer against a large gang of smugglers. They had an-chored out at sea and came ashore in long boats armed with blunderbusses and pistols. There might have been as many as eighty of them.' Pleased at having drawn so much attention, the captain settled back to continue recounting the incident. 'We made a large seizure of liquor at Redcar. The smugglers were a crafty bunch and had tried to get the locals' backing by staving in the heads of casks for the populace to drink what they would. Of course, a crowd of drunks is likely to offer little resistance to them or assistance to us.' He looked about at his audience for their reaction. 'After a savage fight we managed to retain hold of the illicit cargo. A band of stragglers who had not made good their escape tried to ambush a cart at the back of the line as we made our way to the Customs House. They were unsuccessful in reclaiming the casks on it. They were stupid, too, in following us, for they also were arrested. But, most importantly, a number of the ringleaders were apprehended that day. I feel able to boast that ever since the incident it has been quiet along that coastline.'

'Will that peace last, I wonder?' Randolph mused ironically. 'No doubt other men will come forwards to replace those now in gaol. Unfortunately free-trading is part of the scenery all over the country and those who run contraband are often considered heroes rather than villains. Spices, tea, lace, tobacco, liquor…there is temptation for every class and community in their cargoes.'

'Do you hold an apologist's view of smuggling, sir?' Paul Stewart enquired coolly.

'I approve of a practical attitude towards the matter,' Randolph returned with a slight smile. 'It seems to me that as long as a demand exists for duty-free goods the trade will flourish.'

'Then we will renew our fight there or anywhere else the criminals operate,' Captain Stewart stated adamantly. 'You seem to have an understanding of the trade, Mr Chadwicke. Am I correct?'

'The Suffolk seaboard has its smugglers, as does every coastal region.' Randolph gave the earnest young officer a half-smile. 'I applaud your moral stance, Captain, and the fact that you are presenting the free-traders with such valiant opposition. I imagine that instead of allowing you to rest on your laurels your superiors have sent you south to defeat the smugglers operating in this neck of the woods.'

'We welcome your presence here, Captain Stewart,' Deborah quickly interjected, keen to prevent a hostile atmosphere from fomenting. 'Unfortunately I understand Mr Chadwicke's cynicism on the likelihood of ever completely eradicating the trade.' She sighed. 'We have had a lull in activity along this stretch of coast in the past when the dragoons have had victories. But eventually the lights again move through the woods at dead of night. There is much support for the villains in the surrounding villages, and constant demand for their goods.'

Julia leaned across and clutched the captain's red-coated arm with thin fingers. 'You must not leave, sir, until you have done for Hastings an equal service as you did for Whitby.'

'I shall do my utmost for you, ma'am,' the captain charmingly replied.

'Who would like to join us in the music room and listen to a recital?' Harriet had approached the sofa to make that amiable enquiry. 'Mrs Pattinson has agreed to play the pianoforte for us.'

Julia Woodville gave a murmur of pleasure on hearing that musical entertainment was imminent. Immediately she extended a limp, freckled hand to the captain. For a moment he looked at it, then, with a faint smile, which had disappeared by the time his eyes had encompassed the other couple in the group, he helped the widow to her feet. Julia's hand grasped his uniformed elbow and she urged him forwards, giving instructions on how to locate the music room once they'd quit the drawing room.

The two people who remained, one seated, one standing, received from Harriet a winsome smile before she moved on to urge her brother and the other gentlemen to repair to the music room too.

'Come, Susanna,' the vicar called to his spouse, still seated, alone, at the baize table. 'Mrs Pattinson is going to play us a few tunes. Will you accompany her and sing for us, my dear?'

Susanna's sour expression hinted she was unlikely to agree to do so. Her rouged mouth had tightened and it was with some bad grace, it seemed to Deborah, that the woman took her husband's arm. She swished about and went off with him, thus leaving Deborah and Randolph the only occupants of the drawing room.

Deborah sensed a caress on her skin; so light and brief was that fingertip touch that for a moment she thought she must have imagined it. When it came again and zigzagged a fiery trail to a spot behind an ear before removing, a ripple of pleasure passed through her. She turned her head, tilting up her face so that her fair ringlets danced on her nude skin, to look at hard dark features.

'I suppose we should go also,' Randolph muttered huskily, 'although I'd sooner we stayed here.'

'Why? Do you not like music?' Deborah rattled off as she sought to calm a feeling of excitement simultaneously chilling and heating her limbs. She, too, would sooner stay where she was so they might talk privately.

Many unanswered questions had been pricking at her mind since he'd left Woodville Place at dawn. Several times she'd inwardly berated herself for not insisting on having her answers before he'd carried her upstairs and left her at her door. If he *had* caught Seth Luckhurst prowling around Woodville Place's grounds that night, why would he not tell her so? Had he sought to protect her because he imagined she might become as hysterical as had her mother on learning of the villain's proximity? If so, he surely did not know her character—but then, why did she persist in expecting that he might? She had been completely fooled about the strength of his interest in her once before and should have learned her lesson from it.

Seven years ago she'd believed they were in love and had been proved foolish in assuming he returned her finer feelings. She'd put her love and trust in a man who'd conquered his infatuation with her as soon as they'd parted. But she was honest enough to acknowledge that she couldn't put all the blame on him. It hadn't been a callous seduction on his part: at eighteen she had spurned her fiancé and chased after Randolph with as much zeal as he had pursued her. The memory of her brazen immodesty, and her selfish disregard for her parents' feelings in it all, still had the power to make her blush. Youth and innocence had been her undoing; she'd clung to a romantic idyll of her own creation, longing for it to be real.

Still she could not quash her gladness at their reunion, or her need to see desire in his eyes when he looked at her. And this evening he had constantly looked at her despite his well-mannered attention to the other guests when they engaged him in conversation.

This afternoon she had taken some time sorting through her clothes press to choose what to wear for the Davenports' soirée. The grand ball gowns that she'd owned, but not worn for many years, were not appropriate for a cosy evening at the vicarage. Yet she'd known she wanted to wear something stylish to impress him with her appearance. At eighteen she'd frequently been told that she was stunningly lovely; even rival débutantes had admitted to it, albeit with reluctance or envy in their voices. Now she was older and, despite Randolph's compliment that she'd changed little in the intervening years, Deborah knew her mirror did not lie. A tiny dent had appeared between her brunette brows from the sorrows she'd endured and the memory of past laughter was also delicately etched on her porcelain complexion.

When she'd met Randolph in Hastings she'd been garbed in serviceable clothes. When he'd dined with them later that day she'd dressed in a manner befitting to an informal meal with her mother and an unexpected gentleman guest. This evening had been the first opportunity she'd had to dress up and remind him of the vivacious young woman he'd once wooed. She'd wanted to resemble the *seductive little miss* who'd once driven him wild with desire.

The gown she had settled on was one that had been made for her début; fortunately it was of classic Grecian style and thus had not dated too much in the intervening years. A simple blue silk sheath was overlaid with a net of fine Brussels lace. Her figure was fuller now than it had been when she was a girlish eighteen and the snug fit thrust an alluring, rather than a vulgar, amount of exposed pearly flesh above the scooped bodice. The sheeny material clung to her slender midriff and enhanced her small waist, whilst the rich, sapphire colour was undiminished by the gauzy lace and intensified the shade of her eyes.

As though his mind tracked hers, Randolph said in a voice of gravelled velvet, 'You look ravishing tonight. That dress always suited you, perhaps more so now you've filled it out.'

An immediate look was slanted up at him and her soft lips parted in readiness to launch an indignant retort that she thought it always had fitted her very well. It remained unuttered as her gaze locked with mocking amber eyes. Moments later his interest had deliberately slipped to her parted pink mouth before roaming the mounds of milky skin that were, from his vantage point, freely available to a ravening inspection.

'Perhaps we should join the others,' he muttered ruefully.

A thrill of anticipation stalked Deborah's spine as she recognised the frustrated need in him. She realised he could easily move his hand and slide his fingers over the sensitive flesh of her breasts. He had stroked her in such a way once before when he'd been ardently kissing her behind a cool marble pillar. On that occasion she'd been dressed in her virginal bridesmaid's dress and she'd had every silly expectation of soon becoming his wife. Her head jerked down; she was terrified he might guess her wish to have him again fondle her in such a way.

'We *should* join the others in the music room,' she gasped out. 'I recall you used to like recitals and dancing. We often danced together at Almack's.'

'We did much together,' Randolph reminded gruffly. 'I haven't forgotten any of it, not a single thing.'

'You forgot me,' she hissed in an angry, suffocated voice and made to jump up from the sofa. She felt his touch then, two warm palms sliding over her shoulders, curving on fragile shoulder bones to keep her where she was.

'That's the puzzle that remains unsolved, Deborah. I think it's time it was.'

He leaned forwards so their heads were close as she continued to wriggle to get free of his restraint. She turned her head and her wide blue eyes met a fierce feline stare. Suddenly she could sense that anger, as well as desire, was firing him; the fingers curled on her cool flesh were firm and insistent. Instantly they were removed and he'd straightened. A single, negligent hand remained propped on the sofa as he turned to face the door.

Harriet had entered the room and immediately hurried towards the sofa with a frown creasing her features.

'What is it?' Deborah asked at once. She had immediately stood up as she sensed Harriet's agitation.

'Oh…I'm sure it is nothing,' Harriet answered rather shrilly. 'I was just in the kitchens asking Dilys to bring some lemonade to the music room and…' She flapped a hand and giggled nervously. 'It is your driver, Fred. He was in the kitchens and most upset. He had been keeping an eye on the horses and carriages in the yard in between sitting with the staff below stairs and—'

'Fred? Is something up with him?' Deborah interrupted.

'He is in a high old state, I'm afraid,' Harriet replied on a gulp. 'I'd sooner not alert your mother to what he has said. I know she suffers with her nerves and it will ruin her enjoyment unnecessarily if nothing is amiss. I'm sure it is nothing.'

'What is it, Harriet?' Deborah moved towards her friend and

clasped her hands, sensing a niggling apprehension curdling her stomach as she felt Harriet's fingers trembling against her own.

'Fred has said he was returning from the stable and, on looking towards the church, he saw Noose-head Ned up by the lichgate staring down on him.'

Chapter Twelve

'Noose-head Ned?'

'Oh, for Heaven's sake!' Deborah's exclamation had mingled with Randolph's amused quizzical voice for they had spoken together. 'Fred was blathering about that silly tale the other day when I was tending Edmund's grave.' An exasperated sigh huffed out of her. 'I suspect he has allowed his imagination to get the better of him.' Deborah gave her friend an apologetic look. 'I will go directly and try to calm him down before he causes a commotion and spoils the party.'

'Who or what is Noose-head Ned?' Randolph asked. His eyes had narrowed speculatively and the humour was no longer in his tone.

'It is just a foolish tale of a ghostly being rumoured to materialise at night,' Deborah explained. 'According to Fred there are villagers who have become hysterical after the spectre crossed their path. He's said to ride about moaning and groaning and swinging the noose that remains about his neck.' On seeing Randolph's sharpening interest, she told him what she knew about the origins of fabled Noose-head Ned.

'Ned Swinton was a smuggler who was hanged several years ago. Or rather he was in the process of being hanged when some daring accomplices darted out of the crowd to free him. He was still kicking when they cut him down, and they rode hard and got away from their pursuers. By all accounts when they stopped, believing they were in the clear, Ned was found to have expired on his horse, still upright in the saddle with his hands entangled in the reins.' She gave a self-conscious little laugh. 'Folklore has it that Ned believes he still breathes and instead of passing over to a spirit world he's trapped in a limbo between life and death.' A small gesture described her scepticism. 'His body was allegedly dumped out at sea by his cohorts. Now Ned favours haunting the churchyard to look for a resting place, and the lanes around Pump Cottage where he once lived as a young man.' Having told all she knew, she started towards the door with a vexed sigh.

Randolph stopped her before she had time to quit the room. His fingers felt warm and firm on her cool, yielding forearm. 'I'll come with you and speak to Fred Cook just in case there is something in what he says that needs investigation. He might have actually seen a human being.'

He didn't elaborate, but Deborah knew what he was thinking. Her driver might have caught a glimpse of a moon-dusted tramp and in his fanciful state believed the fellow a phantom. A grateful smile accepted his assistance. 'But I don't think Captain Stewart should yet be alerted,' she added in a cautionary way. 'I wouldn't like an innocent traveller to be apprehended because of Fred's hysteria.'

'Amen to that,' Randolph muttered drily. 'I think the captain could be overzealous if he chose to be.'

'I shall go back to the music room,' Harriet interjected, 'and act as if all is well.' The opening bars of another rousing tune could be heard coming from along the corridor and made Harriet smile in relief. 'Mrs Pattinson, bless her, is doing us proud this evening with her performance.' With that she set off in one direction whilst Randolph and Deborah took the other.

Deborah was soon disabused of her notion that Fred might be making a great fuss for little reason. Entering the kitchen, she found her driver ashen and visibly quivering. He was seated in a chair by the scrubbed pine table and the Davenports' elderly housekeeper, Mrs Rush, was in the process of pouring him another shot of brandy whilst crossing herself with her free hand.

Fred immediately took the tot and downed it in a gulp. He gawped at his mistress with wide, terrified eyes that held a hint of apology. 'I told you he were about, miss.' He snuffled against his sleeve. 'Now I seen him with me own eyes 'n' I know Lizzie ain't lying.' He rubbed his quivering palms against his cape-covered arms as though to scrub away a tormenting memory. 'Swinging the end of the noose at me he were as though he might come 'n' use it on me.' He shoved back his chair and sprang up. Having looked about for a place to flee and found none, he instead backed against the wall.

Deborah felt alarm grip her. She knew her coachman well enough; he could not act this role. His distress and shock was genuine. Something had frightened Fred almost out of his wits.

'Come, sit down again,' she urged hoarsely and with a gentle hand led him, quaking, back to the table.

'Where exactly was this, Ned?' Randolph asked. He had so far remained quiet, listening, but now came forwards and, taking the bottle of brandy, poured the coachman another small tot.

'Up…up on the hill by…by the lichgate, sir,' Fred stammered as he again sat down and clasped both hands about the small glass as though to steady them.

'Did anybody else see him?'

Fred wobbled his head about. 'Only me 'n' the squire's coachman been outside tonight, sir. And squire's man been napping in his master's coach most o' the time. He's still out there now.'

'I'll take a look,' was all Randolph said as he stepped past and went out of the side door leading to the stable yard.

All hope that the other guests might remain in blissful ignorance of the brouhaha was to be dashed. As Harriet entered the music room she saw at once that her brother was assisting their maid who had dropped her tray of lemonade on the floor close to the door. The pianist gamely carried on running her fingers over the keys, but as her audience's attention dispersed, the melody faded away to nothing and Mrs Pattinson stood up.

'What on earth is the matter with you, Dilys, to make you so clumsy?' Gerard Davenport demanded in a low voice as he helped the young maid collect glass shards and store them on the tray. He placed a hand on her thin black-uniformed arm to find her shivering. In between snivelling out apologies the nervous girl was dabbing ineffectually with her pinafore at the pool of lemonade on the rug.

'Ned's about, sir,' she croaked in an underbreath. 'Fred Cook's seen him right close just a moment ago.'

Harriet quickly went to help clear up the mess. She gave the maid a frown that made Dilys shrink back and press together her lips. A moment later Captain Stewart had joined the Davenports to politely enquire if he might give assistance. Hot on his heels came Susanna, her attractive features pinched in anger.

A low, sibilant conversation between husband and wife ensued as Dilys continued to quiver, collect crystal and dart saucer-eyed looks up at her employers.

'Noose-head Ned?' In snorting disbelief Susanna repeated the name her husband had whispered, but she'd blanched so violently that her rouged lips became a startling scarlet slash in her powdered complexion. 'Nobody believes that daft tale.' Her scoffing sounded shrill. A moment later she'd recovered composure and explained a bit about the local ghost to Captain Stewart, who had expressed an interest in knowing more.

Julia rose from her chair as the gist of the upset lilted in fragments to her hearing. She passed some of it on to the others, hovering close by, politely waiting for an end to the hiatus in the entertainment.

'Come, we must leave at once,' Mrs Pattinson told her comfortable husband. As though to propel him into action she caught at his arm and urged him up from his chair.

'No need to panic, m'dear,' the squire soothed as he stumbled to his feet. 'It's all just a ploy by those rogues to get their cargoes stashed out of sight. One of them has been covered in flour and is having a fine old time wailing and gnashing his teeth to scare us away. Busy down on the beach tonight, I'll warrant.' When his wife seemed unappeased by his jocularity he placated her, 'I know you believe in the spirits, m'dear, but mark my words, Ned's no more a ghost than I am.'

'It is dark and late,' his wife pointed out querulously. 'We have quite a journey to make.'

John Pattinson gave his wife's hand an indulgent pat. 'I'll tell the vicar we're off, then. No need for you to fret, my love.'

'I'm sure it is nothing,' Harriet said desperately. She was severely disappointed to know that guests were leaving already. It was barely a minute after nine.

'Perhaps we should leave too,' Julia muttered in a quavering voice to nobody in particular. 'I must go and find Deborah and see what sort of state Fred is in. Oh…what a to do!'

Following a brief word with his subordinate Captain Stewart announced, 'Sergeant Booth and I will patrol the area before heading back to barracks. You may all journey home knowing you will remain safe, I promise.' He turned to Gerard and Harriet with a smile and a bow. 'Thank you both for a very fine evening.'

'I'm sorry you've been put to such trouble, Captain,' Harriet said, flustered. 'Would anybody like a hot drink before departing?' she forlornly offered, trailing in the wake of the exodus from the music room.

Moments later a congregation had formed in the vestibule and coats were being found and donned.

Deborah immediately approached her mother on noticing her agitation. 'I'm sure it is nothing to worry about, Mama,' she reassured quietly. 'Mr Chadwicke has been outside and checked for trespassers. He's questioned the Squire's coachman and the fellow insists he's seen and heard nothing untoward.' Briefly Deborah broke off in her reassurance to say goodbye to the Pattinsons who were first to leave.

'I'm not sure that Fred Cook is fit to drive you home.' Randolph had just come in from the stable yard where he'd found Fred all ready atop the coach, but still shivering and starting at shadows. 'It might make matters worse to give him more brandy to settle his nerves.'

'Indeed, we must not! If he's drunk, he's sure to overset us in a ditch,' Deborah muttered.

'Oh, what a trouble he is. What are we to do?' Julia gasped.

'I shall drive the coach and take you home,' Randolph quietly insisted.

'I'm sure there's no need, but thank you…'

'Oh, would you do that, sir?'

Deborah's demurral had been immediately drowned out by her mother's relieved acceptance speech. 'You are so kind to us. Twice now you have come to our assistance because of the wretches who infest the neighbourhood. I think the squire is right. It's the smugglers' intention to scare us indoors so we see and hear nothing.'

'Surely you are heading back to Rye tonight, Mr Chadwicke, and that lies in the opposite direction to Woodville Place.'

Despite Randolph's offer having been made in an undertone it seemed Captain Stewart had made it his business to hear what he'd said.

The captain flushed beneath Randolph's withering look; nevertheless he stepped closer, brazenly unapologetic for having eavesdropped. His eyes lingered on Deborah's face although he spoke to Randolph. 'I know you have your mount with you, too, Mr Chadwicke. It would be no trouble for me to escort the ladies' carriage safely to Woodville Place so you might head directly towards the Woolpack on horseback.'

'There's no need for you to do so, Captain, I assure you,' Randolph drawled. 'But I'm flattered to know that, though you've only recently arrived in Sussex, you have taken the time to acquaint yourself with my business.'

The men locked eyes for a moment before Captain Stewart executed a jerky bow and stepped aside. He went to take his leave of their hostess who was already at the foot of the stairs. Within a moment of saying farewell Susanna was halfway up the treads as though she couldn't be bothered with niceties for the remaining guests and was eager to retire.

'Aren't we lucky to have two gentlemen prepared to get us safely home?' Julia whispered to her daughter.

Deborah's eyes glancingly met Randolph's mordant gaze. From that fleeting contact she gleaned some unsettling information: he was quite aware that Captain Stewart had taken a fancy to her, and he didn't like it. Also, he had more he wanted to say to her. Beneath the hard glitter in his eyes she had recognised a burning frustration that their conversation in the drawing room had been interrupted by Fred's hysteria. A short while ago she, too, had wanted to have some answers to puzzles that long had niggled at her; now she felt too weary to want to enter what was sure to prove to be arduous territory.

'Will you accept the invitation to stay with Marcus and Jemma at Christmas?'

Deborah blinked at flickering flames, then swerved her eyes back to Randolph, seated opposite her by the parlour fire. She certainly had not expected him to raise that innocuous subject. She placed down her cup of warm chocolate and smiled; she was grateful that he seemed to have decided it would be inappropriate—after the shocking end to the evening—to resume a conversation that might lead to them bickering at close to midnight. The Noose-head Ned business had taken its toll on her nerves, although she had thought herself immune to its silliness. She imagined that Randolph also had not remained unaffected by the evening's impromptu excitement, and had decided not to add to it by raising the hazardous subject of their past.

On the journey home from the vicarage, whilst Randolph had driven them, and his horse had clopped docilely behind the carriage, Fred had huddled, wide-eyed, in the corner opposite her and her mother looking like a poor, demented thing. Julia Woodville's anxiety had seemed to escalate the longer she was in close proximity with him. Again and again her mother had shrilled that if it had not been for Mr Chadwicke's great kindness they would be overturned in a ditch, dead by the wayside. Constantly she had peered through the carriage window into the darkness as though to ease her mind that no spectre rode alongside.

On reaching home Julia, though very agitated, had insisted that Randolph must come in and at least take some brandy before setting off for the Woolpack. Once she had arranged for his refreshment and her daughter's chocolate to be brought to the parlour, she'd said her goodnights and gone to find Lottie to prepare her a sleeping draught.

This time Deborah had not found it an unwelcome duty to keep Randolph company whilst he took a warming tot. She had wanted to stay with him despite knowing he might immediately resume the conversation he'd started in the Davenports' drawing room. But he had surprised and pleased her by talking about their mutual friends instead.

'I very much hope to see Jemma and Marcus,' she replied to his enquiry about her Christmas plans. 'It will depend on travelling conditions in December, of course, and my mother's health. Mine, too, I suppose.' She gave a diffident smile. 'I caught a very bad chill last Yuletide and spent the holiday coughing and sneezing.' Her eyes flitted from a sleepy amber gaze. 'It would be very wrong to take our complaints and give them to those two dear children.' She hesitated, garnering the courage to ask, 'Are you to join the Greshams' Yuletide gathering in Surrey?'

'I haven't been invited.'

'Oh…' Debbie glanced at him from beneath her lengthy lashes, trying to gauge whether that meant he'd fallen out with the man who once had been his closest friend and her fiancé. She didn't want to pry, yet had a curiosity to know.

'Marcus isn't aware I'm back in England,' Randolph supplied as though he knew what she wanted to ask.

'I have an unfinished letter for Jemma,' Deborah told him. 'I shall let her know that you are back, and that I have seen you and…'

'And…?' Randolph prompted softly as her words faded away. 'Will you let her know that within a few hours of us being re-united I acted towards you like an uncouth lout?'

'I think I shall let Jemma know that we met unexpectedly when you travelled to Sussex on business,' Debbie briskly said, unsure why she'd avoided endorsing a valid description of his behaviour. Of course, since he'd forced that harsh, lecherous assault on her he'd kissed her again very sweetly, and acted the perfect gentleman in every way. 'I'll also let her know you've been most kind and helpful to us whilst in the vicinity to buy sheep,' she finished on a dubious look.

'I get the impression you still think that might not be the truth, Deborah,' Randolph replied, his light tone belied by the steady scrutiny that accompanied it.

'I… It is just I find your interest in livestock a little…out of character.' She'd thought her wording diplomatic until she heard his response to it.

'And you think you know my character, do you?' he quietly jibed.

'Touché!' It was a muttered aside as she turned away from him to hide her expression. 'Once I thought I did,' she added in a barely audible voice. 'As it turned out, of course, I never knew you at all.'

So, despite her thinking that he would courteously avoid doing so, he had cleverly turned the conversation to provoke her into making a reference to their past. She put up her chin, some of her lethargy dispersing beneath her indignation. If he wanted to issue awkward questions, she could match him with some of her own. 'Why have you not asked me if we have been troubled by Seth Luckhurst since you last were here?'

Randolph lifted the cognac to his lips and sipped. 'Have you been?' he asked, replacing the glass on the table.

'No…but I rather think you already knew that and so have not bothered to enquire. Have you warned him to stay away from me and from Woodville Place?'

'Yes.'

That blunt answer caused Deborah to momentarily catch her breath. 'And what did he say to that?' she eventually asked.

'Nothing that I could repeat to a genteel spinster...even one who is now a woman.' His eyes mocked her though he'd kept his tone mild.

Deborah inwardly squirmed at the reminder of her wrongful claim to worldliness. 'Have you fought over me?' she blurted.

Randolph smiled and a finger traced the rim of his glass. 'Do you want me to?'

'Of course not!' she spluttered, but a blush slashed her ivory cheekbones with colour. 'Why did you lie when you were here before?' she rushed on to cover her confusion. 'I'm sure Seth was loitering out in the grounds the night you and Basham went on watch.'

'I didn't lie. When I returned indoors he'd gone. Why would I worry you about him for no reason? I said there was nobody out there, and nothing for you to fret over. That was the truth.'

'You'd got wet and your knuckles were scraped. You must have had a scuffle of some sort by the stream.'

'I see you've been giving it a lot of thought, Deborah. I'd like to think that's because you're worried about me.' A darkly amused look slanted at her over the rim of his glass. 'Are you?'

'Of course,' she whispered after a protracted quiet. 'I'd be concerned for anybody who had dealings with those ruffians. You have only to look at what they did to Fred to know they're mindlessly vicious.'

'I can look after myself.'

Instinctively Deborah knew it was no idle boast, yet the admission disturbed rather than reassured her. The feeling she'd had since he'd arrived in Sussex that he was no stranger to danger was strengthening.

'Why did you go to the Indies?' she blurted. 'Was it because your brother was in bad trouble? Were you in trouble too?'

'My brother was in bad trouble wherever he was, Deborah,' he said, holding the gently oscillating tumbler between thumb and forefinger. 'After my father died, it fell to me to sort out his messes. Often I became embroiled in them in the doing of it.' Abruptly he put down his glass and stood up as though he regretted having said too much. 'Thank you for the drink. It's late. I should be on my way.'

Deborah rose quickly too. Oddly, she knew that she didn't want him to go yet. When they'd first settled down into their chairs, she'd expected awkward questions from him; now she was the one keen to probe for some more answers. Her tiredness had dispersed and she felt alert again and desperate to solve, once and for all, those frustrating puzzles that constantly pricked at her mind.

'Why didn't you write to me?' It was out before she'd consciously decided to air a grievance that for seven long years had remained locked in a treasury in her mind. 'You promised you would.' Her voice had sounded raw with emotion and immediately his tawny eyes sprang to savage her face.

'I did. You know I did.'

Chapter Thirteen

'Don't lie; please don't lie. It doesn't matter now, of course.' Deborah tried and failed miserably to authenticate her nonchalance with a hoarse laugh. 'I just wondered why you would promise to keep in touch, then not do so.' She swallowed, turned away swiftly, feeling suffocated by unshed tears. 'It's of no importance…thank you for escorting us home,' she croaked. 'Basham will show you out. Goodnight.'

He was between her and the door in two swift strides.

As she came closer to him she sensed her steps faltering, her heart pounding as she remembered how once before he had arrested her in almost the same spot and brutally kissed her. But she forced her feet to keep moving. An innate sense told her he would let her go. And so it seemed. The solid wall of tension had been breached and she was a step past him and expelling the breath caught in her throat when a hand came out. He caught at one of her wrists by instinct, for he hadn't turned about to watch her retreat. Slowly he drew her back until they stood side by side, facing in opposite directions.

'I wrote to you four times. I don't believe all those letters went astray.'

'Neither do I,' Deborah answered in a bitter whisper whilst twisting her wrist in his fingers.

'You still think I'm lying?' His tone was flat.

'I think I don't know you. I think I never did know you, and thus I can't trust you.' She jerked her arm to liberate it, a sob audible as he tightened his fingers enough to make her cease straining.

'Are you frightened of me, Debbie?'

'No...'

The tiny hesitation betrayed her and made his mouth wryly slant. 'You weren't at eighteen. Then I think I was more frightened of you. But I admit I probably knew no more of your true character than you say you knew of mine.'

She pivoted slowly and he mimicked the movement so they stood face to face.

'You were frightened of me?' Incredulity was in her voice and in the misty blue eyes that scoured his features. 'How could I have made you so?'

'In a way you terrified me. You were too beautiful, too popular, too well endowed in every way.' A searing golden gaze flowed over her silk-sheathed figure. 'I was constantly scared of losing you to someone more worthy of you than I was. At one point, when I was truly insane, I imagined it might be a good thing if you went ahead and married Marcus. At least I knew he'd care for you, give you everything you deserved to have.'

Abruptly he released her wrist and thrust his hands into his pockets, for he itched to haul her against him and mould her soft curves against his body. But she could put fire in his loins without them touching at all. The heat and heaviness in his breeches was mockingly insistent despite him now knowing for certain what he long had suspected: she believed him a fraud and a liar. Not once in his life had he acted deceitfully when with her, or lied to her. He'd nothing to apologise for apart from allowing an odious brother's troubles to drive them apart.

But why should he care now what she thought of him? He'd been loyal and true to her for eighteen months whilst waiting for a kind word to arrive from England sealed with the Cleveland crest. Finally he'd come to accept that he'd deprived himself of female company for no reason. He'd come to accept too, a while later, that there was no more need to abandon his brother to the hellish life into which he'd sunk and rush back home. He'd had a letter from Marcus; from it he'd learnt that Deborah had just got engaged to an army officer. It was slipped in amongst other news as though Marcus had known how distraught he'd be to find out he'd lost her and had tried to soften the blow. Yet his friend had understood him well enough to know he'd sooner know than not.

Randolph was tempted to believe Deborah might have lied to him. Had she really not received even one of his letters, sent over that first year? Or was she now ashamed to admit that out of sight had been out of mind and she'd not cared enough to set pen to paper and reply to a note that begged her to wait for him?

When he'd set sail for the Indies Deborah Cleveland had been a vivacious débutante surrounded by fawning gallants. She'd lost her father and her fortune and no doubt some of the fortune hunters had disappeared too at the same time. But she'd fallen for her dragoon and would now have been Edmund's wife but for the fellow's death. She was a woman now…as she'd made a point of impressing on him. Well, he was in need of a woman; he most definitely had a use for her. But perhaps now, with her mother asleep upstairs, was not the right time to seduce her, he reminded himself with sour self-mockery.

'Go to bed,' he ordered hoarsely. 'I'll have another drink and take myself off.'

Deborah suddenly felt quite ashamed. Perhaps he was embarrassed to admit his infatuation with her had quickly cooled, but nevertheless that was all a long time ago. Harping on what might have been seven years ago was sure to irritate him. They were different people now. She knew her appearance and attitude were more mature, and he was certainly different: harder in looks and character.

But he had acted as their knight errant again this very evening and gone out of his way to bring them safely home. Her mother felt always more secure in his presence and for that alone Deborah felt grateful. As he plunged down again in the armchair, temperamentally shoving a long leg towards the fire and a hand to the empty glass on the table, she went to him. Carefully she placed the brandy decanter close by.

'Please, take what you want…'

He laughed, a coarse sound that was little more than a rumble in his throat. Golden eyes slanted upwards as hers darted ruefully down and were immediately captured. She realised that it had been most unwise to come again so near to him whilst his mood was volatile, but try as she might to retreat, her feet felt leaden and seemed to root her to the spot.

He raised a hand slowly, taunting her with its leisurely approach and her chance to escape it. Long dark fingers spread on a pale, fragile wrist and, when still she remained quiescent, manacled it. A deft rotation of his hand had her off balance and tumbling sideways on to his lap.

Finally Deborah was jerked from her trance. Her shrill protest was lost beneath the swift plunge of his mouth on hers. She struggled furiously to free herself; the humiliation he'd inflicted on her once before whilst angry was still painfully fresh in her mind. But despite the imprisoning hand at the back of her head maintaining contact between them there was no savage demand present as his mouth started to move on hers. A persuasive pressure was moulding her lips to his and the slide of his tongue against the clamped line of her lips was not selfish, but seductive. A thumb spread to stroke against her nape with mesmerising softness. When it shifted to caress the sensitive spot behind an ear, she instinctively swayed her head to allow the subtle touch.

It was enough of an encouragement for Randolph to deepen the kiss. Hard fingers cupped her satiny jaw, skilfully manoeuvring it apart so he could tease the plump softness of her inner lips before penetrating further to torment with his tongue.

Deborah sensed the outrage that had inflamed her transforming to something more sensual and betraying. An ache low in her belly was shooting icy fire to her breasts, making them feel tender and weighty. A hand had wound into her golden chignon, loosening it, and she felt a wave of glossy hair sway to bathe her bare shoulders. Tilting back her head, she allowed his mouth to steam warmth against the pulse bobbing crazily at the base of her throat. As he traced a hot moist trail vertically on smooth skin instead of avoiding him, she turned into the kiss, her pulsing lips parted in readiness to receive him.

Randolph sensed his victory and took it. His mouth covered hers again with an erotic barbarity, his tongue plunging and retreating while his artful fingers pushed down her bodice straps and glided over warm velvety flesh.

Deborah gasped as cool fingers enclosed her breast, stroking and squeezing in a rhythm that matched his mouth's pressure on her lips. She felt her feminine core heating and she fidgeted restlessly against him.

With a throaty growl Randolph swivelled her hips towards him so she almost straddled his lap. His head lowered as he pushed the bodice beneath her bare bosom so lush flesh was propped on its silken support. He teased the satiny flesh he'd exposed with mouth and tongue before he gave her what she whimpered for. First one, then the other tense little nipple was taken and suckled until she was sobbing and squirming with need.

A moan escaped Deborah as she surrendered to the outrageous pleasure he was giving her. She locked her small hands behind his head, holding him close as she instinctively rocked to and fro.

It was the clock chiming midnight that jolted Randolph to his senses. That and the discomfort of his tortured body as Deborah writhed against his pelvis. He pulled her head down roughly to his and kissed her whilst his unsteady hands yanked up her clothes, protecting her bruise-tipped breasts from his ravening hands and mouth. Eyes blackened with desire whipped over her; she was languorous with passion; her eyes were a faint blue light behind a web of inky lashes. Her head was lolling to one side and then she moaned and her slick scarlet lips were seeking his again.

He'd wanted to stop her probing more deeply into his past and perhaps asking for answers he couldn't yet give, and to his shame he couldn't deny that a part of him had wanted to punish her for denying knowledge of his letters. But he'd allowed things to get out of control. God knew he desired her now as much as ever he had. When he'd implied to Luckhurst she was his mistress, the idea to seduce her had already seeded itself in his mind. In fact, from the moment their eyes had clashed in Hastings, and he'd felt a strange satisfaction settle on him, he'd known he was lost to wanting her again. When she'd hinted she'd lost her virginity he'd seriously considered doing something about it.

Her mother was keen to return to London; Deborah had admitted she missed her friends and the lifestyle she'd once enjoyed. Randolph was confident that in a short while he'd have the wherewithal to give her back what she missed. He'd be in a position to offer to help her and her mother move back to the metropolis and again have the luxuries they'd previously enjoyed. An isolated property could be purchased where they could discreetly meet and make love, and if her mother guessed what was going on, Randolph had a feeling Julia Woodville might opt to keep her suspicions to herself.

He could muster enough decency and control not to possess Deborah quickly now on the sofa before they were disturbed. A woman she might be—no thanks to Edmund Green—but he could tell from her shy kisses and blushing bashfulness that she was no seasoned mistress. He doubted the dragoon had bedded her more than a couple of times. With a groan that seemed to resonate from deep in his being and was swiftly followed by a curse, Randolph stood up with her in his arms.

The sudden movement roused Deborah. 'What…what are you doing?' It was a befuddled murmur against his shoulder.

Before he could answer Randolph's head jerked up as he heard a tap on the parlour door. He put a silencing finger to Deborah's lips and gently lowered her to the ground, but kept her hard against him as though he were unwilling to yet break contact.

Deborah frowned, still sensually stupefied. A moment later the knock came again, loud enough this time to penetrate her torpor. Her eyes widened in shock before she sprung back from him, blinking wildly.

His deft hands flowed over her, straightening her rumpled skirt and bodice. With a subtle smile, he turned and walked to the door and opened it.

Basham entered and, having flicked a look between his flushed and rather bedraggled mistress and the hard-eyed handsome guest, diplomatically fixed his regard on Mr Chadwicke's cool, quizzical expression.

'A Captain Stewart is in the hallway, sir. He wants to speak to you. Shall I tell him…umm…you're unavailable?'

'Not at all,' Randolph smoothly contradicted. 'Tell him I'll come and find him in a moment or two. I was just finishing my nightcap and am ready to leave now in any case.'

'Very good, sir,' Basham said and, having swung a furtive look between the couple, he clicked the door closed.

Deborah took a step towards Randolph, five unsteady fingers raking through her unruly locks in an attempt to neaten them. A niggling of alarm at the reason for Basham's appearance momentarily subdued some of her acute awkwardness at having nearly been caught *in flagrante* by one of the servants. She realised that she had to be very thankful Basham had had the discretion to wait for permission to enter. Had he not done so… Her cheeks flamed at the excruciating embarrassment she'd just escaped.

Now her sensual daze had deserted her, her wanton behaviour had to be faced. She felt blood fizzing in her cheeks as she realised it might not just be Basham who deemed her disgracefully immodest. What did Randolph think of her now? He had told her to go to bed, yet she had stayed. He had given her the chance to evade him, yet she had remained daringly close until she'd tempted him to pounce.

'Captain Stewart?' she blurted breathily. 'What does he want at this time of the night?' She kept her eyes lowered to her skirt, brushing and adjusting it. 'Do you think he has news of what or who frightened Fred?' She took another step towards him, her nervous hands now occupied in fierce attempts to contain her abundant hair in a neat flaxen coil.

'It's more likely the captain has come to ensure that I'm not overstaying my welcome.'

Deborah's eyes flicked up to his.

'The captain seemed quite taken with you,' Randolph said on

a slight smile. 'I thought for a while we were going to come to blows over who had the privilege of bringing you home.'

'I'm sure he was just being polite,' Deborah blurted on a blush. A chill crept over her. Was the privilege he'd acidly referred to the chance to tumble her on the sofa? Did he imagine she would have allowed the captain a few liberties if he had been the one to linger over a warming drink before leaving?

'I'm sure he wasn't being polite,' Randolph contradicted her as he strolled towards her. 'I'll see what he wants and return to see you another time. There are things we need to talk about.' He raised a cool finger to brush against her warm cheek. 'Lost letters…aged misunderstandings…what does any of it matter now?' he said silkily. 'You're a very seductive lady and undoubtedly we still like one another enough to want to keep in touch, don't you think?'

Deborah moistened her lips. His mocking, lustful tone had lacked the emotion she'd craved to hear. A searching glance at his smouldering eyes told her that with just a little encouragement from her he'd see off the captain and come back to her in minutes, not days. He very much wanted her, but not as he once had, as his wife. Next time when he returned to Woodville Place he would proposition her and to her shame she knew if he did so whilst touching her, she might be tempted to accept an offer to be his mistress.

'Please don't feel under any obligation to return,' she whispered in a brittle tone. 'I know you have business matters to attend to.'

'Believe me, Deborah, I no longer feel obliged to you in any way. But I'll be back as soon as I'm able.' A moment later he was gone from the room.

A few days later Deborah was foraging in the grounds of Woodville Place when Basham came crunching over leaves in an uneven gait. The manservant wobbled to a halt beneath the huge gnarled branches of the walnut tree.

'Gentleman caller arrived, miss,' he puffed out.

Deborah handed her basket brimming with walnuts to Lottie who, after an inquisitive look at Deborah, continued to search amid brittle brown leaves for more crinkly shells to swoop upon.

'Who is it, Basham?' Deborah pushed back behind an ear a stray curl that had tumbled on to a wind-pinked cheek. Immediately on hearing the sex of the visitor her insides had lurched. Then she remembered she was not expecting Randolph to yet call. After their strained farewell she'd decided he'd be sure to let a suitable length of time elapse before returning. But return he would—she was equally sure of that. In addition, he'd further to travel now; she'd heard from Harriet, who'd had it from her brother, that Randolph was no longer lodging at the Woolpack. He'd moved on and was staying with an aristocrat at his hunting lodge. Deborah had guessed the nobleman must be Viscount Stratton, for his name had been mentioned in conversation and she knew he resided in the area.

'A Captain Stewart's in the parlour, miss,' Basham replied. 'Mrs Woodville's taking her afternoon rest in her chamber. In any case he did ask to speak to Miss Woodville.'

Deborah brushed together her palms and with a frown went towards the house.

'It's a nice surprise to see you, Captain.' It was a tactful rather than truthful greeting.

Paul Stewart turned about from where he'd been gazing through the parlour window, hands positioned neatly behind his back and his gauntlets tapping idly against an open palm. He gave her a crisp bow. 'I hope you will not mind this unexpected visit, Miss

Woodville. I hear your mother is indisposed at the moment. I hope she is well.'

Deborah tucked the unruly fair tendril again behind her ear and gave him a smile. 'She is very well, thank you, but she rarely misses her afternoon nap. Sometimes she takes herself off to bed in the late afternoon and I do not see her again until morning.' A curled leaf was picked from where it clung to her plain dimity gown and was let drift to the empty grate. 'Mama likes her novels and her letter writing and her own company.'

As the silence between them lengthened Deborah felt at first unsettled, then vaguely irritated by his taciturnity and fixed stare. She was on the point of prodding him to reveal his business when he spoke.

'It is not lonely for you having no siblings or companion of your own age?'

'I have enough to occupy me.' Deborah managed a faint smile. 'And I have a friend to visit close by if I wish.' She had an intuition that Captain Stewart came not simply to see her, but to have some information.

'You are good friends with Harriet Davenport?'

'Yes, I am,' Deborah replied.

'And Mrs Davenport?'

'We are not well acquainted,' Deborah replied. 'The vicar got married only a year ago and Susanna is not from around here.'

'How did they meet?'

A slightly exasperated look met that blunt enquiry. 'I'm not sure exactly; I believe I recall Harriet saying at the time that it was at the assembly rooms in Brighton. Gerard was there on church business and happened to socialise with friends one evening. I have not asked more as it is not my place,' she commented pointedly. 'Will you take tea, Captain?' she asked out of politeness, but hoped he would decline. Oddly, though, she hoped he'd stay long enough for her to discover why he had come here and had wanted to speak to Randolph on the night of the Davenports' soirée.

'Thank you, no,' Paul Stewart replied to her offer of refreshment, and gave a smile that perhaps conveyed he knew she hoped his visit would be brief. 'Unfortunately, this is not a social call, Miss Woodville. I am here on official business.'

'I don't see how I can help you in any way with that, Captain.' Deborah's open expression displayed her surprise.

'I should like to ask you some questions about Mr Chadwicke,' he said, his pale blue eyes narrowing on her face as though he watched closely for her reaction.

'Please sit down if you wish to,' Deborah said and turned her back on him to approach a fireside chair. She hoped he had not noticed the rush of colour beneath her cheeks, propelled there by the mention of Randolph's name and an odd, but instant, apprehensiveness.

'Have you seen Mr Chadwicke since he escorted you home from the vicarage?' he asked, settling opposite her.

'I have not, sir,' Deborah informed coolly. 'I believe you came here to see him just as he was leaving that night.'

'Indeed I did,' Paul Stewart said.

'And was it official business that brought you here on that occasion?'

A mottling of colour appeared beneath his pale complexion as though he'd not appreciated her pert question. 'I'd wanted to ensure that all guests had got safely home. Also, I'd wanted to question Mr Chadwicke. If he'd reported seeing something suspicious whilst driving your carriage back to Woodville Place, Sergeant Booth and I would have immediately gone to investigate. However, if I'd known then what I do now, I would not have wasted my time.'

'I see—does that mean you now know what caused our driver to have such a scare that night?'

'No…it means now I have delved a little deeper in to Mr Chadwicke's background I'm not sure I could have trusted him to truthfully tell me if he had seen anything suspicious.'

For a moment Deborah simply stared at him in astonishment. 'Will you explain what you mean by that, Captain?' she eventually demanded.

'I have been making a few enquiries about Mr Chadwicke and what I have discovered is alarming to say the least.' He paused. 'I understand from the vicar that you knew him well when you lived in London some years ago.'

Deborah's eyes darted to him in annoyance. 'If you have anything you want to know about my past, I would sooner that you ask me directly, sir.'

'Indeed—that is why I am here,' he answered smoothly. 'You knew him when you lived in London?' he persisted, his tone hardening.

'The Earl and Countess of Gresham are mutual friends of ours.'

'Ah…yes,' Captain Stewart muttered sourly. 'He seems able to foster acquaintance with the high and mighty despite his exceedingly dubious connections.'

'I take it you are referring to his late brother,' Deborah said stiffly, keen to let him know he could not shock her by exposing the fact that Sebastian Chadwicke had been a scapegrace. 'I take it you are also referring to Mr Chadwicke's friendship with a nobleman who lives locally.'

'Stratton?' Paul Stewart barked in contempt. 'It's true Stratton is a viscount, but whether a noble is another matter.' He smiled in satisfaction as he saw a quickening of interest in Deborah's lucid blue eyes. 'Ah, I collect you do not know that Viscount Stratton springs from a clan of Cornish brigands. I am not from these parts so am immune to fanciful tales of his heroics. In my opinion, he was no more than a common criminal. Perhaps he still is.' He settled more comfortably in his chair, looking unattractively smug as he steepled his fingers. He tapped them gently together whilst continuing to watch her through shuttered vision. 'First I shall let you know that Viscount Stratton and Ross Trelawney are one and the same. The Trelawney brothers were once the most infamous smugglers to ever infest the south coast.'

'Ross Trelawney?' Deborah echoed faintly. It was impossible to have lived in the vicinity for more than half a decade and not have heard tales of the Trelawney brothers' exploits. But, if the epic were to be believed, when still young men they had all seen the error of their ways and given up free-trading. They were now well-respected gentleman who had fabulous wealth and legitimate businesses. Ross Trelawney, so she'd heard, had been given a peerage by the king following services to the crown. Deborah had decided that surely indicated he'd atoned for past sins. Yet she had not made the connection between the bucca-neering Cornishman and Viscount Stratton being one and the same. But why would she? She'd had no idea that Randolph had dealings with smugglers.

'Ross Trelawney has a magnificent estate in Kent and owns a good amount of the county,' Paul Stewart continued. 'He has a hunting lodge not far from here. I understand from your friend Gerard that Mr Chadwicke is staying there with Trelawney.'

Deborah's skin prickled icily; her mind darted hither and thither. 'So, they are friends,' she managed airily to say. 'I don't see what any of it has to do with my acquaintance with Mr Chadwicke, or Noose-head Ned frightening our driver that night—'

'Well, let me tell you,' Captain Stewart fluidly interrupted. His mouth curved, yet his pale blue eyes looked icier. 'I have learned from my sources that in the past Trelawneys and Chadwickes have not only been friends, but colleagues.'

Chapter Fourteen

As a debonair gentleman in Mayfair Randolph had been the epitome of polished civility. Deborah feared that Captain Stewart was about to tell her that a moon-dappled beach might rival a candlelit drawing room as his natural habitat. Despite her pounding heart she realised she was not as shocked as she ought to have been. She'd been subduing a suspicion that something sinister about Randolph might emerge.

On the day they'd met in Hastings she'd sensed a latent danger about him. The cool, professional manner in which he'd handled his pistols, and seen off the Luckhurst gang, had alerted her to a menacing undercurrent she'd not before encountered in his character.

'Were you aware prior to his arrival that Mr Chadwicke was coming to Sussex to purchase sheep?' A slight lift to his top lip displayed Paul Stewart's doubts on the veracity of Randolph's claim to have an interest in livestock.

'I wasn't. It was a great surprise to bump in to him in Hastings,' Deborah replied faintly. 'We'd had no communication for many years.'

'It was a happy coincidence, then, for you to meet one another. Or perhaps your chance meeting was not such a surprise to him as you say it was to you. I imagine he is a shrewd fellow and renewing a connection with an esteemed local family might have been to his benefit.'

'You think he would deliberately foster our friendship and use my mother and me to lend him respectability?' Deborah's tone held a mingling of disbelief and muted outrage.

'That's exactly what I think, Miss Woodville.'

Again Deborah felt her insides painfully knotting while her mind ferreted this way and that, examining facts. She had considered whether Randolph had known she was in Sussex and had come with an axe to grind over their ill-starred relationship. Was she only half-right? Had he discovered she lived in the right area and engineered the meeting to callously exploit to his advantage their shared history? It seemed preposterous to suppose him capable of such calculating behaviour, or that he would want her and her mother to tacitly supply his character reference. Yet, if what the captain was implying were true, and he were embroiled with free-traders, she could not deny that she and her mother had endorsed his image as an honest, personable fellow by offering him hospitality in their house. The vicar and his family, and Squire Pattinson and his wife, genteel people generally considered above reproach, socialised with Randolph as a consequence of his friendship with the Woodvilles.

'I think you are mistaken in this, Captain,' Deborah said slowly and clearly. Her snap decision had been easily made. She would not believe any of it without proper proof. In fact, she knew she would not be convinced until she'd heard Randolph admit he was a villain. In her heart she had never believed Randolph a liar. If he said he had sent her letters, then he had done so and they'd got lost. But she *could* accuse him of withholding information. She knew he would do that if he wanted to protect her from distress; he had admitted doing so when he'd discovered Luckhurst prowling about the grounds after dark. He lusted after her, and was careless about her knowing it; but she was equally sure he harboured an ember of affection for her that he was reluctant to display. With sudden clarity she knew she wanted very much to make him love her.

'I know that on the day he arrived in Hastings Mr Chadwicke nearly had a fight with Seth Luckhurst,' Deborah began her defence. 'I was present and witnessed all that went on. Seth had made a nuisance of himself that afternoon and had beaten my driver. Mr Chadwicke was escorting me home when Seth and two of his cronies accosted us. Seth was very aggressive. When Mr Chadwicke got the better of him and frightened him off, his humiliation was apparent. I'm sure Seth can dissemble, but equally I'm sure he is not a good enough actor to fake such a scene. He genuinely had no idea who Randolph was.'

'And how did Chadwicke get the better of three men when the odds were stacked heavily against him?' Captain Stewart interrogated immediately.

Colour rimmed Deborah's cheekbones. In her haste to support Randolph she might have hampered his case. Briefly she said, 'Mr Chadwicke was armed.'

'Was he, now?'

'It would be a foolish gentleman who travelled without a weapon for self-defence,' Deborah offered with some asperity.

'Perhaps you are right. He had a lucky victory on that occasion. As for Seth not liking, or recognising him, that is perfectly possible. I have not said Chadwicke is in cahoots with the Luckhursts. Perhaps the opposite is true.' He paused, unsure whether he ought to continue. In truth, he knew he should not. He was aware the intelligence he was passing to Deborah Woodville was confidential. Yet the more she defended Randolph Chadwicke, the greater became his need to tell her all he knew until he'd painted him so black she turned against him.

He had come under her spell from the first moment he'd spotted her looking angelic in the vicar's drawing room. Her blue silk gown and fair ringlets weren't present today; she was modestly dressed and her glorious hair was windswept; still her pale, unadorned beauty had the power to stir his blood. The fact that Chadwicke had that night subtly signalled she was his had embittered Paul. When Deborah had seemed aware, yet unminding of foreign-looking fingers that had rested so close to her they almost touched her naked shoulder, he'd realised, with a stab of jealousy, that Chadwicke might already have seduced her.

Sergeant Booth had been a colleague of Deborah's murdered fiancé. Booth had informed him of Lieutenant Green's fate, and also that since the dragoon's death Deborah was known to be unwisely vociferous in her hatred of all smugglers. Paul had felt elated to unearth Chadwicke's infamy. He'd felt sure that Deborah must be unaware of it and had wanted to rectify her ignorance and gain her gratitude. But she was not acting in the way he'd hoped for, or expected. She'd appeared shocked by what he'd disclosed, yet still she seemed determined to defend Chadwicke. In Paul Stewart's mind there was only one reason why she would cleave to him at any cost: she was in love with him.

'A newcomer is expected to challenge the status quo,' Captain Stewart announced. 'We've had intelligence from our informants about it. In my opinion Chadwicke isn't in Sussex to join the Luckhursts, but to do battle with them for control of the lucrative trade in contraband on the south coast.'

He had finally unequivocally stated he believed Randolph a smuggler, and Deborah was unable to suppress a breath of despair parting her soft lips.

Sensing victory, Paul pressed home his advantage. 'Almost eighteen years ago Sebastian Chadwicke was the principal in a gang of smugglers operating along the Suffolk coastline.'

Although Deborah heard the captain's damning evidence, it seemed his voice drifted to her from a long way off.

'A particularly vicious band they were, too, by all accounts,' the captain impressed on her. 'It is on record that Sebastian Chadwicke fled abroad to evade capture for the murder of a Revenue man who'd been stabbed in an affray just outside Hadleigh. Even before that dreadful event about eight years ago, his younger brother, Randolph, was involved in the business and was running contraband from the continent. He would liaise with other gangs around the country, especially those on the south coast. He and Ross Trelawney were in partnership for a while.'

'I don't believe you,' Deborah whispered, but her lack of conviction was plain in her unsteady voice.

'Why not? Because you are in love with him?'

Deborah blushed to the roots of her fair hair. Dreadfully disconcerted she might have been, but his impertinence rankled enough to inspirit her. 'How dare you make such a personal assumption!'

'Are you?' Captain Stewart demanded, unmoved by her hissed objection. He gained his feet. 'I'm sure Chadwicke's capable of using you as an unwitting decoy; perhaps he's been taking other liberties too…?'

'I think it is time you left, sir.' Deborah's eyes flashed blue fire at him before she averted her face from his bold, impenitent scrutiny.

'You have not denied that you are in love with him,' he purred. 'Are you going to let him use…perhaps incriminate…you and your mother?' Her refusal to be drawn seemed to irritate him.

His gloves were swiped against an open palm. 'Now I have informed you of the nature of the beast I would not have thought you'd want to defend him, Miss Woodville. I understand you were engaged to a Lieutenant Green who, whilst carrying out his duty, was murdered by a smuggler.'

Deborah's dusky lashes drooped low over her eyes. It seemed the captain knew where to hit. Even before he'd reminded her of that awful fact it had been pricking at her conscience. Abruptly she stood up. Her sharp little chin was elevated to a rather haughty angle and she coolly met his eyes. 'I think what you have told me about the Chadwickes—and I do not know it *is* true, but if it proves to be—it is none the less far in Randolph's past. He has been in the Indies for many years and thus cannot have been running contraband across the English Channel. He has only recently returned following the death of his brother.' She drew in a gulp of air. 'I don't believe he would engage in criminal activity now he is head of his family. His mother is still alive and he has a spinster sister also dependent upon him.'

'And all of them in straitened circumstances, thanks to Sebastian Chadwicke having squandered the family's assets and died in disgrace.' He paused for effect. 'His crimes finally caught up with him, and not before time. He was hanged for treason.'

Deborah's complexion went deathly pale, but she conquered any other sign of her astonishment.

'Chadwicke is in need of funds, Miss Woodville,' Paul Stewart informed her in a poisonous purr. 'And what better way to refill the Chadwicke coffers than to take a tried-and-tested route to riches with Trelawney's backing?'

'I think I must ask you to leave now, Captain,' Deborah whispered.

'I think you forget I am here on official business, Miss

Woodville. I don't want to seek a warrant...' Paul Stewart rattled out the threat in angry frustration. Still she would not desert him!

'Will you arrest me?' Her challenge, spat in a voice of suffocated outrage, seemed to finally temper his vindictiveness.

'Of course not.' He forced a frosty smile. 'I warn you about him for your own good, you know. I hope you understand the gravity of what I've told you. If you persist in being his advocate, and bring shame upon your own and your mother's heads, do not say I did not give you fair warning of it.' With a stiff bow he strode past her and to the door.

For some fifteen minutes after his departure Deborah paced back and forth in the parlour, her head filled with vying ideas of how to proceed. Over and over again a theory, or course of action, was leapt upon, then rejected for none was properly thought through. Her mind darted always onwards to find some new and better way of proving Captain Stewart wrong and Randolph innocent. Finally she went back to the chair she'd sat in and slumped down. Her fair head bowed into cupped hands and she felt tears transfer from her lashes to her palms. Her shoulders hunched forwards to contain a sob swelling in her chest.

The captain surely would not fabricate something so serious. She believed he was malicious, but a liar? No, he had his military career and his reputation to protect after all. She had sensed at the Davenports' soirée that Paul Stewart had taken against Randolph, but he would not jeopardise his future because he had a fancy for her and had sensed Randolph to be a rival. She rather thought the captain was a self-righteous stickler. He would have carefully done his research before presenting her with his shocking findings.

Still she was unwilling to accept that there wasn't a reasonable explanation that would negate what he'd told her. Annoyed with herself for wanting what she could not have, she shook back straggling golden tresses from her damp cheeks. Why would she defend him at all cost? Unless…was the captain right about that as well?

A bittersweet ache fluttering in her chest was her answer. She *was* still in love with Randolph and that, in its way, was as alarming to her as the knowledge of his family's dreadful secrets. Little wonder nobody had ever spoken about Sebastian Chadwicke other than in mutters. Little wonder he had always been addressed as Chadwicke rather than by his title of Lord Buckland. Nobody would believe him worthy of the honour held by his decent father. Had her parents known the extent of his wickedness?

Deborah knuckled her dewy eyes and gazed into space. Her mother had known that Sebastian had fled abroad to escape arrest for murder. Deborah had assumed he might have been embroiled in a duel over a woman. *Nothing quite so noble*, her mother had sourly quipped, and she'd named him a devil. How much did her mother know about Sebastian Chadwicke's wickedness? And was she aware of Randolph's involvement in his heinous crimes?

Deborah got to her feet. She had decided it might be wise to start to find some answers.

Thankfully her mother was at her writing desk, rather than snoozing on her day bed. When Deborah knocked on her chamber door she was immediately summoned to enter.

Julia quickly put her pen on the stand on seeing her daughter's wan face and tense and dishevelled appearance.

'What on earth's the matter? You look as though you've seen a ghost.'

'Noose-head Ned, perhaps?' Deborah muttered, but with very little humour apparent.

'What is it, my dear?' Julia got up and went to her daughter, drawing her down on the edge of her bed.

'Captain Stewart has just visited us, Mama. Basham knew not to disturb you. In any case, he wanted to speak to me.'

Julia moistened her lips. 'Has he intimated he would like to come courting?' She patted at her daughter's hand. 'I could tell he was utterly smitten by you when we were at the Davenports. If you don't fancy him you only have to say so, Debbie.'

A gasp of mirthless laughter escaped Deborah. 'I almost wish that had brought him here, unwelcome as his suit would have been.' She paused, unsure how to begin the sorry tale. 'The reason he came was to say he has been snooping into Randolph's family history. He came to accuse the Chadwicke brothers of vile crimes.'

Julia returned her daughter's stare for a moment, her mind immediately darting to a compartment in her desk in which reposed four unopened letters. A feeling of ultimate vindication comforted her as she stroked again at Deborah's quivering hand. 'I don't know why the captain has done such a mean thing, other than to poison your mind against Randolph.' She gave her daughter a wry smile. 'Oh, yes, I've seen how Randolph looks at you too.' She sighed. 'I know you have always been fond of him and I've been expecting him to approach you again.' Realising her mistake—she wasn't supposed to know of their youthful romance—she hurried on, 'It was a long time ago that Sebastian stirred up so much trouble that it reached the *ton*'s notice. He invariably stayed away from London and did his mischief a hundred miles away in Suffolk. So not all of it became common knowledge.' Julia smoothed her skirt. 'I've told you I very much liked Randolph's parents. They were respectable people. I have to say I don't recall much about their daughter. She must be a young lady now. And you know that your papa and I liked Randolph. He has always been so very courteous and charming…'

'Indeed he has,' Deborah concurred with a tinge of bitterness that made her mother look closely at her. Deborah stood up and fidgeted on the spot for a moment before going to the window. She turned about and noticed a look of quiet puzzlement on her mother's face. 'Sebastian was *very* bad, wasn't he?' Deborah whispered. She watched keenly with watery blue eyes for her mother's reaction. 'Do you know why he fled abroad many years ago? I know you have said that he killed a man…but do you *really* know how the disaster came about?'

Julia began to question her daughter about what the captain had said, then instead stopped and frowned. She could tell from Deborah's poignant sadness that something of great moment had happened whilst she'd been happily writing to her friend in London.

Julia remained quiet and thought carefully before beginning, 'I recall that Sebastian had allegedly been in dispute with a fly-by-night merchant over payment for some foreign luxuries. A shipping matter I believe it was and there was a rumour the cargo might have been stolen. In the ensuing fight the fellow was killed and Sebastian fled to save his neck.' Julia sighed. 'It seemed a straightforward case of self-defence, but whatever it was, nobody was surprised that it had ended that way for him. He was a wicked sort who kept company with like-minded people. When you lie down with dogs…' She made an expressive little gesture. 'But the family, and especially Randolph, for he was of an age to be affected by his brother's disgrace, gained much sympathy. A black sheep can turn up in any family. *There but for the grace of God,* I recall your papa saying at the time the calamity leaked out. The Clevelands, like most clans, have bred their fair share of scapegraces over the centuries.'

'According to Captain Stewart, Randolph has always been part of the Chadwickes' disgrace and is undeserving of our trust and sympathy,' Deborah said hoarsely. 'You are almost correct in what you've related, Mama. A fellow *was* killed in a dispute over shipping. The stock was contraband and the victim a Revenue man. Captain Stewart has told me that the Chadwicke brothers were Suffolk smugglers. He believes that Randolph still is.'

Chapter Fifteen

'Would you bring the trap round to the front in twenty minutes, please, Fred?'

Fred looked up; his mistress had breathlessly gasped out that instruction as though she'd bolted down the back stairs to deliver it. He'd been polishing silver at the kitchen table but, grimacing surprise at Lottie and Mrs Field who were preparing vegetables, he put down the cutlery and got to his feet.

'We shall have just a cold collation this evening for supper,' Deborah told the women. She eyed the mound of carrots and potatoes peeled and ready for the stew pot. 'But, of course, prepare yourselves a proper dinner. I must go out for a while, but should return before nine and will eat then. Please save some stew for Fred.' With that she was gone and soon running lightly through the house towards the stairs. In her chamber she changed into her warm outdoor clothes. She was about to quit the room when she stopped and returned to her dressing chest and sat down before the mirror. She stared intently into solemn blue eyes whilst her mind sped to an irrevocable fact. Whatever came to pass in the next few hours would determine her future happiness.

It was close to dusk when the trap clattered past Woodville Place's iron gates and turned in the direction of the vicarage.

The purpose of Deborah's visit there was to get from Gerard Davenport—if he knew it, and she prayed he did—the direction of the hunting lodge where Randolph was staying with his friend Ross Trelawney. She went on the mission with her mother's blessing and encouragement; but even had she not given it, Deborah had already decided she must contact Randolph without delay and let him know that Captain Stewart had been either casting very grave aspersions on his character, or broadcasting the extent of his wicked crimes. Deborah knew that she still cherished a secret, if forlorn, hope that the former were true.

Her mother had suggested that Fred go alone to get the lodge's direction from the vicar. Deborah had stated, in a tone that brooked no refusal, it would be best that she go in person. Gerard was sure to question her urgent need for Mr Chadwicke's whereabouts, and she'd sooner answer him personally than have Fred give his version of events. Fred was a loyal employee, but not the brightest of fellows. If the captain's recent visit to Woodville Place were to be mentioned, and added to the equation, speculation might ensue. Deborah certainly did not want two and two put together to make matters worse than they already were.

Valid as that argument was, she also had a private reason for wanting to go out that she dared not disclose. She knew it would greatly upset her mother to know that her plan wasn't to return with the address and simply write a note asking Randolph to call on them urgently. If the lodge were situated within a reasonable striking distance Deborah's intention was to confront him in person tonight. Considering how intimate had become their relationship, she had a pressing need to know—a *right* to know—exactly who Randolph Chadwicke was.

Her mother's forceful attitude, on learning that Randolph was accused of being a free-trader in cahoots with a roguish viscount, had greatly surprised Deborah.

'Poppycock!' her mother had angrily snorted. 'He is as different from his brother as two men can be. We might not have known him as well as we knew his friend Marcus Speer, but your papa and I had enough sense between us, and enough dealings with Randolph, to have recognised an honest, decent gentleman when he crossed our path.' She'd then looked a trifle discomposed and muttered, 'Naturally, only to be expected that the poor fellow would suffer a bit of prejudice because of such dreadful connections.' Julia had then gone on to express an opinion similar to Deborah's own. 'Captain Stewart, it seems, is not an asset to us after all. If he is not a mischief-maker, and it is all a misunderstanding, then he is without doubt still a malicious man. He should not have told you any of this. Of course, we must be glad he did and hope it backfires on him.' An eye was cast over her lovely daughter as she announced, 'If he comes here again I shall have something to say to him. And you, miss, must make it clear that his attention is most unwelcome. I won't have such as he for a son-in-law.' A moment later she'd clasped Deborah's hands to her bosom and had endorsed her daughter's wistful thoughts. 'Over many years Randolph has been a very good friend to us. When he recently stayed here, and took charge so calmly, it was as though he were one of the family.'

Now, as Deborah's flitting glance settled on the sun dipping below the western horizon, she wondered what her mother would think if Randolph turned out to be not only a smuggler, but a fellow who harboured dishonourable intentions towards her daughter.

'Hartsmere Lodge is situated just off the road to Green End.' Having answered Deborah's immediate question, Gerard Davenport urged his unexpected visitor towards the hearth and indicated she should sit down in the chair close to the fire. Just as she did so Harriet's entry in to the parlour brought Deborah again to her feet. The two women clasped hands in affectionate greeting.

'What a nice surprise,' Harriet exclaimed.

Deborah could sense her friend's unspoken question. Gerard had already voiced his when Dilys had announced her arrival, thus drawing him from his study to greet her. Deborah guessed that Harriet had just come down from upstairs where she'd been tidying herself before dinner. An appetising aroma of savoury beef was in the air, making Deborah aware of her own hunger. An instant later food was forgotten.

'Deborah was enquiring after Mr Chadwicke's direction.' Gerard satisfied his sister's curiosity. 'She needs to get quickly in contact with him. It is confidential,' he added in a cautionary way.

Harriet blinked and shot a look at her brother as though begging his permission to disclose something. A small nod and lift to his eyebrows sanctioned her wordless request.

'You need not fear worrying us, Debbie. We already know all about it!' Harriet squealed excitedly. 'I know your mother feels safer when Mr Chadwicke is around and Lord only knows it seems we will all need protection if we soon are to be awash with smugglers.'

'Smugglers?' Deborah pounced upon the word and in a whisper echoed it back at her friend. 'I'm not sure…what do you mean?'

'Gerard was in Rye today and there was a buzz going around that a huge cargo of contraband is due to be brought ashore at any moment.' Harriet glanced at her brother in case he might indicate with a frown that she'd said enough.

The vicar gave his sister no such look.

'Gerard spoke to Mr Savidge and he also had heard the gossip,' Harriet rushed on. 'Free-traders are anchored out to sea and are preparing to storm the beach and do battle with the militia to get their goods landed.'

Deborah blinked, darting a look at Gerard for him to confirm the news. A grim nod from him was all that was needed to make Deborah's sense of dread escalate.

'The Luckhursts are not the culprits this time,' Gerard informed. 'Apparently the brothers are seething with rage that a new gang appears to be trying to take over their patch.' He sighed in vexation. 'It was bad enough before. But better the devil you know, I say. What chaos and bloodshed must we endure if two rival gangs start to fight for control?'

'When I visited Rye a day or so ago I noticed that far more redcoats than usual seemed to be about,' Harriet chipped in. 'Now it's suddenly become very clear why Captain Stewart would call in those reinforcements.'

'The militia have their spies and their informants,' Gerard said sagely. 'I'll warrant the authorities knew of this long before we did.'

Harriet turned to Deborah. 'But you had not heard about it, Debbie?' she asked in surprise.

'Mama and I were speaking earlier about some worrying news regarding the smugglers.' Deborah's speedy response was designed to subdue further awkward questions. She was pleased that with hindsight she'd not lied. She quickly unscrambled some facts so she might continue in the same vein, yet without mentioning Captain Stewart's visit. In view of what she'd just learned, many questions from her friends would ensue if they knew the dragoon had that afternoon been at Woodville Place. 'I hoped the tale we'd been given was exaggerated. And you are right—Mama feels happier when a gentleman is about the place for protection. If Mr Chadwicke could be persuaded to call on us soon, she'd like it very much.'

'I didn't see him in Rye today. If you like, I could go to the lodge tomorrow and take a message for you,' Gerard offered pleasantly.

'No! It is not necessary…but thank you. Something smells very tasty,' Deborah quickly tacked on the end to cover her agitation. 'Your dinner is making me feel quite hungry.'

'Why do you not dine with us?' Harriet immediately invited. 'As Susanna is gone unexpectedly there is plenty to spare and we can have a proper chinwag about when the action might take place.'

'Thank you, but I must not stay. Mama will be waiting on my return.' Deborah managed a smile. 'I must get going, and apologise for calling so late.' Harriet looked as though she might use persuasion, so Deborah asked quickly, 'Is Susanna not coming home to dine?'

'She has had to go unexpectedly to her brother's,' Gerard explained in a muted tone. 'A note arrived that the poor fellow is ill again.'

'He seems to be at death's door quite often,' Harriet observed a touch sourly, and drew a reproving frown from her brother.

'Well, he does,' Harriet said snappishly. A moment later her tone had turned impish. 'Not that I mind when she is away…'

Her brother cast another stern look her way. 'I shall bid you farewell then, Deborah. I have just a few more paragraphs to write for Sunday's sermon and I'd as soon get it finished before supper.'

'She is a bit too often with that *brother* of hers,' Harriet darkly muttered, on accompanying Deborah through the vestibule.

Deborah turned an interested glance on her friend. 'You think there is something suspicious about it?'

'It's odd that Gerard has never met him. I wouldn't be surprised if she's drawn to Devon less by altruism than romance…' she hinted on an arch look.

But Deborah, curious as she was to know more, had no time to tarry and chat. With a small wave she was soon down the stone steps and back in the trap.

'Mist's coming in from the sea,' Fred announced dolefully. 'Knew we shouldn't have come out on such an evening.' He flicked the reins over the grey mare's plump rump. A moment later he was gawping over his shoulder at his mistress. 'Green End?' he barked in alarm. 'But, miss, that be a good nine mile off east, and the mist's comin' in fast.' He looked about fearfully. 'Ain't a night to be out. I reckon we should straight off head home.'

'Fred Cook, we are going to Hartsmere Lodge, towards Green End, and if I am not scared of ghosts and shadows, I don't see why you should be.' Deborah gave him a severe look. It transformed to an inspiriting smile. 'Come along, Fred. You know that Noose-head Ned is just a figment of lively imaginations.'

'I know what I saw,' Fred insisted in a hoarse voice. 'It weren't me imagination.'

'Well, I'm sure you *thought* you saw something. If this spectre does pop up now and again, you can bet on it the smugglers are missing a member of their crew while they go about their business on the beach.'

Deborah looked about; the mist was indeed in evidence. As they turned out of the Davenports' driveway a swirl of white shifted sinuously in front of them. She pulled her wool cloak tighter about her and tweaked the hood to shield her complexion from the mist's clammy caress. Sporadic glances up and around told her the fog was becoming more solid as they left the vicarage behind. If what she'd just heard from her friends were true, and nefarious business was imminent, this could be the night the free-traders would choose to do it. But she had now what she'd wanted and a stubborn yearning was subduing the flutter of fear in her chest that warned her to heed Fred's advice. She knew it would be sensible to head directly home. The order to turn about hovered on her lips, but refused to quit them. It seemed she was fatefully determined to run Randolph to ground and force him to answer her questions.

As though he thought the faster they travelled the sooner they'd be safe and sound Fred flicked the whip and set the mare to a faster pace. The trap rattled and bounced over uneven ground as glistening shrubbery flashed past. Deborah held tight to the seat with both hands and, squinting into the distance, saw the signpost at the crossroads. Barely slowing down to steer, Fred urged the mare to the right and on they flew through the night, the mist licking at them until thickets provided a meagre protection and the road was again visible.

It was the horse rather than Fred who first took terrible fright. The animal skittered to the side of the road, snorting and shying and a wheel of the trap plunged into the ditch, throwing the vehicle to the left and its passengers off balance. Fred scrambled back to the seat and instantly one of his quivering fingers pointed to the right. His face was a mask of terror and his mouth worked, but no sound came forth. Deborah swivelled on the seat, struggling to sit upright, and saw a phantom-like figure astride a horse. It was garbed in a hat and cloak that appeared to have been liberally showered with flour. A moment later her wide and terrified eyes were dragged to her driver as Fred slumped forwards in a faint, banging his head on the side of the trap as he fell at her feet.

With palsied hands Deborah untangled Fred's fingers from the reins and tried to soothe the spooked mare with hoarse mutters and tiny tugs on the reins. She knew that if the animal bolted, the trap, listing dangerously to one side, would be broken asunder and she and Fred thrown to the ground, perhaps to be fatally injured beneath wheels and hooves.

A slanting glance was sent to her right; she was hoping Noose-head Ned had had the decency to disappear. Obviously she and her driver, given their perilous predicament, were going to be of no threat to him. He might just as well set about whatever business had him skulking tonight. And she rather thought she knew what it was. The ships idling at sea were coming in.

He was still there, watching. She narrowed her shocked vision on him. He was a stocky fellow, quite tall, she imagined, from his height in the saddle. His face had been powdered to a ghastly luminosity and was half-hidden by a tricorn hat pulled low on his brow. Squinting closely, she noticed that a few strands of his hair had escaped the disguise and looked to be black in colour. As though the fellow had guessed she was not nearly as frightened as she ought to be, he swung the length of rope that trailed off his neck.

For some reason that very much annoyed Deborah. Whilst she and Fred were in mortal danger, he was showing off. 'Do you know how ridiculous you look?' she shouted in an impassioned voice. 'Get off that horse and come here at once and help me,' she demanded, jumping to her feet. It was a senseless move to have made. She gingerly again sat down as the trap tilted further into the ditch and Fred's inert form rolled closer to the side.

Deborah slid on the seat away from Fred to balance the vehicle and wrathfully gazed back at Ned. A soft gasp parted Deborah's lips, for she saw then that he was not alone. The outline of another rider, previously merged with shadows, had become visible. The two men appeared to be conducting a low conversation.

'Who are you? What do you want?' Deborah demanded in a croak. When she gained no response, she stammered, 'If…if you help me get our vehicle back on the road, we'll forget we've seen you and be on our way.'

A booming guffaw met that. 'I'm sure you'd like me to think so, my lovely. But Ned's far too cute to fall for that one.'

Ned spurred his horse closer until he was by the side of the tilting vehicle. Deborah immediately swung her face from his, but thick, floury fingers caught at her chin and jerked it round.

'So...you aren't afraid of me?' he taunted. 'You should be, you know. Pretty, aren't you, sweetheart?' His mouth had parted, and looked to be a dark cavern in his chalky visage. 'I could find a use for you,' he purred and pinched her chin tighter.

'Dragoons are close behind us,' Deborah lied desperately, yanking her face backwards and away from his spiteful touch. 'You'd best be off.'

He rumbled a chuckle. 'Dragoons are hiding by the beach, I'll warrant, waiting for a cargo to come ashore. So will I be very soon and I'll have it if I have to slay every soldier in the doing of it. But first I've got something else to do.' He tilted his head towards her, trying to capture her evasive eyes with his crafty gaze. 'So where were you off too on this filthy night, darling?'

'I'm going to Hartsmere Lodge, to see Mr Chadwicke.' Deborah whispered. 'He's a very good friend of mine and...and is expecting me,' she lied. 'If I don't turn up soon, he'll be out searching for me. You'd best be on your way.'

That information completely changed Ned's attitude: his face set in to shrewd lines that compressed flour in creases about his eyes and mouth. He flicked a glance back at his companion and the fellow, still by the trees, beckoned urgently.

Ned trotted back and stopped alongside his colleague. Deborah noticed then that the other fellow looked to be dwarfed by Ned's thickset frame.

Deborah dragged her eyes from the parleying pair and darted

looks about, dithering uncertainly. Many courses of action raced through her feverish brain. The one that stayed at the forefront of her mind was that she should quickly jump to the ground and bolt into the gloom, but she was reluctant to leave Fred behind, and at their mercy. Yet if she did nothing…what would become of them both? If she escaped, she might manage to get to a dwelling and find assistance. How far was Hartsmere Lodge? Which direction should she take? It was too late! Ned was on his way back towards her.

'Well, Miss Woodville, it's a miserable night to leave you here all alone,' Ned rasped. 'You can come with me and I'll keep you warm…as warm as Chadwicke would, I'll swear.' He grunted a lewd laugh.

'How…how do you know my name?' Deborah whispered. He knew who she was! The spiteful fingers about her heart seemed to have tightened their grip

'You're Chadwicke's doxy,' he answered coarsely. 'I can see why he'd fit you in even on a busy night such as this.' A lascivious glance swept over her, then a hand dived under her cloak, causing her to shrink back from a rough fondling of her bosom.

A moment later Deborah's anger had overcome her fright. She slapped away his insolent fingers, causing a cloud of powder to rise in the air. 'I am no man's doxy!'

'Chadwicke says different, so we heard.'

Deborah was momentarily stunned into speechlessness.

'Done with you, has he?' Ned's leering face was thrust closer to Deborah. 'Never mind. Whether he has or he hasn't is of no consequence. I'm to kill him tonight, but it'd be a shame to have to snap that pretty neck of yours…'

Ice had shivered along Deborah's spine when she'd heard his guttural threats. From the first moment Ned had approached the trap, and she'd clearly seen his features, she'd guessed he would want to silence her. Despite his covering of powder she'd recognise him again, and he knew it. And it was his intention to murder Randolph too! What she'd heard from the Davenports just an hour or so ago was true. Two rival gangs of smugglers were going to do battle for the cargo out at sea. Her immediate need was to warn Randolph that an assassin was on his way. Her frantic brain had sped to the conclusion that, instead of fighting it out fairly on the beach, Ned intended to sneakily ambush Randolph at the Lodge.

With no further thought on the matter, Deborah shoved the heel of her hand hard into his face. As Ned bellowed in surprise and anger his horse reared, giving her the chance she needed. Deborah gathered her skirts in shaking fists and leapt over the side of the trap. She heard the vehicle creak and tumble and momentarily hesitated, for her thoughts were for poor, comatose Fred. But an instant later she'd sped away towards the woods, dodging and swerving this way and that as dark clumps of vegetation loomed in front of her. She felt her hood catch on a low branch and fall away from her fair hair so that it fluttered like a bright flag behind her. Brambles nipped at her bare shins, for her trembling fists had hoisted her skirts clear of her flying feet. On she pounded, her drumming heartbeat deafening her to any sound of pursuit. Finally, when it seemed her lungs would explode if she didn't rest, she dived behind a gigantic tree trunk. She shoved her back against it as her chest pumped painfully with her laboured gasps. Blood was thundering in her ears, yet she strained to detect the telltale sounds of twigs cracking beneath hooves so she might judge how close were her pursuers. Would they have dismounted and given chase on foot?

She drew her cloak about her, drawing up its hood to conceal the gleam of her hair and slid to an edge of the great bole to peer around it. A wall of impenetrable blackness met her questing gaze. She searched about for a route that might circle back to the road where Fred was, all the time listening for sound of pursuit. Having decided to flee to the right, Deborah retreated one tiny step at a time whilst filling her lungs with much needed breath to launch her forwards. She started as her small buttocks came into contact with a man's thighs. She sucked in a breath in readiness to scream just as a hard palm slid across her mouth.

'Quiet,' a voice whispered close to one of her ears. 'I mean you no harm, I swear. Be still and silent, they're very close.'

Something in his authoritative, yet lightly amused, tone made Deborah heed his warning. She swallowed and became as stiff as a board, very aware of her back pressed against a muscular masculine body. Her impaired hearing had prevented her detecting the sound that had alerted him to her hunters. But now the rhythmic tattoo of galloping hooves was audible to her also. Two horses suddenly crashed out of the blackness and thundered past, one carrying Noose-head Ned and the other his skinny companion. As soon as the sound had died away, the fellow loosened his grip, then let her go.

Immediately Deborah spun about, her wild eyes scouring the dark face above her.

A flash of white teeth preceded her saviour's neat bow. 'Viscount Stratton, at your service, ma'am,' he drawled.

Chapter Sixteen

'You're Ross Trelawney?' Deborah gasped.

'You have me at a disadvantage, Miss…?

'Cleveland,' Deborah whispered. The gleam of teeth disappeared and Deborah knew his amusement had suddenly vanished.

At that moment the moon escaped a cloud and silver beams filtered through the trees to highlight his profile. Deborah saw he was of similar height and breadth to Randolph, but his hair was extremely dark and carelessly tousled. The viscount had the look of a handsome gypsy rather than a wealthy aristocrat she realised a moment before they were cast back into blackness. Scudding nimbus had recaptured the moon, but not before she'd glimpsed a large horse tethered some yards away.

'I imagine that Randolph doesn't know you're darting about the woods with Ned Swinton on your tail,' Ross remarked quietly.

'Randolph has told you about me?' Deborah demanded in astonishment.

'Indeed he has, so I'd best get you out of harm's way or he'll have my hide.' He caught at Deborah's elbow with a firm grip and urged her towards the horse. 'Come,' he said without preamble. 'Let's get you to the Lodge, Miss Cleveland.'

'But…but, you don't understand. Ned is out to murder Randolph, he told me so. And my driver is injured and unconscious in our trap. I can't leave him. I must go back and help him. And you must warn Randolph as soon as possible that Ned is going to ambush him.' Deborah wriggled her shoulder to free herself from a determined hand propelling her along.

'Randolph already knows Ned's after him,' Ross said soothingly. 'As for your driver, after I've got you safely to the Lodge I'll go and fetch him and bring him to you.'

His low baritone sounded calm and persuasive, but still Deborah's concern for Fred caused her to pull back. A million questions whirled in her mind, but she knew they must wait. The most important thing had been that Randolph knew his life was in imminent danger. If he were already aware an assassin was stalking him, her next priority was to help her servant. She had thwarted Ned and his accomplice and because of it she was afraid they might return to the trap and vent their spite on poor Fred. If he wasn't already mortally wounded, he might soon be. She explained to Ross her fears.

'Ned and his crew have more important fish to fry tonight,' came his immediate reply. 'They'll leave alone your unconscious driver, you may depend upon it.'

'Where is Randolph?' Deborah asked in a quavering croak. 'Is he by the shore?' Her eyes searched Ross's shadowy face, but the gloom made his expression impenetrable. '"More important fish to fry…"' She quoted his words back at him. 'You mean the cargo out at sea, don't you? Ned's an ally of the Luckhursts, isn't he? They're all Randolph's rivals and will try to kill him before he gets to the contraband, isn't that so?' Her rapid questions gained no replies. In exasperation she shoved at his arm to send him away from her. 'Oh…if you won't tell me anything, at least go and help Randolph without delay.'

'Indeed I must help him without delay,' Ross agreed. 'But I have to get you somewhere safe, or Randolph might be first to commit murder, and I'll be in his firing line, not Ned or the Luckhursts.' As he spoke he extracted a pistol from a pocket of his coat and checked it before putting it back whence it came. 'Come, let us go,' he urged softly. 'I am to rendezvous with Randolph very soon. There is still time for me to get you to the Lodge. I swear Randolph will want you to go with me.'

Her safety was now an unwanted burden on Ross. She realised, too, that she had put other lives in jeopardy this evening by not heeding her servant's advice to go straight home. Shame and guilt flooded her as she acknowledged young Fred had displayed more common sense than had she. Her determination to confront Randolph with his alleged crimes, and have her answers, had made her illogical. She knew her conscience would not allow her to accept sanctuary whilst Fred lay in a ditch. The least she could do was return to comfort him.

'Have you a gun to lend me as protection? I won't hesitate to use it if Ned again comes near me.' She forced up her sharp little chin despite its wobble. 'I can look after myself.' A mere tremor in her voice betrayed how fragile was her bravado. 'I can return alone to the trap whilst you help Randolph. If Fred has regained consciousness, and is able, we shall set off on foot together to the vicarage where I have friends…' Her voice broke. 'Tell Randolph that I hope he stays safe and gets away…'

'You can tell him yourself,' growled an awful, disembodied voice.

Deborah spun about, her heart vaulting to her mouth.

Ross turned more slowly. He blew out his cheeks in an audible sigh before muttering, 'Right, I'll be off. I could do with your assistance at some point.' It was a sarcastic request sent over a shoulder to Randolph as he strolled to his horse.

'What in damnation do you think you're doing here?' Randolph blasted through gritting teeth. He strode up to Deborah and pinned her back against the tree by planting two large hands on her shoulders.

His unbridled fury had the effect of incensing her. All previous tender thoughts for his safety were buried beneath her simmering indignation. 'I might ask you the same thing,' she spat back. 'But I won't, because I don't need to. I know now all about you. You're a smuggler!' she hissed. The dreadful things about his past that she'd learned from Captain Stewart now bombarded her mind. She forced her weight forwards to escape him, but managed only to increase the painful grip digging in to her flesh. 'You've abused our hospitality in the most hateful way. You're a vile criminal, as was your brother, and I don't know why I've risked my life, and Fred's, to come and tell you that Captain Stewart knows all about you, and is probably going to capture you tonight and make sure you get hanged for your crimes.' Her eyes felt hot and gritty with tears that slowly dripped to her cheeks. She was obliquely aware that Ross had spurred his horse forwards, and Randolph knew it, too, for he snapped sideways his head, flicking soft fawn hair against her cheek, to watch his friend disappear.

'Let me go,' Deborah raged and her small fists pummelled his chest before yanking at his muscled forearms. 'I've done what I came to do. I've warned you that the game is up. If Fred is dead or badly maimed because of what I've done, I'll never forgive myself…or you.' She raised her eyes to find his hawkish gaze riveted on her face.

'The captain visited you to tell you I'm a smuggler?'

She nodded and her ineffectual battering at his body ceased. She sank back against the tree with a sob.

'Remind me to thank him,' Randolph drawled savagely.

'Are you not going to deny it?' she demanded in a bitter croak.

'Where's Fred?' he asked, ignoring her question.

'Back along the road that leads to St Andrew's church,' she answered automatically. 'I went to the vicarage to find out your direction from Gerard. Our trap went into a ditch when Ned accosted us on the road and frightened Bessie, our mare.' She drew in a shaky breath. 'Fred fainted and bumped his head. I pray he is not badly hurt.'

'You shouldn't have come out tonight, Debbie.' Randolph touched a shaking finger to her cheek. 'God knows on this of all nights you should be safe at home,' he muttered in anguish.

'Ned is after you, too. He told me he is going to kill you.'

'We'll see about that,' Randolph rasped on a harsh laugh. It seemed being reminded of imminent peril from that reprobate had hardened his feelings for her too. His eyes and mouth tightened grimly as he studied her upturned, mutinous face. A moment later he'd jerked her away from the tree and was on the move.

In two strides he was at his horse, Deborah held off the ground by an arm encircling her waist, and carried along with him because she'd instinctively struggled to go to Fred. He swung lithely into the saddle without releasing his grip on one of her wrists. An instant later he'd reached down and, despite her protests, hauled her up to sit in front of him. Deborah squirmed as an immovable arm girdled her waist and jerked her back against him. Suddenly a hand clamped on her mouth and she quietened immediately—she'd learned from Ross such a warning meant danger might be close.

A moment later Randolph's muffling hand was gone and he'd inclined close to murmur, 'Ross has come back for some reason.'

A horse clopped quietly out of a thicket and Ross brought the animal to a halt alongside. 'Your driver is gone, Miss Cleveland,' he said softly. 'The horse and trap are still there, but no soul about.'

Deborah choked back a sob of dismay. 'Poor Fred. Poor Bessie! Is she lame, do you know?'

'She looks to be uninjured and not too spooked by it all,' Ross said. 'I'm sure she will rest easy until your driver brings help to get the trap back on the road.'

'It's likely Fred has regained consciousness and set off back to the vicarage,' Randolph told her gently. 'I expect he thinks that's where you've gone to get help.'

'Ned or the Luckhursts might have him,' Deborah squeaked, unable to control her misery at the thought.

'It's possible, but more likely that Randolph's theory is correct,' Ross concluded.

'There's no time to take you back to the Davenports, Deborah,' Randolph told her, regret in his voice, yet it also held flinty authority. 'You must stay at the Lodge. You'll be safe until I come to collect you. A couple of trustworthy servants are there. Mr and Mrs Pinner housekeep for Ross at the property.'

Deborah gave a slow nod, but the tears started to sting again. She thought of Fred trekking the miles back to the vicarage, perhaps concussed and unsure of his bearings. She dashed away the wet on her lashes. It was no time for a faint heart. She was feeling sorry for herself because her behaviour this evening had been stupidly rash and now she must face the consequences. Randolph was about to fight for his life, and despite her fears that he was as villainous as his brother, she couldn't stop loving or wanting to protect him.

As he kicked the horse into action and they set off at a canter she plucked the hood of her cloak up to cover her head and turned her face against the warmth of his chest.

* * *

She wasn't quite a prisoner, yet she knew too that if she attempted to leave, Mr and Mrs Pinner would stop her. Mrs Pinner she could no doubt evade, but her husband was another matter. He was a burly chap of about Basham's age, Deborah guessed, but whereas Basham was a middle-aged man of limited strength and mobility Deborah could tell that this fellow suffered no such incapacity. Mick Pinner moved nimbly and his shoulders looked strong and broad.

Randolph had made speedy introductions between them before giving the couple strict orders that they were to open the door to nobody. Miss Cleveland, he'd impressed on them, was not to go out under any circumstances and later he or Ross would return to collect her. He'd then kissed her swift and hard on the mouth, stifling her questions and complaints, before leaving without another word. She'd known then just how much peril he faced; never would he act so indiscreetly in front of servants…unless he thought it might be the final time they would see one another.

'Take a warm drink, miss,' Frances Pinner gently urged and again set a mug of tea in front of her. The woman removed the cold brew that she'd put before Deborah some half an hour ago, but which had remained untouched on the kitchen table. 'Are you sure you won't have a bite to eat?' Mrs Pinner asked in her country burr. 'There's some nice juicy ham and a fresh loaf.'

'Thank you, no.' Deborah managed to follow her immediate declination with a smile of gratitude. She couldn't eat! Her stomach felt tied in knots and nausea afflicted her when her mind returned, as it constantly did, to mull over the evening's horrific events. Her sense of helplessness was the worst to bear.

This couple were simply doing their duty. It wasn't their fault that she was unable to rush out and discover what was going on. And she knew she desperately wanted to still her scampering

thoughts with answers, whether good or bad. 'Do you know...
is the beach far from here? Where exactly is Hartsmere Lodge
located from Rye? I have lost my bearings and don't know which
way is home. My mother will be frantic with worry. I should
dearly love to let her know I'm all right.' Deborah saw the woman
exchange a significant look with her husband as he piled logs on
to the fire.

'No need to fret about any of that now, miss,' Mrs Pinner ca-
joled. 'Mr Chadwicke and the master will soon be back. You'll
be safe home before you know it to see your ma. Then all will
be right as rain,' she lilted.

The gallop through the woods to the lodge, held fast in
Randolph's arms, had taken no time at all and seemed now to
Deborah so long ago. Due to her agitation when first she'd arrived she had repeatedly paced in and out of the Lodge's various
apartments in an attempt to disperse her nervous energy.

Now, on looking about, she reviewed what she'd seen with a
less hectic eye. It was a luxurious property, hardly the spartan
hunting lodge she'd imagined it would be. Of the outside edifice
she'd seen little other than a gabled façade. Internally it was a
spacious and very well-furnished building that comprised several
rooms on the ground floor. A staircase led from the hallway to
a first floor where several bedchambers were situated. It had
been decorated, she decided, with a woman's elegant rather than
feminine touch. She imagined if he were wed, Ross probably
brought his wife here. Then she remembered what she'd heard
about his philandering reputation and realised, married or no, it
might be she was admiring a mistress's taste. That idea led her
to think it would be the ideal place for a discreet romantic tryst,
and her thoughts again turned to Randolph while tears burned
her eyes. She gazed blurrily into her tea and warmed her hands
on the hot china.

'What was that?' Deborah had been about to sip from the mug. Now it banged down on the table and she blinked in alarm at Mr Pinner to ascertain whether he too had heard a rap at the door.

He definitely had. Mick Pinner was already reaching for the pistol on the mantelpiece. Once he had it in his grip he pointed it in front of him and went on silent feet into the hallway. Deborah jumped up from the kitchen table and rushed to watch him as he put a meaty shoulder against the stout oak door and listened.

Deborah swung a glance back at Mrs Pinner to see she hadn't her husband's sang-froid. The woman looked terrified, but Frances put her finger to her lips to warn Deborah to keep quiet and let her husband take charge.

The knock came again more insistently this time and heavy enough to rattle the door on its hinges.

'Who comes calling at such an hour?' Mr Pinner boomed.

'It's…it's Fred Cook. Is my mistress with you? Is Miss Woodville with you? We've had an accident on the road and…'

A shrill, nervous voice, barely recognisable as Fred's, had Deborah rushing towards Mr Pinner. 'I *am* known as Miss Woodville,' she explained immediately. 'Let Fred in,' she demanded and reached past Mick Pinner for the iron key. 'All he has said is true. Our trap overturned… Oh, do quickly let him in. He was hurt in the accident and knocked unconscious.' She shook Mick's arm for he seemed reluctant to yet open the door. 'Fred, are you all right?' Deborah called. 'I've been so worried about you. Wait just a moment, we are opening up to let you in.'

'What's he look like?' Mick Pinner demanded. His beefy fingers tightened about the key to thwart Deborah's attempt to prise them away so she might turn the iron implement.

'He is young and quite short with freckles and light brown hair and…' She gave an impatient gesture. 'Oh, let him in, for goodness' sake. I know my own servant's voice, I can assure you.'

Mr Pinner gave her a dubious look, but he drew the bolts and chains and finally the key grated in the lock. He opened the door a crack with one hand whilst keeping his pistol levelled in the other. Having peered through the aperture to verify Deborah's description of her driver, he stood aside to allow Fred to rush in.

Once over the threshold Fred whipped about to try to ram home the door, babbling incoherent warnings. But it was too late. A couple of fellows barged in after him and the larger of the two lunged straight at Mick Pinner and, having the advantage of surprise, managed to punch him to the floor. Mick's pistol skittered away on the boards. Immediately Fred scrambled after it, but the slightly built intruder sent him sprawling with a hefty boot on his backside.

Deborah felt her heart pumping frantically as she whipped glances between the occupants of the hallway. Mrs Pinner had rushed from the kitchen to kneel beside her husband's prostrate and bleeding form.

'I'm sorry, miss,' Fred moaned miserably as he levered on to an elbow. 'They had guns pointed at me and said they'd blow out my brains if I didn't obey them. I tried to shut 'em out, honest I did.'

Deborah started from her shock and rushed to Fred's side as he pulled himself upright with the aid of a hall chair. She swiftly examined him from head to toe. 'Are you hurt badly?' A finger gingerly touched a gash on his forehead. The blood had congealed and a lock of matted brown hair had stuck to it. 'Have they beaten you?'

He shook his head, wincing when his bump pained him. 'Done that myself when I fainted,' he owned up sheepishly. 'I'm all right,' he added bravely, cuffing his nose. 'I came to pretty quick and started out for the vicarage to get help. Before I could raise the alarm these two captured me and forced me here as a decoy. Sorry...' he mumbled and swiped again at his face.

Deborah turned her attention to the two men who were standing just inside the door, presumably so that nobody tried to escape. The small individual, who was slouching against the wooden panels, had his foot planted on Mr Pinner's pistol. He had his own weapon stuck in to the waistband of his breeches and a hand rested threateningly on the hilt. Noticing Deborah studying him, he swung his coat closed, concealing the gun with rough wool.

He was Ned's puny accomplice on the road, Deborah realised. Now he was closer she saw there was something else familiar about him and she wondered whether she'd seen him previously in Hastings with the Luckhursts. Aware she'd taken an interest in him, he lowered his face and tapped the crown of his hat so the brim covered more of his features. Deborah turned her attention to the other fellow, swarthy of complexion, and with oily-looking black hair, beneath which glinted a gold earring. Unlike his colleague he met her stare boldly, eyeing her from top to toe in a way she didn't like. He turned to his companion and muttered a phrase in French. No doubt he thought she'd not understood that he said she was pretty.

'Are you French, too?' she asked in English of the short fellow. When he didn't reply, she repeated her question in French. Still he ignored her, so she made as though to approach him. A thin white hand gestured her away so violently that she stopped at once, thinking he might be surly enough to hit her if she got too close.

Now she'd satisfied herself that Fred was as good as could be expected in the circumstances, Deborah went to help Frances Pinner get her husband on to his feet. She tried to ignore the woman's accusing look. She knew Mrs Pinner blamed her for her husband being injured. She had insisted he open the door, even though Randolph's last command to the couple had been to admit nobody.

Between them they helped Mick Pinner drag his wobbly body into the kitchen. He collapsed down on a chair by the table and propped his swollen jaw in his hands. Whilst Frances hurried off to get water and a cloth to bathe his injury, Deborah again went in to the hallway and turned her attention on their gaolers. Now they had got inside, what was it they wanted? She knew they weren't here to get her because Ned had taken a fancy to her and wanted to quench his lust. As Ross had told her earlier, this gang had far bigger fish to fry tonight… But these two seemed content to just loiter…waiting…

With an inaudible gasp of horror the dreadful truth hit her with the force of a physical blow. They were waiting for Randolph to return; perhaps Ross Trelawney, too, was a target for their bloodlust. Of course! Their master had no doubt sent them here! If Ned were unsuccessful in despatching Randolph in a skirmish outside, he'd make sure that his henchmen would lie in wait for his return and kill him at the Lodge instead. She put a hand to her throat as a mingling of wrath and fear blocked her voice there. 'What do you want?' she eventually burst out. 'I have some money.' She plunged a hand into a pocket of her cloak and extracted her purse. With shaking fingers she shook out the coins on the floor. They scattered and bounced and she hoped that their greed might make them move to collect the silver and gold. Two half-sovereigns glinted in candlelight and she saw the big fellow eyeing them. But it was the other one she wanted to lure. If she could just get him to move away from the pistol on the floor she might manage to pounce on it.

The swarthy fellow scooped up a gold coin, turned it over in his fingers, then turned his attention to her. He swaggered closer and circled her, looking her up and down with lustful black eyes. *'Très jolie,'* he muttered in a tone pitched so low it was obvious he only wanted Deborah to hear what he'd said.

She glowered her disgust at him. It made him guffaw and reach out a hand to touch her luxuriant fair hair. When she stood her ground and merely slapped away his fingers, he became bolder. He grabbed at her waist to pull her against him and Deborah sensed pungent breath assault her nostrils as he tried to plunge his mouth on hers. A double-handed punch landed on his thick chest and, as he grunted in surprise, Deborah darted around him to freedom.

Her attacker's puny accomplice had moved at the same moment. With a hiss of annoyance the fellow had lunged forwards to drag away his lecherous colleague, but instead he collided with Deborah. Deborah put up her hands to shove him off and froze for a moment as her palms came into contact with two round female breasts.

The woman sprang back spontaneously with a curse, but Deborah determinedly pursued her to knock the hat off her head and expose her as a fraud.

Chapter Seventeen

'*You?*' Deborah breathed in astonishment.

The flustered woman seemed intent on again hiding her long hair that moments ago had been anchored in the crown of her hat. She gathered the auburn hank in a fist whilst swiping her hat from where Deborah had sent it spinning into a corner. But, having realised the futility of further pretence, she hurled the hat back to the floor in temper, and the chestnut coil tumbled about her narrow shoulders once more.

'What on earth are you doing here, Susanna?' Deborah whispered. Her eyes flitted over Gerard's wife from head to toe. She looked nothing like the sophisticated lady who, with her husband, had recently hosted a party at the vicarage. Then she'd been sleekly coiffed, dressed in silken finery and embellished with powder and rouge. This evening her complexion was bare, her features pinched, and her hair tangled. The breeches and rough wool coat in which she was garbed had hidden her slim curves, allowing her to impersonate a youth very well.

'You will regret this night for as long as you live.' Susanna barked a harsh laugh. 'And that will not be long, I promise,' she threatened through taut lips. She jutted her chin and marched closer to Deborah. 'I should have let Pierre take you upstairs, then you'd be none the wiser who I was, would you? Now you've caused trouble that can't be undone.' She seemed to have conquered some of her agitation, but she sent an angry curse flying at the Frenchman who'd caused her to be unmasked.

Instead of retaliating, Pierre slouched off to skulk sulkily against the wall and watch proceedings from beneath lowered lids. Deborah knew then that, hefty as the fellow was, he took his orders from Susanna.

'Tie the two men to chairs in case they are stupid enough to try to escape,' Susanna bawled at Pierre whilst strutting to and fro. 'If the old woman causes trouble, bind her too. Now I am compromised, all here who've witnessed it must be silenced.' Having watched Pierre start to obey her commands, she swung back to scowl at Deborah. 'You see what you've done, Miss Woodville? In jeopardising me you've risked the lives of those servants as well.'

'None of us will tell we've seen you,' Deborah cried immediately. In consternation she watched the Frenchman start to lash Mick Pinner to the chair upon which he'd crumpled. The idea that she had caused death sentences to be passed on three other people made bile rise in her throat. 'Just go now, please; you and your French accomplice can get away. Your other colleagues are sure to be defeated and captured by the dragoons,' she argued in a desperately convincing tone. 'Why put your life at risk for Ned and the Luckhursts?'

'Why?' Susanna parroted nastily. She pivoted about and approached Deborah to jab a finger on her shoulder. 'The Luckhursts are of no importance. But I risk my life for Ned for the same reason you have tonight risked yours for Chadwicke.'

'You are in love with him?' Deborah gaped at the woman, but remembered Harriet had obliquely hinted that she suspected Susanna was cuckolding Gerard. 'You don't have a brother, do you?' Deborah accused. 'When you say you're going to nurse your sick brother in Devon you're really going there to see Ned.' Deborah paused, tried to marshal her chaotic thoughts. 'Why on earth concoct such a deceit? Surely it would be simpler to stay there with him and conduct your evil trade from Devon instead of Sussex.'

'Hah!' Susanna snorted. 'You know nothing! I never go as far as Devon. I might just as well say I am going to Derby as Devon. I have no use for either place. Ned Swinton is very much alive, as you have seen, and remains in self-imposed exile in France. But he comes often across the Channel to visit me.'

'He came over on the night of the party at the vicarage, didn't he?' Deborah stated in dawning comprehension. 'He wanted to be spotted by someone so you'd know he'd arrived.'

'Exactly right, Miss Woodville,' Susanna sourly praised. 'Once you'd all gone, and the coast was clear, I sneaked out to see him.' She threw back her head and chuckled raucously. 'As you can tell, Noose-head Ned is useful not only to frighten people away from the beach when our boats come ashore.' She smiled girlishly, shook back her knotted locks from features now softened by romantic memories. 'When Ned wants a little privacy for us at Pump Cottage, he first dons his eerie disguise and rides about in the vicinity. Sometimes we use the church for our trysts, and he makes sure ghosts roam the graveyard that night.' She laughed at Deborah's disgust. A moment later her face was again set in hard lines. 'You'd like us out of the way, wouldn't you, so you can steal what's rightfully ours and share it with your lover.'

'What?' Deborah shook her head to display her utter lack of comprehension.

'Don't pretend you're unaware of a valuable cargo coming ashore,' Susanna spat. 'All the locals are talking about the free-traders anchored at sea. We'd known for months that a competitor was on his way to try to oust us from Sussex.' Her mouth had flattened to a thin line. 'As soon as I saw Chadwicke at the vicarage I knew he was the one. Handsome, isn't he?' She smirked. 'I'd have liked to get him alone and tease a few bits of information from him,' she murmured suggestively.

'He would never have fallen for your tricks,' Deborah contemptuously cried. 'He's too shrewd to be charmed by such as you.'

'You think so?' Susanna purred, but her features had tightened at the insult. 'Perhaps I might prove you wrong, Miss Woodville. If he escapes our ambush and returns for you, I might take him upstairs before I kill him.'

Deborah swallowed, trying to combat the nausea she felt at the woman's vile talk.

'Chadwicke might have been somebody in Suffolk, but if he thinks he can take over here he's wrong,' Susanna hissed. 'We'll finish him—Trelawney too, if necessary. My husband rules the roost here, and always will.'

'Gerard? What has he to do with any of it?' Deborah blurted in alarm. She glanced again at the gun on the floor. For some time she'd been taking furtive peeks at it. Since Susanna's true identity had been revealed the woman had seemed too distracted to recall a weapon was on the loose.

'Gerard?' Susanna hooted. 'That fool might think we're legally wed, but the authorities will see it differently if they discover Ned Swinton is still alive and conducting his business from France. I'm a bigamist for practical reasons, you see. I'd been looking for someone just like Gerard to marry...a respected pillar of the community living in the right area.' She smiled smugly. 'Gerard is the sort of fellow who is liked and trusted by the local militia. They confide in him about their tactics and movements. With a little persuasion Gerard lets slip that intelligence and I pass it on to Ned. I always could twist the lapdog about my finger. He's easy to manipulate…if you know what I mean.' A small, ribald chuckle emphasised her point. 'He's a randy fellow for a clergyman. But I'd sooner tease out of Chadwicke what I need to know. That wouldn't be a chore at all.' She smiled at the mix of repulsion and puzzlement creasing Deborah's brow. 'Ned and I have no time for possessiveness. Ned would have liked to tumble you on the ground.' She shrugged her shoulders to indicate her indifference. 'I know he has his flings with the *mademoiselles*. Ned doesn't mind the methods I use as long as he benefits from them. Why would he be jealous? He knows he's the only one in my heart and always will be.'

Despite feeling overwhelmed by what she'd learned, a tiny part of Deborah's mind retained some clarity. She knew she had to push aside the shocking news and concentrate on getting to the pistol on the floor. If she were to get close enough to snatch up the weapon, she must make Susanna move away from where it lay against the wainscot.

'Ned will be killed tonight,' Deborah taunted her, moving stealthily closer to the gun. 'Randolph will kill Ned. You might think your husband a clever fellow, but I know Randolph will outwit him. He's got a plan of his own to put into action. He knows very well Ned and his cronies are going to try to ambush him.'

'Shut up,' Susanna snarled through her teeth. 'If Chadwicke escapes Ned, I'll be waiting when he comes back for you.' She grabbed the hilt of the gun beneath her coat. 'I'll kill him or die in the doing of it. There's nothing for me if Ned perishes.'

'Perhaps Ned might get away and save his own skin. Perhaps he might bolt back to France and his *mademoiselles* and let you swing for him for this night's work. People are already getting suspicious about your *sick brother*. Investigations are underway about you, Susanna. You're about to be exposed as a fraud,' Deborah provoked her. It seemed she *had* touched a raw nerve.

'I said shut up,' Susanna screamed and lunged at Deborah to shove her in the chest.

At the same moment Mrs Pinner screeched out because the Frenchman had attempted to force her down into a chair so he might tie her to it. Susanna cursed and sped to the kitchen doorway to see what had caused the commotion.

The interruption gave Deborah exactly the diversion for which she'd been praying. Racing to the gun, she snatched it up and silently crept up behind Susanna.

She jabbed the gun into the woman's back. 'Don't think I won't use it,' she said in a voice so quiet and firm that she barely recognised it as her own. 'I'm a viscount's daughter and since I turned ten have known how to bag a flying grouse. I certainly won't miss you.' She barely paused before continuing calmly, 'I swear if you do not drop that gun in your waistband on to the floor I will shoot you in the back and devil take it if I swing with Randolph. I don't care to live without the man I love any more than you do.'

She sensed Susanna stiffen with regret. The woman was bitterly rueing her oversight in having left the weapon abandoned on the floor. But Susanna was frightened enough of having a hole in her back to gabble in French to Pierre to put down his weapon on the table. He did so, baring his teeth in a snarl.

'Tell Pierre to undo Fred Cook. Tell him!' Deborah blasted close to Susanna's ear and jabbed at her back with the barrel of the gun.

Susanna gave the Frenchman the order in a voice replete with frustration.

As soon as Fred was free, Deborah ordered him to move the Frenchman's weapons out of his reach and untie Mr Pinner. Mick was now a little recovered from his ordeal and levered himself up in a quite sprightly way. With deliberately rough thoroughness he searched Pierre's pockets for more weapons. He gave a grunt of triumph as he extracted another gun and a blade. With much menacing gesticulation he forced the Frenchman down in the chair he'd vacated and tied him tightly to it.

Pierre threw a look of pure loathing at Susanna. Deborah read in his face his disgust; a woman he'd had to obey had made such a fundamental error that lucky amateurs had them captive.

Fred stared at his mistress with mute adoration for a long moment. 'Well done, miss,' he breathed, his eyes dancing with awe. 'Shall I go and fetch help?'

'No need,' drawled a soft, vibrant voice from behind. 'Although I have to say you don't seem to require my assistance, sweetheart.'

Deborah pivoted about and, at the sight of Randolph striding down the hall, her head tilted back and her eyelids drooped in sheer thankfulness. With no further word he relieved her of the gun that now was quivering violently in her hand and drew her tightly against his strength to calm her. The gun was kept levelled on Susanna whilst a low whistle was ejected between his teeth. A moment later the small hallway seemed filled with redcoats clattering past and into the kitchen, but she was aware that Randolph's clasp had loosened. A moment later he stepped away again to shout something into the darkness to Ross.

Deborah sank back against the wall, suddenly shivering uncontrollably. She felt light-headed with shock and her clammy palms clung to the plaster to hold her up. She sensed the candles dimming and strove desperately to hold on to her consciousness. She couldn't faint! Not now! There were far too many questions she had to ask! She tried to call to Randolph, but no sound issued from her throat. She put out a hand to him and instinctively he turned and she saw his expression change: tenderness and fear were burning in his eyes as he dashed back to catch her. As she felt her knees crumple and her lashes fluttered closed, she was obliquely aware that a dragoon had marched past with Susanna and Randolph had lifted her in his arms.

'Gerard's not a *broken* man, thank heavens,' Harriet said with feeling. 'Naturally he is utterly mortified and bewildered,' she added on a sigh. 'He bemoans continually that he allowed himself to be so easily duped. It's shaken his confidence, for he's always believed himself a good judge of character.'

'Your brother should not be too harsh on himself,' Deborah said gently. 'Susanna has been exposed as a wicked woman and a practised deceiver.' Deborah angled her head to try to catch Harriet's eye and give her an encouraging smile. Her friend seemed lost in thought as she slowly stirred her tea.

Deborah put down her teacup and gazed out in to the garden. The trees were shedding the last of their golden garments. A gusting wind was whipping brittle leaves up from the terrace flags to flick against the windows. Soon it would be winter, she realised. Yuletide would be upon them—a time for celebration with good friends. Yet she knew her future would by then be determined and she might not be happy enough to want to socialise with anyone at all.

Three days had passed since Ross Trelawney had delivered her home to her frantic mother. For the majority of the journey Deborah had been supine on a seat, dead to the world. But she had regained consciousness before reaching Woodville Place.

En route, Fred, bless him, had crouched by her side, chafing solicitously at her hands, as the viscount's carriage jolted along the Hastings road. Eventually her servant's ministrations had had the required effect: Deborah had opened her eyes and blinked at a pair of dusty Hessians stretched out in her line of vision. As the night's extraordinary events had shot back in to her mind she'd thrown off the rug covering her and struggled upright. Immediately she'd launched garbled questions at Ross, lounging in the opposite corner, the most persistent of which was regarding Randolph's whereabouts.

Before satisfying her curiosity, Ross was determined to have from her an assurance that she was feeling properly recovered so he might relay it to Randolph and save himself an ear bashing. Having convinced him that she was in fine fettle, apart from a headache, she'd finally managed to extract some information from him in the last minutes of the journey.

Ross had told her that Randolph was well enough, but had suffered a minor scratch in the successful battle against Ned and his gang. Instantly Deborah had felt panic rise in her chest. When Randolph had stormed the hallway at the Lodge her desperate relief at seeing him had blinded her to the fact his robust appearance might only be superficial. She'd felt guilty she'd not immediately checked him over rather than swooning like a fool.

She had demanded Ross tell her exactly what he classed as *a minor scratch*. Ross had proceeded to roll back a sleeve, then had bared his other forearm. Having judiciously examined a variety of criss-crossing blemishes, he finally pointed to a scar that, in his opinion, was of about the size and severity as the one Randolph would eventually have on his ribs as a reminder of his heroics. No more questions had been possible, and Deborah had realised Ross had intended they run out of time for full and frank explanations of the night's shocking events. The carriage had reached the top of the avenue leading to a circle of shingle before Woodville Place's portals. Even before Mick Pinner could bring the coach to a proper halt, Julia Woodville, with Basham bobbing in her wake, had come flying down the stone steps, tearfully demanding an explanation for her daughter's dreadfully long absence.

Ross had not stayed. Following hasty introductions he'd set off again almost at once, having used an excuse to escape that would ensure an unimpeded departure. In fact, Deborah had prodded him to go without delay when he'd said he ought to make sure a doctor had been found to stitch Randolph's wound.

Once inside the house, Julia had calmed herself enough to comprehend nothing other than mental and physical exhaustion ailed her daughter. She had then drawn Deborah into the parlour, her interrogation becoming more probing and insistent.

Knowing an explanation must be given if ever they were to get to their beds, Deborah had proceeded to sketch her part in the night's excitement whilst hoping not to induce an attack in her anxious mother. The brandy decanter had been brought, and two shots quickly despatched by Julia. Deborah had sipped more slowly at her drink, but she'd felt pleasantly warmed by it. Mrs Woodville had praised Fred as a treasure and Basham had been commanded to find Lottie to fetch hot water and unguents to soothe the gash on their driver's head. Mrs Field, too, was roused from her slumbers and ordered to prepare Fred anything from the kitchen that he felt up to consuming.

But now several days had passed and the shocking truth of what had occurred that night had travelled far beyond the Woodville household. All of Sussex—it was rumoured the thrilling tale had already travelled as far as London—knew of the Machiavellian plot played out in their midst.

That afternoon Harriet had come to visit Deborah for the first time since the extraordinary news broke and naturally their conversation had immediately turned to Susanna's treachery.

'Thank goodness my brother's marriage is not valid,' Harriet said. 'I never did like Susanna, or trust her, and felt at times uncharitable because of it.'

'Your prejudice has been well and truly vindicated,' Deborah wryly replied. 'I hope Gerard will find somebody else in time.'

'I think he is too wounded to contemplate marrying again.' Harriet's tone was melancholy.

'He must not become a cynic because of the likes of Susanna,' Deborah said with some asperity. 'The evil witch doesn't deserve to weaken a good man such as Gerard.'

'Gerard doesn't think he *is* good. He is racked with guilt that perhaps a private conversation with a woman he thought was his wife might have lead to Lieutenant Barrow being badly injured.'

'It is not shameful to trust one's spouse.'

'I know…but Gerard thinks he ought to have acted more cautiously.'

'When love and passion take hold,' Deborah mused huskily, 'caution often flies out of the window.'

'That came from the heart, Debbie.' Harriet gave her friend a penetrating look. 'You were incredibly brave to have gone alone to warn Mr Chadwicke that night. And you outwitted Susanna, too, and held her at gunpoint,' Harriet added with frank awe. 'You put your life at risk in a way that was most definitely incautious.'

'Foolhardy is more apt a description for what I did,' Deborah said on a hoarse chuckle. 'I feel very guilty that I might have made matters much worse by my impetuous meddling.'

'But you did not,' Harriet reminded her. 'And now you are quite the heroine. And Mr Chadwicke is, of course, the hero. You make a perfect match.' Harriet leaned forwards and, taking one of Deborah's hands, gave it a squeeze. 'You might have been apart for many years, but I could tell there was a bond of emotion between you from the moment I saw you together in Hastings.'

She gave a smile. 'With that in mind I think a *perfect match* would be a wonderfully fitting end to the drama.'

Wistfully, and with a poignant ache squeezing her heart, Deborah inwardly acknowledged there was nothing she wanted more. But she was preparing to make light of Harriet's insightful comment when a tap at the door interrupted her.

'A gentleman to see you, m'm.' Lottie bobbed up and down on the threshold.

Deborah's heart leapt to her throat. She had been longing for, yet dreading, Randolph's arrival. She owed him at the very least her humble apologies. In the heat of the moment, she'd said dreadful things. Yet her knowledge about his past was still incomplete. There were a host of questions that buzzed in her mind from morning 'til night and to which she desperately needed answers.

'Who is it, Lottie?' Deborah finally forced out.

'Viscount Stratton,' Lottie said with a rather saucy smile that betrayed the maid deemed the visitor attractive.

Deborah felt a twinge of disappointment, although she knew she would like to see Ross. She owed him her humble thanks for all his assistance. Not only had he gallantly escorted her home; the following morning, bright and early, Mick Pinner had turned up driving a newly repaired trap. The vehicle had been pulled by Bessie, watered and fed, and looking none the worse for wear.

'Perhaps he has brought news of Mr Chadwicke's recovery,' Harriet whispered. 'I will be off now in any case,' she rushed on. 'I have to go to the drapery for a few odds and ends...' Her words tailed off as Ross entered the room and she gazed, entranced, at the dark-haired gentleman fortunate enough to possess the mien of a buccaneer in a gothic romance. A few minutes later, and before Harriet quit the parlour, her cheeks were glowing pink with pleasure from being dazzled by Ross's good looks and easy charm.

Ruefully Deborah realised that her friend was already regretting her tactful offer to take her leave.

Chapter Eighteen

'I believe I owe you my apology, sir.' A mottling of colour flared in the fair complexion of the gentleman who had just made the stilted announcement.

'I believe you do,' Randolph silkily concurred as he rose from his seat in the magistrate's office to confront the dragoon who had just entered.

On noticing Randolph's fists curling at his side, Mr Savidge burst out, 'Perhaps some refreshment, gentlemen?' He rose to hover above his chair and reach the brass bell on the edge of his desk. A clerk appeared, having been summoned by its clatter, and withdrew again with an order to bring a bottle of port and three glasses.

'I tried to track you down at the Woolpack, but to no avail.' Paul Stewart stiffly explained why he'd interrupted official business between Randolph and the magistrate. 'I am returning to Yorkshire within the hour and was determined to speak privately to you before I started the journey.' Despite his bitterness Paul was determined to do his duty. He knew he was fortunate to still have a military career and a position in Yorkshire to take up. His superior officer would expect, and no doubt check to find out, that he had abased himself sufficiently to atone for his serious breach of conduct.

'I have a matter to discuss with the bishop,' Mr Savidge offered diplomatically, if rather reluctantly. He would dearly have loved to stay and hear what went on between these two gentlemen who, it was alleged, had clashed because of Miss Woodville.

The door had been closed barely a minute before Paul Stewart sprawled on the floor, clutching his bruised chin.

'I was going to say I regretted telling Miss Woodville you were a vicious lout no better than the Luckhursts,' the captain snarled, 'but it seems I was right about you after all.'

'I don't give a damn what you think about me,' Randolph bit out, 'but I do care that you put Miss Woodville's life in danger for no more reason than to try to discredit me. You deserve far more than that as punishment for what you did.'

Paul dragged himself to his feet with the help of Savidge's desk. His eyes blazed at Randolph. 'How was I to know she'd be so foolhardy? I should have been informed of what was going on,' he snapped. 'Had I been a party to the scheme and had understood your involvement...'

'We would have suffered a serious defeat,' Randolph finished mordantly. 'It was precisely because of the risk from people like you that the operation was kept strictly confidential. Still you managed to meddle and almost destroy many months' work and put in jeopardy several lives.'

The stinging rebuke brought raging heat to Paul's face. He knew, resentfully, that the charges against him were true. He'd learned that not only had Deborah Woodville been at Susanna Swinton's mercy that night, but several servants too. Yet, an intrepid heroine, Deborah had managed to capture and hold the fort until her hero appeared to rescue her.

To his squirming shame he knew now that Randolph Chadwicke

had never been a contender for the lucrative contraband trade in Sussex, though his association with Ross Trelawney, undisputed smuggler par excellence in his day, had added quite intentionally to the impression that the opposite were true. The Chadwickes' link to Suffolk smuggling had also given the scheme credibility. Only the most senior courtiers and army officials had known of the plot—even the local judiciary had been unaware of the intrigue being played out in their midst. Undercover agents had been planting rumours for months: a new smuggling ring was ready to fight for supremacy in the area and with Trelawney's colossal backing it was sure to succeed in taking over.

Ned Swinton had fallen hook, line and sinker for the plot, and in his desperation to retain control, had broken cover and exposed himself and his accomplices to capture. In the ensuing affray Swinton had been mortally wounded. His wife had been taken off to Horsham gaol to await trial. The Luckhurst brothers and a few others were languishing, red-faced, in a Martello tower awaiting their fates.

Captain Stewart knew it had been a magnificent victory…but none of the glory was his. When Chadwicke and Trelawney had appeared by the beach that night he had attempted to have them arrested. He'd been relieved of his post by Colonel Montague who'd arrived to oversee operations that morning. Later Paul had discovered that the Colonel had been instrumental in hatching the trap with Chadwicke. Paul's humiliation had been unendurable. Had he not been offered a transfer to the other side of the country he would have had no option but to resign. He'd never have been able to bear his subordinates sniggering behind his back over the episode, perhaps for years to come.

Once he'd got completely back on his feet, Captain Stewart swiped his gauntlets over an unsteady palm, adjusted his uniform, and stalked from the magistrate's office without another word.

* * *

'It is very nice to see you, sir,' Deborah said warmly. Ross was now seated and a tea tray, brought by a blushing Lottie, covered the table set between their fireside chairs. 'I'm glad to have the opportunity to properly thank you for your help. I must also thank you for your kindness in having our trap repaired and returned to us. Your manservant drove it back the following day and Bessie looked none the worse for her adventure.'

'It was my pleasure to be of service, Miss Cleveland…or is it Woodville?' He chuckled. 'It might be simpler if I call you Deborah unless you quite rightly object to my scandalous lack of etiquette.'

Deborah smiled wryly. They barely knew one another yet, oddly, she found his suggestion refreshingly unconventional rather than improper. She imagined that Viscount Stratton was quite used to flouting the rules.

From the moment in the woods when he'd firmly, yet gently, clamped a hand on her mouth to quieten her, she'd intuitively trusted him. Even when he'd revealed himself to be Ross Trelawney, infamous rogue, her opinion had not altered. By the time he'd delivered her safely home, and helped placate her mother, she'd known how easy it would be to like him. 'You may call me Deborah if I may call you Ross,' she boldly declared. 'It's only fair; it is equally confusing for me to know how to address you. Do you prefer Viscount Stratton or Mr Trelawney?'

'I prefer Ross, so that's settled then,' he grinned. 'We shall be shockingly informal with one another.'

Having taken a sip of tea, Deborah clattered down her cup. 'Is Randolph's wound healing well?' she burst out.

'He is very much on the mend. The wound had a bit of an infection in it, but—'

'*An infection?*' Deborah gasped anxiously. 'He has a fever?'

'Not any more,' Ross soothed her. 'And the doctor is pleased with his progress.'

'I didn't know,' Deborah cried in alarm. 'I...I thought he simply had much business to attend to, or was still very angry with me, and that's why he had not yet come to visit.' She looked at the hands clasped in her lap and blinked to clear an abrupt stinging heat in her eyes. She knew now that Randolph had every right to be angry with her for accusing him of being up to no good that night. Nothing could have been further from the truth, as everyone in the locality now knew.

'Randolph's not too angry to want to see you, trust me on that,' Ross said gently, interrupting Deborah's introspection. 'But he has much business to attend to, you can trust me on that also. Lord Buckland is a sought-after chap. He has had to attend meetings with all manner of lofty officials and courtiers. Despite being under the weather he has attended them all to get matters finalised as soon as he can.'

'*Lord Buckland?*' Deborah frowned her confusion. 'Surely he has no right to use the title.'

'I knew it,' Ross sighed. 'Already I *have* said too much.'

'And Randolph has told you to say nothing at all to me,' Deborah guessed.

'Randolph thinks it is for him to explain things to you,' Ross said mildly, settling back in his chair. 'And I wholeheartedly agree with that. So might I ask you to forget what I just said?' An appealing look from unusual green-flecked eyes was levelled on her.

'Of course, I won't say anything. I know you are a roguish gentleman, but I don't wish to get you into trouble. I think you are a very good man.'

'I tell Elizabeth so quite often,' he wryly quipped.

'Elizabeth? Your wife?'

'Yes, my wife,' he confirmed softly. 'Are you surprised I have one?'

'Indeed, no. She is a lucky woman.'

'I tell her that too.'

'From which, *Mr Trelawney*,' Deborah said with an ironic inflection, 'I think you believe *you* are the lucky one.'

'The most fortunate man alive—and that is why I am keen to set off home. I have come to say goodbye for now, although I'm sure we will soon see one another again. I know Elizabeth would dearly like to meet you.' He paused before adding without a scrap of self-consciousness, 'I have not been away from Stratton Hall for long but already I miss my family. My children have birthdays to celebrate this week.' Seeing her surprise, he added with a throb of pride, 'They share the same birthday; they are twins.'

'How old? Boys or girls?'

'Five. One of each.'

Deborah nodded, smiling, feeling a little prickle behind her eyes, for his pure emotion was infectious. 'You must go without delay and I wish them both the happiest of birthdays,' she said simply.

'Oh! He has not gone already! Really, Deborah! I would have liked to see Viscount Stratton. I hardly got to properly thank him the other evening when he brought you home. He seems such a charmer. Would he not wait a few hours to dine with us? You did invite him to stay for supper, didn't you?'

'He wanted to go home, Mama, and be with his wife and children. Nothing—not even Mrs Field's finest dinner—would have persuaded him to do otherwise,' Deborah wryly explained.

With a frown of disappointment Julia stripped off her gloves. She had just returned from visiting the Pattinsons; she'd had a fine time gossiping about the recent intrigue that still absorbed everybody. On entering the house, she'd met Lottie coming from the kitchens. The maid had told her that the handsome Viscount had come to call while she'd been out. Julia had immediately hurried to the parlour to see him. But she'd just learned from Deborah that Basham had shown out their guest just ten minutes since.

'I'm surprised Randolph hasn't yet paid us a visit.' Julia levelled a penetrating look on her daughter.

'The viscount told me Randolph's wound became infected. He suffered with a fever for a while. By all accounts he is much better now,' Deborah added quickly, not wanting her mother to worry unnecessarily.

'When I was with the Pattinsons this afternoon the squire said he'd heard on the grapevine that Randolph's brother had died. Randolph's name cropped up in conversation many times and once or twice the squire named him Lord Buckland.' A delicate shrug of her shoulders preceded, 'I didn't know whether to correct him; I recall that Randolph said his brother had produced a son.' She put her bonnet and gloves on the table and continued peevishly, 'I wish he would come. It is best to have all the news straight from the horse's mouth.'

Deborah went to the window and looked out at grey skies. She couldn't bear to wait longer to see him. She felt as if she might explode with tension if she did not talk to him today. If he wouldn't come to her, then she would go to him and force him to tell her everything. She must hear from his own lips who he was now and who he had been when younger. She tilted back her head a little and sighed at the ceiling. She should have asked Ross if Randolph was staying alone at the Lodge or whether he had moved back to the Woolpack. She had no idea where to start in running him to ground. But do it she would.

Having watched her daughter's fraught expression for a moment, Julia drew in a deep, inspiriting breath. There was a weight that had lain too long and too heavy on her shoulders and she knew this was as good a time as any to finally be rid of the burden. 'There is something making you sad, Debbie, and I think I know what it is.' She started her confession about the missing letters. 'I have guessed you and Randolph have been fond of one another for a very long time. I suspected you jilted Marcus Speer because you had fallen in love with his friend,' she added. 'But Randolph went off abroad, didn't he, and things… went awry between you.'

Wistfulness twisted Deborah's rosy lips as she stared through the glass at the leaden heavens. 'He sent me letters,' she said softly. 'I received not one. I know he thinks I am lying when I say so. He knows I think he is lying and believe he sent me nothing.'

'The matter can be put right,' Julia began in a croak. 'It is not an insurmountable hurdle at all for neither of you has lied…'

'It does not matter any more,' Deborah interrupted sharply. She turned to gaze at her mother with blue eyes that blinked back tears. 'It really doesn't matter about a few letters,' she said in a tone that apologised for her brusqueness. 'There are now worse hostilities between us than a dispute over lost notes. Randolph thinks I class him as a vile criminal, and no better than his treacherous brother.'

'Who told him such rot?' Julia barked. 'Captain Stewart?'

'No…I did.' Deborah pressed a few white fingers to her lips to stifle a hysterical laugh.

Julia frowned, seemed about to speak. With a despairing shake of her head she gave her melancholy daughter a fierce hug, then quit the room with a quiet, 'I think I shall take a nap.'

Determined she *would* go, Deborah prepared to leave the house with a frenzied speed. Not only did she fear losing her nerve, she realised that Randolph's business might take him directly home and she'd lose her chance to speak to him. Perhaps he already *had* gone away. She comforted herself with the memory of Ross, just an hour or so ago, reassuring her that Randolph wanted to see her. But surely if he *did* want to see her as eagerly as she wanted to see him he would have found the time to come? With that thought spurring her on—and subduing a prickling sense of pride that demanded she take off her cloak and boots and act with some sense and dignity—she checked she had enough money to hire a ride and hurried from her room.

Speeding lightly down the stairs, she tried to ignore the thought that never in her life had she chased after a man. She was a viscount's daughter and a pretty one at that, so she'd been constantly told throughout her life. In the past—and not just in her heyday—she had been under siege from many gentlemen. After she'd jilted Marcus she'd received six marriage proposals in rapid succession and turned down every one because she was waiting for a letter from Randolph. With just a paragraph to encourage her she would have turned down suitors for a decade. She knew that Edmund would have been amongst them.

On she flew through the vestibule. She was sure that if she could just get out of the grounds and on the road that insistent voice of conscience would cease whispering hatefully in her ear about the lateness of the hour and the impropriety of her mission.

She drew her warm cloak tighter about her as she marched along the shingle towards the gate with the clouds hunched on the horizon behind her. She prayed Lottie would not forget to give her mother the note she'd written explaining that she was going out to see a friend. She knew her mother would assume she'd gone to the vicarage. Without slowing her pace she turned and headed briskly towards town, fervently hoping the breeze would hold off the rain.

On reaching her destination, dry but chilled, Deborah made straight for the blacksmith's forge. She knew Donald Smith hired out a dogcart for short journeys and his son, Simon, would be fetched to drive if required to do so. It would be safer for her to be a passenger; she was not at all sure of her own skill with the reins. She had on occasion, and in clement weather, taken out Bessie pulling the trap over the short distance to the vicarage. But the blacksmith's horse might not be a Bessie. It might be an awkward animal with a mind of its own. Besides, if she drove off unaccompanied, such peculiar behaviour would certainly stir gossip. Equally tattle would start if it leaked out that Simon Smith had driven her from place to place so she might track down Mr Chadwicke.

The dilemma on how to approach the delicate subject of her need to locate a man who was considered either a hero, or a Judas, depending on personal viewpoint, made Deborah hesitate.

Whilst changing into her outdoor clothes earlier she had dismissed the idea of Fred bringing her in the trap; now she wondered if she might have done so too readily. She had forgone transport and walked to town to keep knowledge of this trip from her mother. Julia would be horrified at the idea of her daughter stooping to chase after a gentleman, albeit one she now considered a paragon.

Yet how was she to explain to the Smiths that she'd need to be taken on to Hartsmere Lodge near Green End if Mr Chadwicke were not at the Woolpack in Rye? She scoured her mind and came up with no plausible excuses. Conscious that a few passers-by had amiably acknowledged her, but were continuing to give her speculative looks, she turned to stare sightlessly at the wares in the draper's shop window so she didn't appear to be aimlessly loitering.

After a moment a reflection in the glass caught her eye and she focused, unblinking, on it. She turned with thumping heart to look again at the forge.

Only weeks had passed since they'd stood in almost exactly the same positions as they did now and stared at one another, yet it seemed so very long ago. She dearly wished she had not come. She should have been patient and waited at home. Despite the wounding things she'd said to him he would have called to say goodbye, she was sure of it. Now their parting might be limited to a few stilted words exchanged on Hastings High Street whilst inquisitive locals watched.

Curbing her instinct to rush across the street and launch herself against him, she waited as Randolph handed cash to the blacksmith. A moment later he was at her side.

Chapter Nineteen

'It's late to be out shopping,' he said softly, a smile in his voice. 'Are you waiting for your mother?' He glanced at the interior of the shop. It appeared to be deserted and the dark figure of the draper could be seen moving about, extinguishing the lamps.

Deborah shook her head. His abrupt, powerful presence had set her pulse racing and stolen her voice.

'Is your mother with you?' His question now held a sharper edge, yet the flare of desire in his eyes was undiminished.

Again Deborah's fair head quivered in reply.

'Who is? Fred?'

She'd recognised a hint of rebuke in his voice this time and his authoritarian attitude rankled enough to embolden her. Up tilted her chin and she challenged his censure. 'I'm alone,' she said clearly.

'I thought you'd promised me never again to go about on your own.'

'So I did, but that was before you made your ruling unnecessary,' she reminded him with acid sweetness. 'Thanks to you there are no Luckhursts about now to ambush me on my walks.'

'You sound disappointed. Would you have them back again, Debbie?'

'Of course not,' she whispered. Heat bled into her cheeks; she felt ashamed her tumultuous emotions had made her petulant. For days she'd yearned obsessively to see him. Now she understood why that was. Whatever he'd done, whatever he was or had been, she still loved him. But she was unsure of how he felt about her. Oh, she knew he wanted her still. But did he love her? Had he ever loved her?

'Why are you out alone, Deborah?' he asked with deceptive calm.

She shrugged in the hope it might convey she'd simply wanted a constitutional. Her pride would certainly not allow her to admit it had been her intention to track him down.

'Why are *you* in Hastings?' she countered quickly. 'I imagined you'd be found at the Woolpack in Rye or perhaps at Hartsmere Lodge.' Inwardly she squirmed. She was aware she'd betrayed herself even before she'd heard his mocking response.

'Have I saved you the trouble of searching for me by turning up here?' His amusement faded. 'You weren't intending to walk to the Woolpack in Rye?' When she didn't answer he glanced over his shoulder at the smithy. 'I've been staying at the Lodge in any case. Were you on your way to hire Donald's cart?'

To avoid his shrewd assessment she discovered a renewed interest in the drapery's wares. Her eyes collided with the shopkeeper's and she wondered how long he'd been peeking through the glass at them. Realising he'd been spotted, he jerked back behind the blind. Before he'd concealed himself Deborah had recognised a grudging respect in the merchant's eyes. And she knew what had put it there.

In common with all the people for miles around, Deborah now knew that a mercenary working as a government spy had outwitted Ned Swinton and finally brought about his and his wife's downfall.

There had been no free-traders at anchor offshore waiting to storm the coast and do battle with dragoons and Revenue men. It had all been a calculated plot, right down to the assembling of ships at sea and troops on land. To some Randolph Chadwicke was a knight in shining armour; to others he was the villain of the piece.

'I imagine he is blaming me for the loss of his cut-price supply of French lace.'

'I imagine you're right,' Deborah agreed, aware from Randolph's irony he'd known they were under observation. 'And there are others who feel the same way, and will be glad to see the back of you.'

'Do you count yourself amongst them?'

'Of course not!' It was a spontaneous cry as her eyes swerved to tangle with his.

'Of course not?' he echoed through lightly set teeth. 'The last time we had a conversation I believe you named me a vile criminal who'd abused your hospitality.'

'And are you? Were you?' she flung back. 'I don't know who you are, or who you ever were, that's the trouble.' Her voice keened with frustration and she bit her lower lip to stop its wobble.

'And so you thought you'd come looking for me to find out?'

'Yes!' she stormed. 'I…I wanted my questions answered in case you again went away and left me waiting and wondering…'

'Do you really believe I would go away without first coming to see you?' He jammed his hands in his pockets and strode off a few paces before pivoting about. 'Do you think I'm callous enough to use you and your mother for sinister, selfish reasons?'

'No,' she murmured miserably and dropped down her face to

frown at her intertwining fingers. 'I truly didn't believe that you'd stoop so low. Captain Stewart was annoyed that I refused to believe him and denigrate you. After he visited me that day I came to find you to make you tell me your side of it,' she whispered. 'I'm none the wiser on many things. So again I've swallowed my pride because I couldn't wait longer to know the truth,' she admitted. 'I know that you were sent here as a government spy to break up Swinton's gang. Ross came to see me to say goodbye before he went home. He wouldn't tell me anything. He said you'd rather explain things to me.'

He came back to her and a dark hand was raised to gently cup her quivering cheek. 'He's right. I would. I'm glad you came to find me, sweetheart,' Randolph said hoarsely. 'I'm pleased, too, you care enough to want to hear my side of the story, having had Stewart's version. But you shouldn't have come out alone.' He took her arm to draw her with him towards the forge where his stallion was tethered under the porch. 'Come, I'll take you home.' A rueful chuckle cluttered his throat. 'I don't want to unearth all the Chadwicke skeletons at such a time and place as this. It would be wiser to wait and find somewhere private. There are a lot of them rattling about.'

Despite his mordant humour his expression remained sober and Deborah knew he was not wholly joking. The knowledge sent a shiver of foreboding rippling through her. The hood of her cloak was tweaked forwards by Randolph as protection from the drizzle that descended from the sullen-looking sky. By the time they'd reached the shelter of the porch, the rain had become persistent enough to make him curse beneath his breath.

'I don't relish getting soaked to the skin.' His narrowed, tawny eyes scanned the gloomy scene. 'If we wait under here for a while, it might pass over.'

Randolph huddled them close to the wall of the building in

order that he might protect them from the elements. The wind had strengthened, too, and flapped Deborah's skirts against her boots, and he shifted position to shield her slender form with the breadth of his body.

'Excuse me, sir.'

Randolph half-turned to see Donald Smith at his shoulder, tugging at his forelock.

'If you'd like to step inside and have a warm till it blows over, you be most welcome.' The blacksmith deferentially stepped back a few paces, inviting them to enter his workshop.

Donald was one of many locals who'd been relieved to see the end of the Luckhursts' reign. In his estimation they'd got far too big for their boots and Seth especially had been throwing his weight about. Besides, Donald was an honest businessman who paid his dues and his opinion was that other folk should do the same. His resentment of the smugglers had peaked when his daughter Lizzie had been scared half to death by the Noose-head Ned character on the evening she'd walked home from Rye fair.

'I'm finished for the day and I've a bit of a thirst.' Donald untied his leather apron and hung it up. 'I'm off to the tavern, sir, but stay 'til the rain stops, if you've a mind.' With another tug at his forelock Donald positioned a rough stick-back chair close to the fire for Deborah.

A smile and murmured thanks rewarded him as Deborah perched on its rickety edge. A few moments later Donald had donned his jacket and hat and, with a mumbled farewell, had dashed out into the wet afternoon.

Deborah pushed back her hood and flicked at her golden hair to remove droplets from her fringe. She put her hands to the glow of the fire and felt a little more relaxed. The odour of hot metal and leather mingled with a hint of horseflesh to create a peculiarly pleasant ambience. A flitting glance at Randolph was arrested as she noticed him gingerly press a hand to his side. At once a wave of guilt washed over her. So concerned had she been with protecting her pride and launching her interrogation, she'd forgotten to ask how he was.

'Are you in pain? She quickly got up and approached him. 'Ross told me you'd been injured and that an infection had set in.' Automatically she raised a slender hand as though to soothe his hurt. 'Where…?'

Her small fingers were held, then directed to his lower ribs, where he touched them briefly to a wound dressing beneath his jacket.

'Is it healing well?' she asked anxiously.

He nodded slowly, his low-lashed eyes seeming to smoulder with as much heat as the brazier close by.

'I wish I hadn't set out this afternoon to see you. I should have stayed at the Lodge and let you come to me,' he murmured huskily. 'Had we met there instead of here I think we'd have resolved many things.'

'You were coming to see me this afternoon?' she blurted, blushing at his sultry suggestiveness. She recalled she'd thought the lodge would be an ideal place for a romantic tryst. It seemed he had also recognised its potential.

'As soon as I'd settled with the blacksmith I intended travelling on to Woodville Place. I've wanted to talk to you, too, Debbie.' He lifted her slender fingers to brush them against his lips. 'I wanted to come and see you straight away and satisfy myself you'd recovered from your ordeal that night. But I've been needed at one meeting after the other to file reports with the authorities. Also I was delirious with fever for a day or two.' He smiled slightly. 'I thought it best not to come and risk collapsing or talking drivel.' He gave her a significant look. 'I wasn't sure how my visit would be received. But I was determined to thank you for bravely coming to warn me Ned Swinton and Captain Stewart were out to get me.'

'Had I known Ned Swinton's gang was about that night, I doubt I would have found the courage to set foot outside the door.' She glanced up bashfully. 'I'm sorry I made dreadful accusations before giving you a chance to explain. But I was overwrought after the trap came off the road and angry, too, in case…'

'In case…there might have been some truth in what Captain Stewart told you?'

'And was there?' Apprehensive blue eyes glanced on his watchful gaze.

'Yes.'

The immediate, unadorned admission stunned her for a moment. The next instant her fingers, still held by him, squirmed for freedom, but he tightened his hold on her. The glow from the forge seemed to highlight one side of his face to devilishly sharp angles whilst his eyes remained in shade, their expression unreadable.

'You were once a smuggler?' she whispered.

'Yes.'

A little mew of misery cluttered her throat and she jerked aside her head. Long fingers curved on her nape, drawing her close again, smoothing soothingly on her satiny skin.

'And now?' she gasped.

'And now I'm a smuggler catcher,' he said drily.

'I see…' she croaked and tried again to slip free of his clasp.

'I don't think you do see. You have to let me properly explain, Debbie,' he hoarsely pleaded. 'People aren't always completely good or bad, right or wrong. Sometimes something in between is all that's possible given their breeding and circumstances.'

'Captain Stewart told me your brother killed a Revenue man

and fled abroad. Were you involved in that dreadful crime? Is that
why you also went to the Indies for so long?' Her voice sounded
shrill with distress.

'Hush…' His palms enclosed her cheeks and two slow thumbs
circled calmingly on her complexion. 'I swear I was by then a
reformed character. I was not even in Suffolk that night. I was
in London with Marcus and some other friends.' He tilted up her
chin so she couldn't avoid his eyes. 'Do you believe me?'

She nodded, but her eyes seemed to float in unshed tears.

'I want to tell you why I went to the Indies seven years ago,
sweetheart. I want to tell you about Sebastian and the havoc he
wreaked on my life and that of my mother and sister.' He sighed,
throwing back his head to grimace at the beamed roof. 'I'd hoped
for somewhere more comfortable and private than this when I
explained. But I want no more delay, and no more secrets or misunderstandings between us. Before I tell you the worst of it, let
me say that Sebastian was an incorrigible villain, but he wasn't
the first of the Chadwickes to smuggle. For centuries my ancestors have been plundering vessels and shipping illicit cargoes.'

'But…but you're aristocrats,' she stuttered in confusion.

'Our peerage was not got through noble victories on the battle-
field, sweet. Though it was got through fighting for King and
country. My great-great-grandfather's talent as a bounty hunter
was rewarded with a barony. He was an accomplished privateer
based in the Indies who disrupted merchant ships and stole treasure and hostages for ransom. English as well as foreign traders
came under his attack, and he made a small fortune in the doing
of it. When the King found he had no commander able to thwart
him, he offered Vincent Chadwicke a lucrative deal. For land
and a title he bought my ancestor's loyalty and Vincent worked
for the Crown instead of against it.' Cynicism skewed his smile.

'Sebastian would always say it wasn't his fault he was a reprobate, it was in his blood.'

'And yours too?' she breathed.

'Maybe…' Randolph agreed softly. 'But we were never alike and I saw the error of my ways before I turned twenty. I tried until the day he died to make Sebastian see the shame in lawbreaking too.'

'He killed a government officer for contraband!' Deborah hissed in sheer disgust. 'And then fled abroad to avoid arrest. Why did you go after him?'

'I went to stop him pilfering from the fund that my father had intended be used for my mother and sister's comfort. I didn't have sufficient income to keep us all and run the estate, and my mother was distressed by the idea of losing it.' He paused. 'Sebastian had lived abroad for about three years when our financial hardship became so acute that I had to confront him in person. I had no intention of staying away more than a matter of months. But when I arrived I found my brother had little of worth to sell to make reparation. He had purchased a plantation, but it was badly run and unprofitable. I took over and forced him to work, though he showed little aptitude or enthusiasm. Slowly we started to make enough money to send some to my mother.' He sighed, his eyes distant. 'But unbeknown to me Sebastian had been an opium eater for some while. He had a secret, debauched life in a den of iniquity and after a few years spent with him I accepted that I could not help him conquer his addiction, nor did he want to.'

'But you stayed so long. Why?'

'Because by then I knew two things,' Randolph began quietly. 'I'd discovered my brother had dependants living in squalor, and I'd guessed from a lack of post there was no reason to swiftly return.'

'I swear I did not receive one letter from you.' Deborah's gaze clung soulfully to his face, willing him to believe her.

'And I swear I sent four during the first year I was there.' He snapped aside his face, presenting her with a hard profile. 'What does it matter now?' A rasp of laughter preceded his next words. 'What was it you said when first we met in Hastings? A lot of water has passed under the bridge since then...'

Deborah watched a muscle leap rhythmically in his lean jaw. She had long ceased straining to free her hand. For a time it had lain warm and still in his. Now she turned her fingers, wound them about his broad palm in mute support and encouragement as he resumed his story.

'It was hard to feel sorry for Sebastian despite his corrosive affliction. But his children were a different matter,' Randolph said. 'He rarely showed remorse for what he'd done or rued the debauched lifestyle that had deprived his mother and sister of a comfortable existence in England.'

'Captain Stewart said he was hanged for treason,' Deborah murmured, her eyes brimming with sympathy.

'He was. Within a short while of him arriving in the Indies he'd joined a gang of brigands. He spent less time with them after I joined him there. But one day he managed to thwart my vigilance and disappeared. About a week later I learned he'd been captured with some of his pirate friends trying to board an English vessel. Members of both crews had been killed in the battle.' Randolph abruptly let her go. He jammed his hands in his pockets and paced aimlessly. 'I wish to God I'd never gone there!' he ejaculated through gritted teeth. 'It was pointless. I had to come home and tell my family the worst possible news: that Sebastian was dead, hanged like a cur in a foreign land and his body left on a gibbet as a deterrent to others.'

Deborah felt her eyes prickle with tears; despite his savage speech she knew how terribly hurt he was. He felt guilty for not saving his brother from the gallows, and his family from the distress and disgrace of such a dreadful punishment. After a quiet moment she softly enquired, 'What became of his wife and children?' Her balmy blue gaze bathed his harsh features. 'I remember you said that Sebastian had a son and a daughter.'

'He had two children, but he didn't have a wife. In common with everything else in his life, he stole one. Claudette was married to a neighbouring landowner, but she lived with Sebastian as his mistress.'

'And what has become of them?' she gasped. 'Are they destitute?'

'I sold the plantation and used the majority of the money to bribe her husband to take her back and rear my brother's bastards as his own.' He turned about to look at Deborah. 'He accepted the offer, and why should he not? Forgiveness for being rejected in favour of a drug-addled criminal has its price. I thought him a reasonable fellow. Actually he appeared a far better father to the children than was my brother.'

'As the boy is illegitimate I suppose you *are* Lord Buckland,' Deborah mused beneath her breath.

All that broke the ensuing silence was a patter of gentle raindrops and the hiss of flames in the forge. Having concentrated for some minutes, Deborah ventured, 'Did you agree to work for the King to atone for Sebastian's sins, and polish the title you'd inherited?'

'Nothing so noble, sweetheart,' he said sardonically. 'I did it for the money.'

'You're rich now?' Deborah asked quietly.

'Rich and respectable,' he admitted with a grimace. 'It's a pity the opportunity to become so didn't arise seven years ago.'

'Why didn't you tell me you were working undercover for

the authorities?' she asked with a hint of indignation. 'I would have kept your secret, I swear. Didn't you trust me enough to tell me?'

'I couldn't tell you, Debbie,' he said forcefully. 'God knows I wanted to, but I couldn't. I'd trust you with my life, but I'd never risk your safety in such a way.' He came towards her, smoothed a shaking hand over her soft cheek. 'Nobody apart from Ross knew the truth. Even Captain Stewart and his men were kept in the dark.' He paused. 'We knew there was someone in the area who was passing on confidential information. I don't blame Gerard; he was not to know his wife was a sly trickster.' He frowned. 'Had I hinted to you what I was up to, you might have unwittingly let something slip to Harriet. That information might have found its way to Gerard and then on to Susanna...' He sighed. 'I do trust you, Deborah, but if my cover had been blown before the mission had been successful, it would have put you and your mother in dreadful jeopardy. It was common knowledge that we were friends who'd known one another years ago. Swinton and his wife might have abducted you, dreadfully mistreated you, to get information from you.' He drew her in to his arms, rocked her gently. 'You saw how ruthless was Susanna Swinton. Believe me, her husband was doubly evil and vicious. He would have spared you nothing. I still can't bear to think what might have happened had you been left too long at the mercy of that bitch. I was mad with worry. I nearly aborted the mission to come back and rescue you.'

'Hah! You'd no need! I was a match for her!' Deborah snorted against his shoulder, although she clutched at his arms for support. The dreadful memory of that night still had the power to weaken her limbs.

He chuckle stirred her golden hair. 'Yes, you were,' he slowly, softly praised her. 'In fact, we make a good team, you and I—'

Abruptly he stepped away. 'It's stopped raining. I'll take you home now.' With a hand on her arm he urged her to the open doorway and together they surveyed the dripping landscape.

'There's more to say, but I'd sooner we talked somewhere else.' He gazed at the washed skies whilst speaking.

'I don't want to go home yet,' she said huskily, drawing his eyes immediately to her sweet, upturned face. She was sorry the rain had stopped and he'd interrupted their heart to heart to say he'd take her home. She had sensed he'd been on the point of saying something significant. 'I haven't yet told you I'm sorry I said you were a vile criminal. I want you to know, too, that I believe what you've told me, and I trust you were always sincere in your dealings with us.'

His eyes narrowed, grew dark with desire as he sensed her meaning.

'I want you to take me to the Lodge,' Deborah whispered.

Chapter Twenty

Bunched muscle was visible beneath the gauzy lawn of his shirt as Randolph attended to the fire. Deborah watched him patiently coddling small sparks into flames, then, once the glow was strong enough to stamp his shadow on the wall, he stood in a fluid movement and came to sit opposite her at the kitchen table.

She sensed the strength of his stare on her profile, but felt suddenly too shy to meet his eyes. As her pulse accelerated, making more acute the painful thump beneath her ribs, she tried to subdue her apprehensiveness. She had suggested they come here. She'd understood what he would read into her offer to go to the woods with him. She'd understood, too, that her reputation would be irrevocably damaged if ever it leaked out what she'd done.

On the journey from Hastings, seated in front of him on his horse, she'd felt relaxed and cosy. Randolph had told her about his youth as they'd travelled at a slow trot towards Hartsmere Lodge. She hadn't turned once to look at him, nor had she interrupted; but an inner tranquillity had settled on her as she had quietly listened, resting against his chest with his words resonating against her cheek.

'I wasn't a smuggler for very long,' he'd begun his story. 'As a boy of fifteen, I wanted to experience the excitement of going on night runs with my older brother. My parents discovered I'd become involved, but didn't stop me. In an odd way I think they hoped my presence might moderate Sebastian's craving for danger. In fact, I was another pair of hands and so he took more risks. It wasn't the jeopardy that brought me to my senses. By the time I was nineteen, and despite the cash to be had, I'd been sickened by the evil in the adventure.' He'd paused at that point as though the memory of that evil still had the power to disturb him. 'But I'd made Ross's acquaintance.' An unseen smile had lightened his tone. 'We became colleagues and firm friends and for that alone I don't rue all my misspent youth.' A stream had been splashed through and dry land again encountered before he'd carried on. 'Sebastian didn't enjoy the camaraderie as did I. He could be violent and greedy, so had few friends. The turning point for me came one night on a French beach when Sebastian ejected *émigrés* from our craft so he might load on more kegs of brandy. A count had begged passage for himself and his wife and young son. They had no money and Sebastian would only take those who could pay. Ross and I brought many French refugees to England on night runs for no more than a *merci beaucoup*. Sebastian was contemptuous of the fact we refused to make a profit out of those poor souls.' His voice had faded away and he'd tilted up her chin so their eyes had merged. 'Am I a vile criminal?' He'd sounded defensive, uncaring of her answer, yet his feral eyes had demanded her acquittal. She'd simply touched her warm lips to the stubble on his cheek, making him groan and kick the stallion in to a gallop.

'Do you want to go?'

His toneless enquiry made her start from her reverie. Her wide eyes quit the fiery dance in the grate to clash on his knowing gaze. He understood her fears and because of it she felt obliged to deny them. There had been no coercion on his part. It had been her idea to come here, she again reminded herself. Still she felt nervous, overpowered by the force of his virility. She pressed together her lips to still their quiver and shook her head. 'No,' she murmured gruffly. 'I…like this little house. I…I'm glad we came.' She smiled slightly and again avoided the eyes that seemed to gleam in the firelight. She was very susceptible to his masculine appeal, she realised with a pang. His white shirt, gaping at the top, exposed a strong, brown column of throat. On the table a dark hand lay idle, fingers lightly curled, their length and strength partially hidden. 'But I…I can't stay long. My mother will be terribly worried if I am again very late home,' she stammered.

'Where does she think you are?'

'I left her a note that I was visiting a friend. She will think I'm at the vicarage.'

'Did you use similar excuses when you were with Edmund?'

'Oh, if we were not socialising in company, Edmund always courted me at home.' Her answer was artless, ejected on a single breath.

'Always? A woman surely wants some private time with her fiancé?'

The hard irony in his voice thrust to her attention something that had been niggling at the back of her mind. On the day they'd met in Hastings she'd deliberately hinted she was no longer chaste. She felt foolish and regretful at having done so; she'd no experience of carnal pleasure other than what Randolph had taught her. She was ashamed, too, to have made it seem Edmund had taken advantage of her. Edmund had always treated her with the utmost affection and respect. He would have dissuaded her, for her own good, from a discreet tryst with him. Wistfully she realised she'd never wanted one, and had been satisfied with his brief goodnight kisses.

When Randolph had kissed and intimately caressed her on the night of the Davenports' soirée she had wished the bliss never to end. Obliquely she'd been conscious her mother's presence in the house would protect her from a full seduction if her self-control were defeated. But she was on her own now.

Soon she might be exposed as a fraud. But there was more bothering her than that he'd discover her lack of experience and sophistication.

Within hours of their reunion Randolph had told her it was his intention to remain a bachelor. But he'd wanted her again that first day, and he still did. The strength of his need seemed to suffocate the space between them.

She'd guessed Randolph had warned off Seth Luckhurst by saying they were lovers and Ned Swinton had come to hear of it. The beast had called her Chadwicke's doxy. Randolph had hinted at propositioning her when he'd called her a seductive lady and remarked they liked one another enough to want to stay in touch. Deborah knew if she asked Randolph to take her home now he would do so; but she couldn't make him say he loved her. The reason for her bittersweet heartache was clear: she didn't want to be Randolph Chadwicke's mistress. She wanted to be his wife.

'Being a smuggler must have been very dangerous. Have you killed a man?' she burst out to break her plaintive mood and the pulsating silence.

'I killed Ned Swinton.'

Deborah blinked at that news, her eyes darting to his shadowed face. Despite knowing against what sort of villain Randolph had been pitted, still she found his admission rather shocking.

'If I hadn't shot him he would have stabbed me to death,

Deborah,' Randolph said quietly. 'He had a good try at it—I've got the proof.'

'Are you in pain?' she asked in concern as his hand quit the table to probe his ribs.

'Not from that,' he muttered drily. He cast a glance on her from beneath his brows, as though considering before speaking. 'Before Swinton died,' he began slowly, 'he boasted how he'd long outwitted the authorities. He claimed to have killed a dragoon a few years ago and pinned the blame on a man called Snowy.' Randolph paused, frowning his regret as lines of strain crinkled Deborah's pale brow. He'd wanted to put to rest for her a ghost, not upset her. It was a moment before he resumed. 'Swinton said he'd clubbed another dragoon more recently. He believed Lieutenant Barrow had perished. He showed no remorse for either crime.'

'He admitted he'd killed Edmund?' Deborah whispered.

'He used Snowy as a scapegoat. No doubt he then murdered him to keep him quiet.'

Deborah nodded slowly; she had long been sceptical of Snowy's guilt. 'I'm glad you avenged my fiancé's death,' she said simply and gave him a small smile.

'Did Edmund bring you somewhere like this?' Randolph asked softly, insistently.

'Did you tell Seth Luckhurst that I was your mistress?' Deborah countered his question with one of hers.

'No.'

'I think that's a lie,' Deborah said hoarsely. 'Swinton called me Chadwicke's doxy.'

'I don't lie to you, Deborah, I've told you that before.'

'You lied about being in the area to buy sheep.'

A hand plunged into a pocket in his breeches and drew forth a paper. 'A bill of sale for the purchase of three rams and a dozen ewes to be delivered to Buckland Hall in Suffolk.' He skimmed it towards her and it drifted to rest between them on the table. 'I told Seth Luckhurst that you were mine,' he said abruptly. 'Are you?'

'I…it depends what you mean by that,' Deborah returned in a barely audible voice.

'What do you want it to mean?'

'I want it to mean that you *have* lied to me…just the once… when you said you were happy to remain a bachelor.' The silence seemed interminable and she was unwilling to raise her eyes from the table to try, pointlessly, to study his concealed expression. Deborah struggled to her feet so abruptly the stick-back chair clattered on to its back. She put a hand to her flaming cheek. She'd virtually proposed to him and he'd said nothing. At least he hadn't laughed. She couldn't have endured his scorn.

'I should go,' she blurted with constrained cheerfulness. 'My mama will be sending out a search party if I don't soon appear…' She headed to the dresser in the corner where her discarded cloak lay.

Before she could don it the garment was taken from her quivering hands and dropped back on to the pine wood. A moment later a tanned sinewy arm had banded her waist, hauling her against his hot hard body. She felt cool lips brush an ear making her shiver. 'Please don't, Randolph,' she gasped. 'I know I've made you think I'm a shameless hussy by letting you kiss me and touch me the way you do. I know I've hinted that Edmund also had… But he was too gentlemanly to ever compromise me in such a way, and…'

'And I'm not?' The complaint was tinged with humour and affection.

She twisted about in his arms and tilted up her face, then regretted having done so. Her earnest eyes merged with a blazing black gaze; their mouths were merely inches apart. Her eyelids drooped, shielding her from the power of his subtle silent seduction. 'I know you've considered asking me to be your mistress,' she breathlessly said, 'but...I won't, so don't say anything. I expect, now you're rich and influential, it was your intention to bribe me with an offer to live in town if, in return, I agree to sleep with you.' The wistfulness in her voice was betraying and she frowned in confusion. She'd never before considered he'd use coercion of that sort, or that she'd be susceptible to such a lure. 'I know I'll be twenty-five soon and that's an age to be a woman, but in truth—' She broke off, unable to conclude the confession.

'But in truth you're still a girl,' he finished huskily. 'And a beautifully gallant one, too.'

She shook her head, but whether to deny her courage or her innocence she was unsure.

'I'm glad Edmund wasn't lucky enough to have possessed you, but I envy him none the less,' Randolph said softly. 'He had your affection and respect. Why did you want me to believe you were lovers?'

'I don't know,' she muttered raggedly. 'I suppose so you would think me worldly,' she carried on with a hint of defiance. 'I didn't want you to see the same naïve little girl you left behind, pining for you to return.'

'I loved that naïve little girl. For a whole year, she kept me sane, gave me hope that she'd wait for me to return and become my wife.'

'You loved me?' An incipient glow was in her eyes as she raised her lids to look at him.

'Of course I loved you.'

'You never said so!' she stormed, tears springing to her eyes.

'I couldn't, Debbie,' he groaned. A hand cupped her face, caught tears on a thumb. 'A marriage proposal should follow such a declaration, or at the very least an explanation for its delay.' His arms tightened about her, his chin rested on the crown of her silky golden head. 'Tell me honestly, Deborah, what you would have thought had you known then what you know now about my family and my past.'

'I would have waited for you to sort it all out,' Deborah insisted, thumping a small fist, twice, on his shoulder in despairing emphasis. 'I waited years to hear from you,' she keened. 'I accepted Edmund's proposal despite knowing I would never love him as a wife should love her husband.' She read the demand for an explanation in his hungry eyes. 'He was kind and he loved me and I would have liked a family before I got too old. I would have waited for *you*,' she raged. 'You should have told me why you had to go away.'

'I believe you would have waited, sweetheart.' His lips brushed her brow, soothing her. 'But your parents—quite rightly—would have been horrified at the thought of it. You were a beautiful débutante with dozens of suitors to choose from and a huge dowry to bestow on the fortunate fellow.' He bowed his head and soft strands of fawn hair tickled her cheek before he turned to sweep a kiss on her briny cheek. 'I was scared if you learned too much about me…before I had a chance to put right the worst of it…you would not only reject me, but despise me, too. I couldn't stand that, Deborah.' He paused to reflect. 'Marcus offered me a loan so I might immediately propose to you. I wouldn't take it. I wanted your affection and respect, I told him. I went away determined to do everything in my power to be worthy of you.'

Abruptly he let her go and took a pace away, his head thrown back as he gritted at the ceiling, 'I damned my pride to perdition so many times. I'd rant at myself for not taking the loan Marcus had generously offered.' His head was snapped down and he looked bleakly at her. 'By the time I was ready to admit defeat and take Marcus's money, it was too late. I'd heard by then of the changes in your circumstances. I knew your father had died, and your mother had remarried. Then I heard you'd got engaged to a dragoon and I knew I'd lost you.'

'*Did* you lie to me on the day we were reunited?' Her words were little more than a sigh. In the fire-daubed room she waited with bated breath for his answer.

'Yes.' His mouth moved and when he raised his long lashes she saw the smile was in his eyes too.

'Say you love me…' she threatened, but her lips were curving too.

He was back at her side, hauling her into his arms, his amusement gone. With fierce passion his mouth swooped on to hers. Immediately she clung to him, coiling her slender arms about his neck, her lips parting sweetly beneath his insistent pressure.

'I love you,' he murmured against her pulsing mouth. 'God knows I love you, Deborah. I've loved you in my mind night and day for longer than I care to remember.'

'I love you, too,' Debbie sobbed against his cheek. 'And I've lost my dowry,' she said sorrowfully. 'I've nothing much now to bring to my husband. You should have married me and taken my money to help you when you most needed it seven years ago. I swear I would not have minded.'

'But I would,' he said vehemently. 'I'm sorry you lost what your father wanted you to have. But I never wanted it. It was a barrier between us. I hated that you had so much when I had so little. I knew I would be thought a fortune hunter if I married you with nothing but debts and disgrace to my name. Now I can give you anything you want and I'm glad.'

'But I've nothing to give in return…'

'I'll think of something,' Randolph told her mock-solemnly, his eyes dangerously wolfish.

Deborah blushed beneath his sultry amusement. 'I wish you'd told Luckhurst I was your unofficial fiancée.'

A choke of laughter met that demand for decency. 'I think we've been unofficially betrothed for a long, long while. And soon everybody will know it.'

Her heartfelt thanks were immediately bestowed. She went up on tiptoe and touched her mouth to his, sliding her soft lips back and forth. She slipped her tongue tip to his lower lip, mimicking the loving he'd just showed her, revelling in the growl of pleasure she drew from him.

A furnace ignited in Randolph's loins; he returned her passion with a force that bowed her back and sent her, held in his arms, retreating a few steps. He continued the erotic onslaught until her thighs were against the table edge and he was supporting her spine close to its top. Gently, urgently, he hoisted her upon it, following her down so his torso hung above her and his weight was on an elbow. A hand rushed over her silhouette, caressing her soft curves. When it reached her thigh a fist spontaneously pulled up her skirts so his hands could luxuriate in the sensation of silky skin slipping beneath his palms. When he turned the backs of his fingers to skim the sensitive flesh of her inner thighs, a trembling sigh broke in Deborah's throat.

Randolph looked down in to her beautiful features, taut with desire. He tilted his face to her throat and his tongue flicked moist heat against the crazily bobbing pulse before his mouth moved lower to nuzzle against the little nubs hardening beneath her blouse.

A ragged pant broke in Deborah's throat and she sank her small fingers into his soft fawn hair and dragged his face up to hers. Randolph kissed her gently, gripping the edge of the table to keep his hands from her beautiful body until he'd said what he must.

'Do you know what I thought about a lot, Debbie, when I was in that godforsaken hellhole with Sebastian?' he murmured against her soft, slick lips.

'Me…' she sighed beatifically.

'Apart from you,' he growled.

She swayed her head and her arms coiled about his neck to make him again kiss her.

'I thought about our wedding night,' he told her hoarsely. 'It was going to be perfect…a feather bed, silk sheets, champagne, beautiful night finery for you… I wanted to give you everything your heart desired. I still do.' He put a shaking finger against her bruised lips, then drew her up so she was held hard against his shoulder. 'I wanted your first time to be magical.' He smiled wickedly. 'If I'm truthful, I wanted to savour it too. I'd waited so long for you I dreamt of feasting on you for hours and hours…' He held her against him, feeling the thunder of her heart shaking his painful ribs. 'So…shall we stay or go, sweetheart?'

Deborah blinked languorously at him, and a gentle smile softened her features into a study of serenity. 'My mama *will* wonder where I am, but…' She saw the self-mocking regret enter his eyes. 'But if we're quick…'

He roared with laughter and in a fluid swoop had her off the table and in his arms. 'Trust me, sweetheart, if we were, you'd never forgive me.'

He dropped a kiss on her cheek and swayed her for a moment in his arms. 'Will you marry me, Miss Woodville, or should I say Miss Cleveland?'

'Indeed I will, sir,' she replied, quivering with happiness. 'And I know it is most confusing knowing how to properly address me.'

'It won't be for much longer, Deborah,' he returned tenderly. 'I'll get a special licence. Soon you'll be Lady Buckland and I'll be the proudest, happiest man alive.'

Julia Woodville awoke with a start, feeling a little chilled for the fire had fallen low in the grate. She immediately looked at the clock on the wall. It was almost ten minutes to eight. Rubbing her eyes, she clucked her regrets whilst swinging her feet to the floor. She had not meant to sleep so long. Deborah would be waiting downstairs for her company at dinner. Julia sighed. It might be no happy meal. She had an unpleasant task to do, but do it she must. She couldn't countenance waiting any longer to make her confession. She had seen this afternoon how dreadfully sad her daughter was. If it was within her power to heal the rift between Deborah and Randolph, she must swallow the bitter pill and hand over the letters.

Earlier that afternoon she'd come to her chamber and, in readiness to finally do the deed, had withdrawn from their hiding place the letters. She approached the bureau and picked up the little ribbon-tied bundle.

Hearing a noise, she twitched aside the curtain, wondering who was at the stable at such an hour. Peering out, she saw Basham leading away a large horse. An incipient smile twitched her lips and her heart soared in hopefulness; it looked, to Julia, to be Mr Chadwicke's mount. About to drop the curtain, Julia's hand stilled as a movement near the torch caught her eye. As the flare by the stable door wavered in its sconce she saw highlighted the silhouettes of an embracing couple. A glint of gold was visible as the breeze stirred her daughter's flowing tresses. A moment later Julia watched Deborah rest her head on Randolph Chadwicke's broad shoulder as, arm in arm, they strolled towards the house.

A joyous smile bathed Julia's face and she hastened towards the door. She hesitated with her hand on the doorknob and retraced her steps to her desk. She abruptly snatched up the letters and, with a silent prayer, fed them to the fire, waiting until the flames danced about them before she quit the room to go and welcome home her family.

HISTORICAL

Novels coming in January 2011

LADY FOLBROKE'S DELICIOUS DECEPTION
Christine Merrill

Confronting her errant husband after being snubbed, Lady Emily Longesley finds that he has been robbed of his sight and doesn't know her! Emily longs for a lover's touch. If she plays his mistress, can he finally begin to love his wife?

BREAKING THE GOVERNESS'S RULES
Michelle Styles

Governess Louisa Sibson was dismissed for allowing Jonathon, Lord Chesterholm to seduce her. Now she lives by a strict set of morals. But Jonathon *will* get to the bottom of her disappearance —and will enjoy breaking a few of her rules along the way…!

HER DARK AND DANGEROUS LORD
Anne Herries

Exiled Lord Stefan de Montfort rescued Englishwoman Anne Melford from the sea, taking her to his French château. The spirited beauty fires within him a forbidden desire. Now he's determined to break one last rule and claim her as his bride!

HOW TO MARRY A RAKE
Deb Marlowe

Mae Halford mended her heart after rejection by Lord Stephen Manning. Now she's ready to find a husband—only the first man she bumps into is Lord Stephen himself! Romance may blossom once more—but will their adventure lead to the altar?

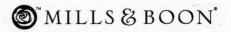

MILLS & BOON

HISTORICAL

Another exciting novel available this month:

LADY ARABELLA'S SCANDALOUS MARRIAGE

Carole Mortimer

You are cordially invited

to the marriage of

DARIUS WYNTER, DUKE OF CARLYNE

to

LADY ARABELLA ST CLAIRE

What is Lady Arabella letting herself in for? Sinister whispers surround the death of Darius' first wife—could Arabella be in jeopardy? Or will the infamous Duke prove all Society wrong?

One thing's for sure—after the compromising situation that led to this marriage, Arabella will soon discover the exquisite pleasures of the marriage bed…

The Notorious St Claires

HISTORICAL

Another exciting novel available this month:

BOUND TO THE BARBARIAN

Carol Townend

Out of her depth and into his arms…

Sold into slavery, maidservant Katerina promised one day to repay the princess who rescued her. Now that time has come, and Katerina must convince commanding warrior Ashfirth Saxon that *she* is her royal mistress.

Spending balmy days and long sultry nights with this man make Katerina's task increasingly impossible. How long will she be able to keep up her deception? And how long before she finds herself willingly bedded by this proud barbarian?

Palace Brides
Beauties of Byzantium—claimed by warriors!

MILLS & BOON

HISTORICAL

**Another exciting novel available
this month:**

BOUGHT: THE
PENNILESS LADY

Deborah Hale

Her new husband may be handsome—but his heart is black.

Desperate to safeguard the future of her precious nephew, penniless Lady Artemis Dearing will do anything – even marry the man whose brother ruined her darling sister!

Forced to wed a gold-digger—or a loving wife?

Hadrian Northmore's suffered enough heartbreak—he will not lose his brother's son too. Calculating and deceitful as Lady Artemis may be, he *will* marry her if he must! But Hadrian isn't prepared for overwhelming desire, or his new wife's sweet disposition. There's been some mistake…his hard-built defences are crumbling before his very eyes!

Gentlemen of Fortune
*Three men with money, power and success…
Looking to share life with the right woman*